CROSS-CHECK

A DARK ENEMIES-TO-LOVERS HOCKEY ROMANCE

BLACKWOOD BLADES
BOOK TWO

ISLA VAUGHN

ARROWSCOPE PRESS, LLC

Cross-Check

(p) ISBN-13: 978-1-951919-77-1

(e) ISBN-13: 978-1-951919-76-4

Publisher: Arrowscope Press, LLC; www.arrowscopepress.com

Editing— Taylor Anhalt, Editor

Cover Illustration—Audrey Anhalt https://audreyanhalt.com

Cover Design—T.E. Black Designs; www.teblackdesigns.com

Interior Formatting & Design— Arrowscope Press, LLC; www.arrowscope-press.com

PROLOGUE

MILA

Waves crashed against the sand while my mother's warning still echoed—*Stay away from him. That family's not safe.* But I couldn't forget what came after: Lorne standing over Darren's body, the gun, the erasure of our names. It was too much to keep buried. Luke deserved the truth—unless he'd been living it all along. My mouth went dry, and I curled my hands into fists to still the slight tremble. Fear would've been smart. I just wasn't feeling smart tonight.

The locker room was probably empty by now, the echo of pucks and whistles fading into the night. I'd already checked my phone twice, reread his text—*I'm up. Meet me.*—and still couldn't calm the tremor in my hands.

The drive to the academy from the beach blurred past in a wash of headlights and second-guesses. By the time I parked in the arena's lot, I'd almost convinced myself it was just a conversation. But conversations with Luke King had a way of changing everything.

It was getting late, and most of the players had already left. I hurried across the lot and slipped through the metal doors that would take me to Luke. After climbing the main levels, I hit the older part of the building. The stairwell to the roof creaked under my shoes, as if it remembered every secret this town had swallowed.

When I pushed the final door open, the rooftop and skyline spilled around me in smoky dusk hues. Everything resembled one of my charcoal sketches—shades of gray, truth smudged until shadow and what was real blurred together. Fitting. We'd both been living in half-erased lines. And there he was— standing near the edge, back to me, the set of his shoulders tight beneath his hoodie.

For a heartbeat, I almost turned around. Because facing Luke again meant pulling every lie into the light. I'd spent enough time running—from this town, from names, from truths that wouldn't stay buried. I squared my shoulders and tilted my chin up. Tonight wasn't about escape. It was about finally turning around to face the thing that had chased me away.

He turned, eyes catching the last streak of gray-blue sky, and it hit me how exhausted he looked. Not physically—emotionally. As if the weight of Blackwood itself had been pressing on his spine. I tread forward, leaving a foot between us. Close enough, but not to invite touch. I needed the space to stand on my own and tell him the truths he needed to hear.

"I wasn't sure you'd show." His deep voice rumbled across the space between us.

"Neither was I." My voice didn't shake, but the rest of me did. I wanted to start easy—small talk, a joke, anything—but the words clawed their way out before I could stop them. "I overheard Elise after school on the phone today."

His gaze sharpened, all predator focus.

"She's unraveling, Luke. Whoever's pulling her strings... it's bad. She actually said 'drug him.'"

The disbelief that flickered across his face almost hurt to watch. I wished I didn't have to be the one to confirm how ugly this world could get.

But that wasn't why I'd come. Not really. He notched his head toward the blanket laid out, waiting for us to claim it and the memories of all the past times we'd found sanctuary together up here.

I sank onto the edge of the blanket, knees folding beneath me. "There's more. And I need your word before I say it—that you'll protect my mom and me."

He hesitated then nodded once. "You have it."

The words steadied me enough to continue. "I don't even remember why I had to meet Mom at work that night over a year ago. Doesn't matter. I followed her location, and when I got there…"

Luke shifted. His muscles rippled beneath the taut fabric of his hoodie, and I shivered.

"There was blood. A body. We got the hell out. I inhaled deep then pushed onward. "Back at our place, she wouldn't tell me who pulled the trigger. The person who was killed… it was my mom's boyfriend. Darren Langley."

Recognition flashed in his eyes. "The VP," he said slowly.

"Yeah. And that was the night we fled. But there's something else." My throat went dry, and I had to clear it before I could continue. "My mom… she saw Lorne that night. Standing over Darren's body. Gun in hand." Even saying his name made my pulse stutter. The memory was branded into me—the way Mom had shaken as she told me to grab my things. We didn't say goodbye. We ran.

"There must be some mistake." Luke's expression hardened, disbelief fighting realization. "You're here now. Your school records are back. No one's coming after you."

Silence swelled between us, thick and dangerous.

"Your mom thought my family did it," he said finally.

"She still does." The confession scraped raw, and I threaded my fingers together until my knuckles turned white. "They made her come back. Whoever's behind Dunn Industries—or maybe even Lorne—forced her into a job she couldn't refuse. Told her we'd be safe if we played along."

Luke looked as though he wanted to argue, to deny, but the fight in his eyes dimmed.

I pressed a hand to his chest, felt the uneven rhythm of his heart under my palm. "That's why I can't fight Elise openly. She's her father's weapon, and my mom works for Dunn now. If I push too far, it blows back on both of us." I swallowed hard. "We're stuck playing by rules we don't even understand. And I don't want to have to leave again."

"Who is they?"

I shrugged. Wasn't that the question of the hour? "I-I don't know for sure. Only that Mom told me to stay away from you. Said the King family's not safe."

Luke didn't break eye contact, his face frozen in that impossible-to-read way of his. "Darren isn't dead."

My breath caught. The world tilted, and I curled my fingers into the blanket.

"There was never any notice about his death. No news, no whispers. Your mom doesn't have the full story."

My stomach twisted. I searched his face, daring him to break the promise he'd just made. "You said you would trust me. Give me the benefit of the doubt."

"I did. I do. Look… if there was a cover-up, and he is dead? Then I get why your mom ran."

He leaned back slightly, and my hand fell away. I missed his heartbeat beneath my palm instantly.

"But, Mila… I was told your mom stole from us."

I flinched before bracing for the possibility of it, because we did have money when we ran. "I-I don't know about that. Maybe she stole from her boyfriend. I don't think it was from your family's company."

"Okay." His features hardened the way they did on the ice when he was about to take on the opposing team. "You need to keep your head down." He scrubbed a hand over his jaw, gaze narrowing. "Don't poke the beast. Don't give them a reason."

That was it? Was he pulling away from me? It wasn't what I wanted, not even a little. "And what about us?"

His pupils flared wide, something that I hoped was desire swirling in those depths. "I've got your back. We'll figure this out. But we do it together."

I nodded, my gaze locked on his. "Together."

"No more secrets."

"That goes both ways." My voice dropped to a dare.

"We're in agreement then. A team."

I drew back, and he caught my wrist, holding it there.

"You won't lose me."

For a moment, I believed him. His gaze dropped to my mouth, then back to my eyes—as though he was giving me one last chance to pull away. And then he kissed me.

It wasn't gentle—it was years of grief, fury, and need colliding into something between forgiveness and war. His hand tangled in my hair; mine fisted in his hoodie. One touch and I went up like a fuse. Raw, powerful, and potent. An addiction I couldn't quit. The sound that escaped me didn't feel like a choice—desire, relief, and warning tangled together.

When he pulled back, our foreheads stayed pressed, breaths uneven. "This changes things," I managed.

"Damn right it does," he murmured and kissed me again.

Slower. Deeper. More of a claim than a kiss. We lost ourselves in one another until a car horn blared below and we pulled apart, reluctantly.

The stars blurred above us, a thousand silent witnesses.

Luke reached into his pocket. "Might as well mark the night." He unfurled his hand to reveal a delicate silver chain with a star pendant.

I blinked back sudden tears at the sight of the necklace he'd given me long ago. I never thought I would see it again. "You kept it?"

When he fastened the necklace around my throat, something shifted. A circle closed; a wound sealed.

He didn't answer. Just brushed my hair aside.

My fingers drifted up, grazing the tiny silver star. "I left it in your bag before the game. For luck. I wasn't supposed to leave that night. I thought I'd be there to get it back from you the next day."

His nostrils flared, and guilt hit me hard for never being able to tell him why I'd left. I knew exactly what he'd thought—I'd left him without a word, thrown all our hopes and dreams away, the ultimate betrayal.

"Still suits you."

I melted inside at his simple words, because I knew what they meant. Forgiveness. Acceptance. For the first time since I came back, we were on the same page. Not publicly as a couple, but here. Now. Whenever we were alone. And still, a quiet fear threaded through the warmth—because this time, there was so much stacked against us, and wanting him didn't make any of it safer.

We sat there, the night folding around us, two ghosts pretending we could start over. But underneath the sweetness of his promise, I could already feel the storm building.

Because if what I'd told him was true—and I knew it was— then the danger wasn't outside us anymore.

It was in his family's blood.

And the moment we chose to stand together, we drew a target on both our backs.

The necklace was cool against my skin, a reminder of what we'd reignited. The same star that once represented us and our dreams for the future. Now it meant war. Maybe Mom was right—Luke King was dangerous. But so was I, now that I wasn't afraid anymore. We weren't just rebuilding trust. We were lighting a fuse.

CHAPTER ONE

MILA

The necklace was warm against my skin when I woke—an anchor and a warning.

My pulse kicked into high gear, as if my body knew sleep had been a mistake. Luke and I called a truce last night. Morning made it feel like a dare. I wasn't running. Not this time.

The stairs groaned under my weight when I headed down for breakfast. Sunlight bled through slatted blinds, striping the worn, outdated living room in gold and shadow. Our rental always smelled faintly of salt—California air sneaking through the cracked windows no matter how tightly you pulled them shut.

Mom was at the kitchen table, straight-backed, coffee steaming beside her. Not the woman who used to work for King Enterprises in neat pencil skirts and polite smiles. Now she wore Dunn's polish as armor—silk blouse tucked into a charcoal skirt, blazer draped over the chair, heels already on. Dark hair pulled tight from her face, gray-green eyes so similar to mine studying whatever glowed across her tablet.

Her eyes flicked up as soon as I entered. "You talked to Luke." Not curiosity. A verdict.

My grip tightened on my backpack strap. "Yeah."

Mom's gaze lingered. "And?"

"He said he believes me," I muttered, staring past her shoulder.

Her mouth thinned. She nudged the tablet aside with one manicured finger. "That's not the same as safe."

Heat climbed my throat. I pressed my palm flat to the table to ground myself. "I'm not lying to him."

She leaned forward, elbows on the table, voice even but cold enough to cut. "Don't confuse honesty with protection." Her nail clicked against the table. "Dunn didn't pull us back here out of mercy. They wanted leverage."

A chill slid through me. "Have they asked for anything yet?"

"Not yet." Her tablet chimed. She flipped it face down. "But they will. And when they do, we won't have the luxury of saying no." She pushed her mug away, the scrape loud in the quiet kitchen. "The Kings are worse. They don't need favors—they take. And Lorne?" She leaned forward again, voice dropping lower, each word a warning. "He's the one we can't afford to provoke."

I unclenched my fist and forced myself to meet her gaze. The name clawed down my spine. I swallowed it and kept my voice even. "I'm not the same person who left," I forced out. Because I wasn't. Back then, I had stars in my eyes, head over heels for a future Luke and I had planned out. Then reality crashed in, and I did what Mom and I always did—survive. And this time, I wasn't going in blind.

Her nod was tight. Controlled. "Good. Because that girl won't survive what's coming."

I couldn't hold her stare. The necklace burned hot against my chest.

By the time I made it to Blackwood Academy, the sun had

burned through the fog, leaving the air clean but bracing, eucalyptus and salt biting with every breath.

The courtyard buzzed—crowded benches, voices too loud, eyes shifting when they thought I wasn't looking.

Elise Dunn's laugh cut through the crowded space—too bright, too sharp. She stood on the steps, glossy as a poster, black hair sleek and shimmering in the light with that small closed-lip smile that made people lean back.

Logan lounged against the rail, one boot braced, watching me without pretending otherwise.

Nina glittered at Elise's shoulder, all diamonds and deliberate sparkle. Tori's strawberry-blond hair curtained her face. She missed a step and grabbed her slipping backpack, eyes on the concrete.

Our enemies weren't gone, just waiting for the next hit.

Avery's blond ponytail flashed as she cut through the crowd and slid in at my side, shouldering me a path as though it was muscle memory. "Rough morning?" Her gaze skimmed the hall, already running interference.

I shoved a book into my locker, voice clipped. "Overslept." I didn't want to get into the conversation with my mom this morning, or the fragile truce between Luke and me.

Her brow arched, but she didn't push. She leaned against the metal, casual on the outside, but her eyes tracked the hall, ready to intercept whatever was coming my way. I didn't have to look to know Elise was still watching. Or that whispers were already trailing us, carrying Luke's name in their wake.

The necklace weighed heavy against my skin. Last night's kiss replayed in my head—a secret I shouldn't touch. The star pressed hot against my skin, useless as a shield and bright as a target. Promises weren't armor. Not here. Not when the Kings still sat at the top of the food chain and Dunn Industries had us pinned in place.

The war hadn't ended. It had only drawn its battle lines deeper.

CHAPTER TWO

LUKE

Practice had been routine—drills, conditioning, Coach barking orders until his voice went hoarse. The locker room after was the same—Theo ran his mouth, Chase acted as though the world couldn't touch him, and Jax threw jabs that were too pointed to be jokes. Same rhythm. Same noise. Except it wasn't. Not with Elise prowling the halls earlier and Logan lurking at her side, muscle disguised by a grin. And not with Mila, two rows over in class—a temptation I couldn't reach.

Every time I passed her, I wanted to touch her—brush her arm, thread my fingers through hers. Anything. But I didn't. Couldn't. Keeping her safe meant distance, at least in daylight.

But after what she told me on the roof, distance was a lie. We were already tangled. No space was big enough to undo it.

The sky looked different from the pool deck. Too open. Too still. I sat on the edge, arms draped over my knees, sneakers planted on warm travertine that held the day's heat. Underwater lights hummed, turning the pool into a pane of dark glass. The wind whispered through palm fronds overhead.

On the surface, peace. Underneath, nothing close.

Not when I could still taste her. Not when her voice looped in my head.

According to Mila, Darren Langley was dead. There was blood on King Enterprises property—Lorne holding the gun, Dunn pulling Adriana, Mila's mom, back on a leash.

None of it added up. But it didn't feel like a lie. Not from Mila. Her voice broke on his name. Her hands wouldn't stop shaking until I held them.

Except Langley isn't dead. At least, that was what I'd been told.

My father brushed off his absence with a shrug—consulting overseas, a better fit for his skill set. I hadn't questioned it. Why would I? People moved on.

Then Mila looked me in the eye and bared her soul. She gave me Lorne with a gun in his hand, the reason they'd vanished. Staying could've gotten them killed. And now they were back. Not because it was safe, but because someone decided they should be.

I dragged my hands over my face and exhaled. What the hell was happening? She swore he was dead. Dad swore he wasn't. One of them was lying.

Adriana Callahan had worked for King Enterprises before her life went to hell. Now she was at Dunn Industries—the company quietly buying pieces of us, snapping up properties and stock through shells, waiting for the right moment to squeeze. Dad and my brother, Drew, were already running that play on the chessboard. Countermoves. Mitigation. Reports. Their world—company strategy, boardroom fixes—not mine. Not yet.

But Dad had pushed at breakfast. *"Sit in on the call tomorrow."* My fork paused. Drew didn't. *"I've got it,"* Drew said, steady as ever. *"He's got early ice. I'll walk him through the details on Sunday."* Dad's mouth thinned, eyes cutting to me, then away. Drew held the stare until the tension bled out. Relief slid under my ribs. He took the hit. Again.

But Mila. Her mom. Langley bleeding out on our property—that wasn't theirs to fix. That was mine.

I tipped my head back. The stars lay flat above. Orion's belt hung clean over the roofline. Weight pressed under my ribs. Not betrayal. Obligation. The kind you couldn't outrun without hating yourself later.

I thought about Mila again on the blanket we'd laid out on the roof. Lips swollen. Chain catching the moonlight above her collarbone. Haunted eyes before she told me the truth. *No secrets. No power plays. We don't disappear on each other when it gets ugly.*

She wasn't just the girl who left anymore. Or the future I thought was mine until it slipped away. She was the key to something bigger—something people would bury bodies to protect.

And she trusted me. Maybe not with everything. But with enough.

I leaned back on my palms. Night slid cool across my forearms. If I closed my eyes, I could feel her weight in my lap again, the way she fit as though she'd always had a claim there.

Dangerous thinking.

We weren't together. But not strangers either. There was no label for it, just emotions—tension, hunger, fractured trust. Too much of everything else. I was addicted to the contradiction.

Earlier, the school had handed me a reminder I hadn't asked for. During the lunch rush in the courtyard, Elise's gaze had cut to Mila, tracking her every move as if she was already plotting the next strike. Then during practice—ice still fresh, edges crisp. Logan finished a drill and clipped my skate in the turn. A nothing contact. Except his stick caught my shin just enough to bite. He smiled—easy, harmless to anyone who didn't know better. I did. That wasn't an accident. It was a warning dressed up as nothing.

Elise played angles. Logan pressed pressure points. Different tactics, same goal—waiting for the crack they could split wide open.

My reflection floated on the pool's surface. Eyes darker in the blue. A stranger if I stared long enough. Part of me wanted to sink back into that rooftop kiss with Mila, forget the rest. The other part—the one raised where every glance was leverage, every handshake was a threat—knew better.

Theo was already in motion. I'd told him to keep Tori talking. She was one of Elise's closest friends, had that Dunn internship, and was into Theo. She heard things from Elise. Saw the quiet stuff. If there was a campaign building, if midlevels were moving, if personnel got shuffled—Tori would catch a piece of it without knowing why. Theo could get it out of her without tipping her off. We would meet, match it against what Mila gave me, then cross-check with what Drew flagged on the business side.

Find the thread. Pull until the whole thing unraveled.

I pushed to my feet and looked out across the water. The surface stayed calm. My face blurred in the dark sheet, a shadow carved across my jaw.

Mila was right. This town had a ruling order. And if she was in danger, then maybe it was my turn to tear it down.

CHAPTER THREE

MILA

My phone buzzed on the nightstand, screen flaring against the dark. I checked the time. Midnight. The kind of hour that made everything feel lonelier, heavier, more dangerous.

Luke: *You awake?*

A jolt shot through me—sudden, electric, low in my chest, sparking everywhere I didn't want it to. My fingers hovered above the screen. I stared at it a beat too long before answering.

Me: *Yeah.*

Three dots blinked, disappeared, blinked again.

Luke: *What are you doing?*

Me: *Trying to sleep. Failing.*

A pause.

Luke: *Same. Pool deck. Stars are too loud tonight.*

My lips twitched despite myself. Stars, too loud. That was Luke—athlete and poet in the same breath, without even realizing he was both.

Me: *Still your favorite spot, huh?*

Luke: *One of them. Hard to top all the nights we stargazed. Remember the lifeguard tower?*

The memory slid in uninvited—me tucked against him, the hiss of the waves, his hand pointing out constellations while I pretended to care more about Orion than the way his heart beat against my shoulder.

Me: *Yeah. I remember.*

Luke: *We had some big dreams back then.*

"We"—the word was a bruise and a balm all at once.

Me: *Dreams are dangerous.*

Luke: *So are you.*

My fingers hovered over the keyboard. Dangerous wasn't wrong. I was dangerous to him—in ways deeper than kisses and late-night texts. To his family. To his future. To the legacy he was supposed to inherit. But he wasn't running from it now.

Luke: *Have you drawn anything lately?*

I was halfway horizontal and then I wasn't. My knee hit the nightstand hard enough to sting. Barely anyone asked me that or ever saw that part of me. Only Avery did. And him.

Me: *Why?*

Luke: *Because I know you. You sketch when the world gets too heavy.*

My throat tightened. I didn't respond. If I did, it would let him in further than he already was. And that part of me—the part wrapped in charcoal lines and oil paint—wasn't just a hobby. It was my core. My truth.

Luke: *I saw you. The other night. At the boardwalk studio.*

My stomach dropped. The boardwalk studio was the only space in this town that felt like mine—rich with color, untamed waves visual through the windows, and canvases stacked higher than my shoulders. A place I could breathe without someone watching.

Me: *You followed me?*

Luke: *Yeah. After the Grill Shack. After the parking lot.*

The night of that kiss. The one that still burned when I let myself think about it too long. I'd been at the Grill Shack with Avery and her friends, doing my best to fit in when Simon, one of Chase's buddies, slid into the booth beside me. Across the restaurant at Luke's table, Elise pressed herself against him as if she owned him, her hand bold on his thigh. I'd bolted before I could stomach another second of it. He followed me out into the dark lot, words clipped, anger taut—until all of it snapped and his mouth crashed into mine.

Me: *You're insane.*

Luke: *I was worried. You disappeared fast. I just... needed to make sure you were okay.*

I chewed my lip. That was Luke, too. Protective to a fault.

Me: *And what did you see, exactly?*

Luke: *The sea. The storm you painted. I could feel it from the doorway. As if you'd poured yourself into the canvas. It was...*

He didn't finish. He didn't have to. The fact that he admitted he'd been standing there, watching, meant more than the words.

Me: *You don't get to spy on me, King.*

Luke: *Then show me what you're working on. No spying. Just you and me.*

I hesitated. Then I snapped a picture and sent it before I could second-guess. The sketchbook lay open on my bed, pencil smudges across the page. Not the storm. Not the sea. Luke's hand. Holding the star necklace—my star.

Three dots blinked again. Then stopped. Started. Stopped. Finally—

Luke: *Mila...*

The single word carried too much. Memory. Longing. Promises made on the roof that felt as if they were a lifetime ago. I shut the sketchbook as though that could stop the ache. It didn't. The graphite came off on my fingers anyway.

Me: *Don't read into it.*

Luke: *Too late.*

My fingers froze, hovering, but I didn't answer. Couldn't. Because he was right. For both of us, it was already too late. Telling him about Lorne had been dangerous, but this—letting him see the part of me that breathed through charcoal and canvas—felt as if I was handing him my unguarded heart. And that was a risk I wasn't sure either of us could survive.

CHAPTER FOUR

LUKE

I could feel Mila watching me before I even turned around. It wasn't the usual kind of glance—the quick ones you clock in the corner of your eye and dismiss. This one cut through hallway noise, branding the back of my neck with heat and suspicion.

I didn't move. Just leaned casually against the locker bank outside Econ, as if I wasn't breaking the fragile trust between us. From her angle, I was.

Elise stood two feet in front of me, flipping her dark, glossy hair as though she still ruled this place. Her voice was lower than normal. Less shrill, more deliberate. Calculated.

And Mila saw all of it, even the brush of Elise's hand on my forearm. I didn't need to see Mila's face to know the gears were already grinding. If I'd watched that scene from thirty feet, I would've walked over swinging too.

The guys and I iced Elise out after she had Logan lay hands on Mila. That was the line, and it was non-negotiable. She'd already been setting people up, trashing reputations. Rachel—a girl in our grade last year who'd since transferred out—almost hadn't survived Elise's bullying. But this was different. Exile stood. If keeping her within arm's length got us information, I'd stomach it. The mandate didn't change. The method did.

Not that Mila would see it that way.

The conversation hadn't even been planned. I'd gotten two sentences out with Tori before she froze, as if I'd asked for nuclear codes. Then Elise slid in, moving as though the hallway belonged to her, smile polished and lethal as glass.

"Looks like your friends are warming back up." Elise's nails skimmed the strap of her bag, casual but deliberate. "Funny how fast things shift when the right people remind them who's in control."

I didn't answer Elise. Just tilted my head as though I gave a damn.

But to someone across the hall who couldn't hear the words or read the tension, it probably looked as though we were catching up. Maybe even friendly.

Shit.

By lunch, the storm had arrived.

I spotted Mila before she saw me—charging across the quad, long brown hair wild from the wind, gray-green eyes locked on me. A dark storm cloud in denim. No tray. No food. Just fury.

"King," she snapped the second she reached our table. Chase and Jax cut off mid-sentence. Theo raised an eyebrow.

I pushed to my feet. "Mila."

"Walk. Now."

The guys didn't move. They blinked as though they were watching a soap opera play out in real time.

I leaned down, close enough that only she could hear me. "You dragging me off to yell, or is this foreplay?"

"Keep talking and I'll drag you off to bury you," she growled.

God, she was pissed. And fuck me if it didn't do something to me.

We ended up near the back of the courtyard, under an old tree that didn't do much against the sun. A couple underclassmen sat on the lawn nearby, so we kept moving—until we hit the chain-link fencing behind the gym.

"Want to tell me what the hell that was?" she demanded, arms crossed tight.

The vintage olive-green shirt she wore stretched across her breasts, the deep V-neck dipping just enough to drag my eyes where they shouldn't be. Distracting as hell. I forced my gaze back up. "Elise?" I played dumb. Badly.

"You think I didn't see it? You didn't exactly look like a hostage." Her mouth twisted. "Pretty rich, considering you kissed me as if I was the only thing that mattered last night."

Her words punched into me. Because the taste of her—salt, heat, defiance—was still on my tongue every damn time I let myself think about last night. I sighed. "Mila—"

"She's dangerous, Luke. You said it yourself. So what? That doesn't count if she shows up in lip gloss and batting lashes? You think I forgot what I overheard? Her talking about drugging you if she had to?" Her eyes flared. "We're supposed to be a team. Not letting her crawl back into it."

I stepped forward. She didn't move. "If you're going to accuse me, at least make it interesting."

"I'm asking," she shot back. "Are you double-crossing me?"

That landed harder than I wanted. Still, I let her come at me, because every jab, every accusation, meant she cared enough to fight. And I would take her fire over her silence any day. "No," I said, voice low. "But you're assuming a lot for someone who said this isn't about us."

Her index finger tapped against her arm. "It's not."

"You sure?" I leaned in. "Because you're acting jealous."

She let out a sharp laugh. "You wish."

"I don't need to wish." I held her stare. "You wouldn't have stormed over here if you didn't care."

Her head tilted. "I care about not being played. There's a difference."

"And I care about not having a move I make questioned as if I'm some pawn in your trust issues."

Her mouth opened. Closed. Then opened again. "Maybe if you shared the plan, I wouldn't have to guess."

That shut me up for half a second. Because she wasn't wrong.

She folded her arms tighter. "So explain. Why were you talking to them?"

I dragged a hand through my hair. "Tori is an intern at Dunn. And interns overhear things—shifts in staff, whispers about projects. I wanted to ask if she liked it—see if she noticed anything off. But she shut down. Especially when Elise showed. She's Elise's friend," I admitted. "Doesn't mean she's loyal. She's scared. And she's not going to talk to me."

Mila studied me. "So? What's the plan then?"

"I saw an opening, tried to push, but she shut down. So I handed it off to Theo. He can get her to talk."

Her brows rose. "Theo?"

"He's already close with her. And she lets him in."

Mila's hesitation was obvious, her eyes narrowing. She knew exactly what "close" meant. Still, she weighed it, then gave a curt nod. "Fine. But Tori's not the only thing going on. Elise?"

I smirked. "Still an outcast. Trust me. No one's inviting her to hang out."

Mila didn't look convinced. "Yet she's still walking around as though she's untouchable."

"People like Elise survive by twisting situations until they work in her favor. She calls it a favor while she steals your chair."

"And you're what—letting her get close to feed the illusion?"

I grinned. "Would that make you mad?"

Her eyes narrowed. "You'd enjoy that, wouldn't you?"

She huffed, turning away—but not quick enough to hide the flush climbing her cheeks. When she looked back, her eyes cut to mine, cool and defiant. "Don't flatter yourself, King. You're not worth the heartburn."

A grin stretched my mouth wide. Funny, because I could still taste her on my tongue, that wildfire heat she swore didn't matter. If she really didn't care, she wouldn't be chasing me into the courtyard to reprimand me.

Silence stretched for a beat before she spoke again, softer this time. "So what's the plan now? Besides siccing Theo on Tori and letting Elise hang all over you."

I exhaled. "We meet again after Friday's game. You talk to your mom. See if she'll slip anything. Doesn't have to be about Dunn directly—just watch for names, patterns, new staff."

"And you?"

"I'll keep my eyes on Elise. Her dad's still pulling strings. He wants something, based on what you overheard the other night. We just don't know what yet."

Her lips pressed tight. "You sure you're not being played?"

"Only one person I'm worried about playing me right now," I said. "And you're standing two feet away."

She shook her head, a half-laugh escaping. "If I was playing you, you would already know."

I leaned in, close enough my breath skimmed her ear. "Yeah? I'm not so sure."

She walked off before I could push it further, star charm catching sunlight—a dare I hadn't earned the right to take. But I would. Eventually.

CHAPTER FIVE

MILA

Avery caught up to me before the next bell, her bag bumping against her hip as she slid into stride. "Okay. Spill."

I kept my eyes forward, hugging the strap of my backpack a little tighter. "Spill what?"

She arched a brow. "Don't play innocent. You marched across the quad at lunch and dragged Luke off as if you were about to execute him behind the gym. Half the courtyard saw it."

My throat went dry. "It wasn't—"

"Subtle? Definitely wasn't." Her blue eyes cut over me, worried underneath the teasing edge. "So? Elise again?"

Her name alone was enough to knot my chest. "Something like that," I muttered.

Before Avery could push, a familiar shadow crossed our path. Jax.

He moved with that easy, cocky swagger—dark hair perpetually mussed, hockey hoodie half-zipped, broad-shouldered confidence that made girls sigh and trip over themselves. His smirk barely tugged at his mouth, but his gaze snapped—on

Avery—and stayed two beats too long. Too obvious. Until he broke contact and kept walking, as though it never happened.

Avery's inhale hitched. She buried her face in her phone as though the screen suddenly mattered.

I almost smiled. "You two ever going to talk like normal people?"

Her head snapped up, cheeks flushed. "We *do* talk."

"Sure," I said dryly. "If you count flirting in the parking lot after the hockey game and then pretending it never happened."

Color crept higher on her cheeks. "It was nothing."

"Looked more than nothing to me."

She blew out a frustrated breath, shaking her head. "Nothing's gonna change, Mila. Jax being friends with my brother is the real problem. He'll joke, flirt, and stare at me as if I'm the only girl in the world one second—and then the next, it's as if I don't exist. Because God forbid he pisses off his buddy by going after his sister."

The bitterness in her voice made me stop short. I was annoyed for her. "That's bullshit. If he wanted you, really wanted you, Chase wouldn't matter."

Her laugh came out bitter, disbelieving. "Exactly. But apparently, I'm not worth that kind of trouble to him."

The words stung more than I wanted to admit. Because wasn't that what I'd been asking myself about Luke? If I was worth the fallout? If he was willing to risk what it could cost him?

I forced the thought down. "Jax is an idiot," I muttered.

Her mouth twisted, half a smile, half a grimace. "Tell me something I don't know."

The bell blared overhead, cutting the moment short. We split for class, but her words clung to me the rest of the day—settling under my skin, restless. Jax holding back because of Chase. Luke holding back because of… what? His family. His name. Elise circling. Maybe me.

By the time I got home, the sun had already dipped below the hills and the house was mostly dark, but none of it shook loose the tension knotted in my chest.

I should've let it go. The locker scene. Elise. Luke's annoyingly smug grin. All of it. I should've walked past the lunch table and pretended I didn't care who he talked to or how close he stood when he did it. I should've remained cool, mask in place, upper hand intact. But I hadn't. And now my pride felt bruised, my chest tight, and I couldn't stop replaying the way he'd looked at me before I stormed off.

Like he'd won something. As though he knew. Which… maybe he did.

Because the worst part wasn't Elise standing too close, her jet-black hair shining as if some shampoo commercial while she smiled up at him. It wasn't even that Luke hadn't looked uncomfortable. No, the worst part was that it bothered me. And the fact that I'd just admitted that to myself? Infuriating.

Maybe that was the inheritance no one talked about—not companies or money, but the same poison that ate at my mom. Secrets, jealousy, survival disguised as strength. And now it was inside me too.

Later, dusk crept in, streaks of orange bleeding into indigo. The days were shrinking, closing in, and it felt like a warning. Winter was coming fast—and with it, more trouble I could already feel pressing at the edges.

The house was mostly dark except for the soft glow of a lamp in the kitchen. My mom had left dinner on the table— salmon and some couscous dotted with herbs. Reheated, sure, but better than her usual toast-and-coffee default.

She was already there, sitting at the table with a glass of white wine half-full, her phone face down beside her plate. Her blouse was a silk cream button-down that I hadn't seen before, the sleeves rolled up neatly to her elbows. Her hair was twisted into a low chignon that made her look more boardroom than

Mom. Her posture was stiff, shoulders locked in tension, jaw tight, as if she'd been holding her breath all day.

Good. She wasn't in the mood to talk either.

I dropped my backpack by the door and slid into the chair across from her. For a while, we ate in silence. That uneasy quiet we'd perfected since moving back to Blackwood. There had been moments, here and there, when it felt like the old us— the two of us against the world, surviving, even thriving—but the weight of secrets always pulled her away again.

Halfway through my plate, I broke it. "Long day?"

She looked up, startled, as though she'd forgotten I was there. "Mm. Just tired."

Right. Because nothing said casual burnout like working for the rival company that dragged us back here, job offer and threat braided into a leash. No longer King Enterprises—the place she worked at back then, the one whose walls she saw blood spill behind—now it was Dunn pulling the strings.

I stabbed a forkful of couscous. "Everything okay at work?"

Her hand froze around her wineglass. "Why?"

"Just wondering," I said lightly. "You've seemed... tense lately."

She didn't respond right away. She took a long sip then set the glass down with exaggerated care. Silence thickened between us. Finally, she spoke, voice pitched lower. "There was a new audit team brought in this week. People I haven't seen before. They're asking a lot of questions."

That was all she gave me. But it was more than I expected. My fork paused. "Audit team?"

She shrugged, pushing couscous around her plate, appetite gone. "They said it was standard. Something about consolidating legacy accounts. Cleaning up numbers. But no one's explaining anything clearly. It just feels... off."

Legacy accounts. Cleaning up numbers. That was exactly how they'd worded her new position when they dragged us back—bookkeeping dressed up as financial consulting. Pretty enough on the outside. Rotten underneath.

And now an audit team shows up? My gut twisted. What if they weren't here to clean anything—just to pin the rot on her and call it done?

"What kind of questions?"

Her gaze snapped up, sharp enough to slice. "Mila."

I blinked. "What? I asked. I didn't say I was going to do anything."

"You need to stay out of this," she murmured, but her eyes didn't soften. "Do you understand me?"

I nodded. But I didn't mean it. Because I could feel it in her voice, in her body—something had shifted. She was scared again.

We finished the meal in silence, plates scraping, the hum of the refrigerator filling the spaces where words should've gone.

Later, I sprawled across my bed with the lights off, my laptop open in front of me, pretending to study. Not that my brain was cooperating. All I could think about was her voice at the table. *Audit team. Legacy accounts. Questions.*

Someone was stirring up dust. Which meant either they were cleaning house… or trying to bury something before it resurfaced.

I opened the encrypted messaging app Luke and I had set up.

Mila: *Mom said a new audit team is digging around old accounts. No names, but she looked spooked. She didn't say it, but I think she's worried. Something's off. We definitely need to talk after the game.*

I hesitated. Then added: *And no more locker chats with Elise unless you want me to burn down your side of the courtyard.*

Three dots appeared instantly.

Luke: *So you were jealous. Noted. Also… you still owe me a thank you for not laughing when you stomped across the quad like a five-foot hurricane.*

Mila: *Keep talking and I'll prove hurricanes do more than stomp.*

Luke: *Already felt it. When you kissed me as if you wanted to drown me the other night.*

My stomach jolted.

Mila: *Careful, King. You'll choke on your own ego.*

Luke: *Not ego. Memory. I can still taste you, Mila. Salt and fire. You didn't seem as if you wanted to stop.*

Heat rushed up my neck. My fingers hovered. Stupid to answer. Stupider not to.

Luke: *I know I didn't.*

Mila: *That was last night.*

Luke: *And tonight?*

I stared at the screen, pulse hammering.

Mila: *Tonight I'm trying to survive calculus.*

Luke: *Liar. You're thinking about me.*

I bit my lip hard enough to sting, but my fingers betrayed me.

Mila: *Delete my number.*

Luke: *Cute. Pretend you don't want me.*

Three dots blinked again, then disappeared. Reappeared. Stalled. As though he had more to say but wasn't sure if he should.

I set the phone down before I could be the one to cave. But the truth had already sunk its claws in. I wanted him, had always wanted him, and pretending otherwise was just another lie waiting to shatter.

CHAPTER SIX

LUKE

There was something about post-practice exhaustion that made truths come easier. Maybe it was the sweat. Or the fatigue. Or the bruises we never talked about. Or maybe it was just the fact that no one wanted to be the first to leave.

The four of us lingered outside my SUV, hockey sticks leaning against the bumper, gear bags dumped on cracked pavement. The lot had mostly cleared, overhead lights buzzing faintly, throwing shadows that made the asphalt look even rougher.

Theo tossed his water bottle into his unzipped bag, the plastic bouncing off a pile of pads. He leaned back against the fender, lazy on the outside, but I knew better—there was always calculation running under the surface with him.

"You gonna say whatever's eating at you?" Chase asked, stretching his long arms overhead, "or just keep pacing trenches in the asphalt?"

I stilled, realizing I had been pacing.

Jax smirked, cracking his knuckles. "Told you. He does that when something's up."

I rubbed the back of my neck then dropped my voice low.

"Dunn Industries is moving. Quiet, steady—funneling assets through shell companies, buying up King Enterprises stock, positioning themselves for something bigger." The words felt heavier out loud than they had in my head, but keeping it to myself wasn't an option anymore. I couldn't keep the guys out of the loop, not when their families were tied to King Enterprises just as tightly as mine. If Dunn was coming for us, they were in the line of fire too. "Doesn't matter if it's side contracts or hidden acquisitions. They're building leverage, and they're doing it under the radar."

That got their attention. Silence stretched, heavy, different. No smirks. No jokes. This was where we stopped being just teammates and became what we really were—sons of the ruling circle, each one of us carrying shadows bigger than our own names.

"All of our families are tied to King Enterprises," I pressed. "You think that makes us safe. But what if it doesn't?"

Jax shifted his stance. "How far is the movement?"

"Far enough," I answered. "And it's not just the properties. Mila told me her mom was brought back for bookkeeping. Old accounts. Legacy ones. Now Dunn's got fresh auditors digging around."

Theo's brows rose, but he didn't crack a joke. He knew what that meant.

"My dad and brother are already circling the wagons. Chase, your dad's on the board, so maybe he's aware. The rest of you?" I shook my head. "I can't say for sure. But Dunn's playing a long game, and if they're buying up King stock, that makes all of us collateral damage whether our families admit it or not."

Chase's jaw flexed, the easy grin gone. He gave a short nod—confirmation.

I turned toward Jax. "Your dad handles contracts for King's construction arm. He'd know if something's shifting with the land grabs."

Jax's eyes narrowed. "He hasn't said anything. Yet."

"Then either he doesn't know," I muttered, "or he's not saying."

Theo's mouth curved wryly. "That's our town, isn't it? Even family only tells you what they want you to know."

"Exactly," I said. "And right now? Dunn's moving under the surface, and Elise is still lurking."

Chase leaned forward, voice lower. "You think she's feeding intel to her dad?"

I shook my head. "She doesn't need to. He moves the pieces —she just plays the role. That's what makes her dangerous."

Theo shifted against the bumper, arms folding tighter. "And that's where Tori comes in."

I nodded once. "She's inside Dunn. She might not have declared a side, but being with you? That puts her in our orbit whether she realizes it or not. And that makes her visible. Exposed. Elise has been watching her closer—as if she's keeping score."

Theo's jaw ticked, the muscle working as he looked away. He didn't argue.

"She's got a weakness where you're concerned," I pressed. "That's leverage. Use it."

Theo's head came back around, eyes narrowing a fraction. Not denial. Not agreement. Just that guarded middle ground that said he'd already thought about it. Or maybe that flicker in his eyes meant something else was going on that he wasn't ready to put into words.

I caught it. The way his jaw tightened a moment too long, the way his shoulders pulled back as if bracing for a hit that hadn't landed yet. Not about Dunn. Not about Elise. This was Tori. And Theo.

I didn't press. Not here. But I filed it away. Whatever Theo thought he was keeping casual, it wasn't. Not anymore.

"You want me to push," he muttered.

"I want her to choose," I corrected. "Not drift. Not dodge. Make a decision—and make it with her eyes open. With you, not against you."

Chase gave a low whistle, leaning on his stick. "Guess that means you've got homework, Theo. Hope you brought your charm."

Theo shot him a look, but it was without his usual edge.

Jax cracked his knuckles. "Just don't shove too hard. Push someone like Tori, you risk snapping the line instead of pulling her in."

Theo's mouth twitched, the ghost of a smirk. "I know what I'm doing."

But the way he said it—clipped, deliberate—told me he wasn't talking to us. He was trying to convince himself.

"I want you to keep that door open," I said. "Not just about Elise. About Dunn. New hires. Visitors. Security. Anything. Even whispers."

Theo's eyes stayed steady, but his tone carried weight. "And what if she won't talk?"

"Then you get creative," I said evenly.

His jaw flexed again. "She talks to me more than anyone. But don't confuse that with leverage."

I held his stare. "I'm not. I'm asking you to listen."

The silence that followed wasn't just about strategy. Chase's gaze slid toward Theo, measuring. Jax shifted too, catching the tension.

Theo kept his expression even, but his shoulders stayed rigid, arms locked too tight at his sides. "It's just information," he muttered at last. Then, quieter: "For now."

For now.

Jax gave a low whistle, half-smirk tugging his mouth. "Sounds as if you've got your own angle, my guy."

Theo didn't rise to it, just stared past him at the dark line of trees beyond the lot. Which said more than words.

I let it drop—for now.

Chase rubbed the back of his neck, gaze drifting as Jax shifted beside him, arms crossed tight. The crackle between them wasn't about Dunn or Elise. I saw it in the way Chase's jaw tightened—and in the way Jax hadn't bothered hiding where his attention kept landing earlier that afternoon.

Avery had caught up with Mila outside school before practice, blond hair flashing in the sun as she laughed at something Mila said. Jax's gaze had tracked her more than once, and Chase had seen it.

Now the silence stretched, heavy with the argument neither of them was ready to have.

This wasn't a conversation I wanted to light on fire tonight. Not with Dunn circling. Not with Elise playing shadow games. We needed to close ranks, not fracture them.

Chase cleared his throat, breaking the silence. "So… Mila."

Theo smirked faintly. "Trading secrets or trading tension?"

Jax's grin tugged, all sharp edges. "Enemies to something."

I rolled my shoulders, letting it slide. "Not enemies. Not a couple either. Just… complicated."

"That was the question," Chase murmured.

"And that's the answer."

We stayed longer, hashing out details—Theo confirming he'd keep his angle with Tori, Jax agreeing to watch for whispers through his dad's contacts. Chase offered to filter what he overheard at home—his dad never kept his phone calls quiet, and sometimes boardroom talk spilled into the living room whether Chase wanted it or not. It wasn't a plan, not fully. But it was enough to make sure none of us were blind.

I drove home, mind whirling. By the time I pulled in, the night had settled heavy around the house. I cut the engine, stepped out, and leaned against the SUV, gear bag digging into my shoulder. The tinted glass threw my reflection back at me—tired eyes, bruised cheek, jaw wired tight. Mila's necklace still burned in my memory, silver star at her throat. Not mine. Not yet. But there.

Headlights swept the drive. Drew's car rolled in, tires humming low over concrete. He killed the engine, climbed out, and shut the door in one sharp motion.

"Getting in late?" I asked, shifting the bag higher. "Something going on at work?"

He didn't bother with small talk. Instead, he crossed the distance and clapped a hand to my shoulder as he passed. "Nothing you need to worry about." His chin flicked toward the bag, hockey carved into every line of me. "Keep your head in the game. Coaches are watching; college is next. Stay focused. I'll deal with the family crap."

My jaw flexed, but I let it ride. He was right. The business wasn't something I wanted, but he did. He kept moving, shoes scuffing toward the porch, his words affecting me more than I wanted to admit. He made it sound simple. Hockey, coaches, college. But my life didn't split that clean anymore—not with Dunn hovering, not with Mila in the middle of it.

My phone buzzed.

Mila: *You still standing around the parking lot brooding, or did you finally go home?*

A smirk broke across my mouth. She didn't need to text. It wasn't about strategy. This was... casual. Dangerous in its own way.

Me: *Depends. You watching me from the shadows?*

Three dots blinked, then—

Mila: *Please. If I was watching, you would never know.*

I shook my head then shoved a bag into the backseat.

Me: *So you admit you think about watching me.*

Pause.

Mila: *Don't flatter yourself. Just making sure Elise isn't glued to your side again.*

The smirk widened.

Me: *Jealousy looks good on you.*

Another pause. Longer this time. Then—

Mila: *Next time you talk to Tori, I want to be there.*

Me: *Jealous and bossy. Noted.*

Mila: *Occupied. By you. Don't make me regret it.*

The screen glowed in my hand, the words hitting deep enough to carve their place. My chest tightened.

Me: *You won't.*

The screen dimmed, but her words still lingered.

Scouts and boardrooms couldn't touch me the way she could. And that made her the bigger risk.

Not a couple. Not enemies. But definitely a problem.

CHAPTER SEVEN

MILA

The moment my mom slid the cream-colored envelope across the table, I knew something was off.

She didn't say a word at first. Just sipped her coffee, nails tapping against the counter as if the rhythm could fool me into thinking this was a normal Tuesday. But her posture told on her —too stiff, too controlled.

I stared down at the Blackwood Academy seal pressed into the flap. Raised lettering. Heavy cardstock. A letter that carried both expectation and dread.

"What is this?" My voice came out flat, already braced.

Her lips pressed together before she answered. "It's a committee assignment. You've been asked to help plan this year's charity gala."

I blinked. "By who? And why do you have it?"

"A few of the parent sponsors." Her words were even, but her shoulders ticked tighter. "It's a joint effort this year—Dunn Industries and King Enterprises are co-hosting." She paused then added with forced lightness, "Someone in HR reached out. My boss made it clear it wasn't optional. They want me involved. And you too."

My stomach dipped. Why me? Why now? The second both names hit the air, every instinct screamed set-up. This wasn't coincidence. It was placement. I leaned back, eyes narrowing. "So I was asked... or told?"

Her silence was all the answer I needed.

This wasn't a choice. It was a calculated move. And it had been decided without either of us in the room.

"It's expected," she said finally. Her voice softened but not enough to hide the tension in it. "And it's good optics. For both of us."

There it was. She didn't have to say the rest—I heard it anyway. We weren't invited. We were maneuvered. Back in Blackwood on terms. Don't break them.

The envelope sat on the counter long after I left the kitchen, its weight still dragging at me through the morning. School passed in a blur I barely registered. Teachers droned. Notes filled margins. Whispers floated. I went through the motions, but my head wasn't in any of it.

Every glance felt loaded, every hallway too narrow. I couldn't shake the thought that this was another chess move— Dunn and the Kings dragging me onto a stage I didn't ask for, pulling strings through my mom until I danced by default.

By lunch, I'd already rehearsed three different ways to get out of it. Pretend sick. Claim overcommitment. Ignore the invite entirely. Each one unraveled the second I thought it through. There was no way out—not without consequences.

So by the time the committee met after school, all I had left was resolve.

The conference room reeked of perfume and catered cookies, the kind someone thought passed as "hospitality." A long, polished table stretched down the center, lined with stacks of papers and clipboards—and little branded tote bags stuffed with glossy brochures and overpriced floral samples, proof that even charity came gilded in Blackwood.

Tori sat near the middle, fidgeting with her pen until it clicked. Quinn, one of Elise's outliers, leaned forward, eager and bright-eyed as though she was auditioning for extra credit. Stefanie, puppet number two, twirled her dirty-blond shoulder-length hair, her expression flat with boredom. Two other girls giggled and scrolled through their phones at the end.

And at the head of it all was Elise Dunn. Front and center. Smiling as though her exile had never happened. As though she hadn't been iced out recently for crossing lines no one should've. Elise thrived on second chances she didn't deserve, and somehow, she always slithered back in before the door slammed shut.

Her eyes landed on me instantly. "Oh. Mila." Her smile spread slow, deliberate, saccharine dripping from every syllable. "Surprised to see you here."

I didn't bite. I just took the clipboard one of the moms slid across the table and scanned it. Venue. Tables. Décor. PR. Entertainment. My name wasn't listed. Not once.

I raised a brow, the corner of my mouth tightening. When I looked up, Tori's gaze darted away, Quinn pressed her lips tight, and Stefanie smirked. Elise was already leaning forward, tapping her pen against the table like she was chairing the whole thing, talking over one of the moms about how the silent auction should be structured. Acting as if this was her committee to run. Acting as though her social status had been restored.

That was enough. "Elise," I said, tone cool, deliberate. "I thought I was supposed to be part of this committee."

She blinked, faux innocence painted across her face. "Really? Huh. That must've been an oversight."

"Convenient one."

Her head tilted, glossy hair catching the light—weaponizing charm in motion. "Don't look at me. Maybe people just don't like you."

My grip tightened on the clipboard until the edge cut into my palm. Rage rippled beneath my skin, begging to be unleashed. But I didn't flip the table, didn't storm out. Not here. This wasn't just sabotage. This was a message.

So I sat. I listened. I pretended to take notes while Elise dictated centerpieces and Quinn scribbled silent auction ideas. Every laugh Elise let out made the coil inside me wind tighter.

By the time I walked out, I knew two things: Elise had her claws back in. And she wasn't going to stop until she buried me.

***

The fallout started before first bell the next morning.

My phone buzzed. Unknown number. No contact photo. Just a message: *Bold move talking shit to the wrong people. Screenshots don't lie.*

Cold slid down my spine. My thumb hovered over the screen, pulse hammering. Screenshots? Of what? For one beat, I almost didn't open it—as if not looking could keep it from being real.

Then I tapped. Attached was a screenshot. My face in the DM header. The message:

Quinn's such a try-hard. Can't she take a hint and shut up?

I froze. Not because I believed it, but because I knew everyone else would.

Another buzz.

Stefanie's nothing but a knockoff. Wish she'd get the memo.

Then another.

Avery only hangs with me because she needs someone to make her look better.

Each one burned hotter than the last.

By the time I reached the locker bay, my phone wouldn't stop buzzing—pings stacking one after another as screenshots flew. Girls forwarding them. Group chats lighting up. By the time I shoved it into my pocket, the damage was already every-where. The screenshots made it look as though I'd trashed repu-tations. Sent threats. Spread lies. Elise's name was carefully absent from every single one.

The whispers started before I even rounded the corner. Several pairs of eyes cut toward me, wide then narrowing. Conversations dropped low, punctuated by stifled laughter. A group by the lockers broke into quiet giggles, one girl holding her phone out as a spotlight, angling it so I would see. My face glared back at me from the screen.

My jaw locked. Fury burned low and steady. Not fear. Not shame. Rage.

I shoved my books into my locker harder than necessary, the clang echoing. If Elise thought this would make me crumble, she hadn't learned a damn thing.

But the circle tightened anyway. Girls pressed closer. "Guess she thinks she's untouchable again. Some people never learn."

One of them reached out, nails catching the light—claws aiming for my arm.

"Hey." Luke's voice sliced through the noise. He didn't shout, but every head turned.

And then he stepped in beside me, tall, steady, all command.

"If any of you believe that crap," he said, calm but edged in steel, "you're dumber than I thought."

The silence was immediate. They froze then peeled away one by one, unwilling to meet my eyes.

I exhaled slow, the rage still simmering in my chest. I wanted to swing back on my own. I didn't need saving.

Luke's eyes locked on mine. "You good?"

"I'm pissed," I said flatly.

The corner of his mouth tugged upward. "Better answer."

We moved farther away from some of the students. When we stopped, he was a few feet away. Not touching but close enough I could feel the heat rolling off him.

I tilted my head back, staring up at the sky until the words scraped out of me. "I don't need a knight. I need someone who won't throw me to the wolves." My throat burned. I knew I was lashing out, but I couldn't stop myself.

His voice came low, steady. Softer, but heavier for it. "I'm trying to be both."

That made me look at him. His eyes didn't waver. He meant it. Every word. And that was the problem. Because I believed him. And believing him was worse than doubting—because if he broke that promise, it wouldn't just hurt. It would gut me, the way it had my mom when trust turned into blood on the blacktop.

The star charm at my throat pressed heavy against my skin, a reminder of every promise we'd whispered under the stars. No secrets. No power plays. No running.

But promises didn't survive long in Blackwood. They broke. They shattered. And this one was already bleeding at the edges. Because Dunn Industries was circling. Because Elise wasn't finished. Because the Kings had their own secrets—and Luke was tangled in all of them.

This wasn't strategy anymore. It wasn't even just survival. It was him. It was me. It was dangerous.

CHAPTER EIGHT

LUKE

By sixth period, Elise's little rumor campaign was already bleeding out. Blackwood never ran on truth—it thrived on perception. And Elise had bet wrong on who still owned the school.

It started with Jax. Loud enough for half the row behind him to hear, he leaned back in AP Physics and asked Mr. Carson if a phone's IP address could be faked. He didn't even wait for the answer before muttering, "Guess it's easy for burner accounts and petty girls to look the same," his eyes sliding to Elise's table.

The ripple started there.

By lunch, Chase dropped into the senior group chat with a gem: *Crazy how the fake DMs stopped sounding like Mila halfway through. Someone forgot to keep the insults specific.* He even added a shrug emoji. Subtle as a hammer.

Phones buzzed across the tables—one ping, then another, then a flood. Screens lit up. Heads bent low, whispers spiking as the messages ricocheted through the room.

The cafeteria erupted in noise and whispers, the story spreading faster than anyone could stop it. No one cared about fake screenshots anymore. They were too busy picking apart Elise's history with surgical precision—every cover-up, every spin job, every stitch in her airbrushed life suddenly fair game.

Later, drifting through the hallway, Theo sealed it. He let it drop for anyone listening, "Didn't Elise disappear sophomore year? What was the excuse that time? Nose job or leadership retreat? Hard to keep the cover stories straight."

Mila's name? Already dropped from conversation.

I waited until the courtyard thinned and Elise sat alone at one of the stone benches, stabbing at her salad as if it might fight back. The stone looked too polished, too pristine—like everything in Blackwood, perfection on the surface, hiding the cracks underneath.

Her friends had scattered. Even Nina. That told me more than anything else.

She spotted me immediately. "Here to gloat?"

I stopped in front of her, shadow spilling across the table. "No. I'm here to warn you."

Her mouth curled tight. "You think you've won something?"

"I'm not playing a game," I said evenly. "You are."

She tilted her head, her usual smugness creeping back in. "People forget fast. Mila's still the girl who left without notice and then waltzed back in. You didn't exactly welcome her with open arms, Luke—so don't act like she belongs."

I leaned forward, voice low. "You ever wonder what would happen if people found out why you disappeared sophomore year? The truth. Not the nose job excuse. Not the retreat."

Her fork froze. Everyone knew Elise had vanished sophomore year, but no one knew why.

"Remember your roommate?" I asked. "The one who couldn't handle what she saw—the cracks behind your perfect mask? I don't need to invent anything." My voice dropped as I leaned in, steady and biting. "I just have to remind people that perfection doesn't mean untouchable."

Her throat worked, but she forced the words out anyway. "You wouldn't."

I bent closer, the words a blade. "Try me again. Touch Mila—publicly or privately—and I'll show you what happens when everyone finally sees the cracks you hide."

She gripped her phone as though it might save her. "You think this makes you strong? Blackmailing me?"

"No." I straightened. "This is me protecting someone who's done being your punching bag."

Her composure faltered—just for a second. That was enough. I left her sitting there, nails digging into her palm, pretending she wasn't shaken.

Logan passed as I stepped into the hall, laughing with a couple teammates, voice too loud on purpose. His eyes cut sideways, smirk crooked, like he'd been waiting to see if I'd bite. I didn't. Not here. Not with an audience.

Theo waited near the back wall by the gym, hands shoved in his hoodie, eyes tracking me.

"She gonna crawl under a rock now?"

"Hopefully."

He smirked, tilting his head. "Tori's cousin was her roommate in the treatment clinic back then. That's how I heard it."

My jaw ticked, but I didn't engage.

"She's been carrying that secret a while," Theo added. "She looked wrecked walking out of there."

"Good. Can Elise get to Tori through her cousin?"

Theo shifted. "Tori's pulling back from her, but she hasn't torched the bridge. Elise might still try."

"And you?"

He gave a short laugh, but it didn't hide the tension in his jaw. "Don't start."

"You like Tori." Not a question. A fact. "Make sure it doesn't become about that. She's still straddling sides."

Theo muttered something under his breath, but I let it go.

This wasn't just about Elise. This was about all of us. About Dunn positioning themselves to bleed King stock dry. About my dad and brother circling, trying to lock down shares before the floor dropped. About Mila—back here under a leash she didn't choose, her mom's job already tangled up in the mess.

Protecting the company mattered—but protecting her mattered more. King Enterprises could survive a hit. I wasn't sure I could survive losing her again.

I leaned against the gym wall, closing my eyes for a second. The cost of choosing her over everything else pressed down heavier than any practice bruise. I'd held back when every part of me wanted to pull her closer. I'd chosen her safety over the one thing I wanted most.

And still—when the gym went quiet, when no one was watching—I let myself wonder. Did I still love her? Did I deserve her—after everything? Or was I just setting myself up to break when she left again?

The thought gutted me. Because the truth was, I wasn't afraid of Elise. Or Dunn. Or even my father. I was terrified of losing Mila a second time.

Later, by the lot, I stood next to my SUV and watched her leave the building. She didn't see me. Didn't see the way the star necklace caught the last edge of sunlight, silver bright against her throat. A reminder she was still tethered to me—but not mine. Not anymore. Not until it was safe for us to be together.

My phone buzzed in my pocket. It was a message from her, no name attached—just the encrypted app we'd set up.

Mila: *You looked way too pleased with yourself in sixth period. Try not to enjoy being right too much.*

A grin broke across my mouth before I could stop it.

Me: *Watching me now? Should I be flattered?*

Three dots appeared. Then:

Mila: *Don't flatter yourself. You're just hard to miss—and impossible to ignore.*

I typed back, fingers hovering for half a second before hitting send.

Me: *Good. Don't miss me.*

Her reply didn't come right away. But when it did, my chest tightened.

Mila: *I won't.*

I slipped the phone back into my pocket, the echo of her words humming through me long after she was gone.

Not together. Not apart. Tangled somewhere in the middle —dangerous territory. And I was already in too deep to crawl out.

CHAPTER NINE

MILA

The day had been a wildfire of bullshit rumors—snaps of laughter in the halls, Elise tossing shade until half the school was running with it.

And Avery—she'd been dragged into it too.

By the last bell, my skull ached from the constant static of it all. Avery and I walked side by side down the corridor, backpacks dragging at our shoulders, straps slipping as we made our way toward the lockers.

"People suck," she muttered, spinning her lock with more force than necessary. "You would think they'd get bored."

I leaned against the cool metal next to her. "The fake DMs—they're not buying that crap, right?"

Her mouth twisted. "Some are. Some aren't. Doesn't matter. Once it's out there…"

"Hey." I touched her arm, waiting until her eyes met mine. "I get that it hurts—what they're saying, the way things have been. But it matters. None of that noise is who you are. And anyone who really knows you gets that."

Her throat worked, and for a second, I thought she would

deflect. But then she whispered, "It still feels gross. Like they got inside my phone."

Anger sparked low. "What did your brother do when he saw it?"

Avery finally cracked a small smile. "Yelled loud enough to scare half the football team. He wanted Elise to regret ever touching my name."

"And Jax?"

She shook her head, tucking a strand of hair behind her ear. "Didn't say much. Just sat with me. That was… enough."

"And Chase didn't have a problem with Jax hanging around you?" I asked carefully. If Jax had been there for her, I hoped Chase had noticed—and maybe started to accept them.

Her eyes flickered, almost relieved. "He wasn't as mad as I thought. Still pissed, but… he didn't get in the way. That has to count for something."

It did. More than something. My chest ached for her—for how fast confidence could be cut down by a lie and how slow it was to build it back again.

I should've said more—told her she didn't have to face it alone. But the weight of my own day pressed too hard, the endless spin of Elise's games tightening around my ribs.

So instead, I said, "I think I'm going to go home. Screw the committee."

Avery gave a half-snort, slamming her locker shut. "Best idea you've had all week."

Maybe she was right. My feet carried me toward the exit, intent on disappearing before anyone could drag me back in.

That was when my phone buzzed.

Mom: *You're back on the committee. Don't argue. Go straight to the meeting. It'll be "corrected."*

I stopped outside the school, arms folded, staring at the concrete walkway like it might tell me what to do. Confront Elise again? Walk away completely?

The message glowed in my hand, insistent. *Corrected.* As though this wasn't sabotage at all. Like this wasn't Elise. I didn't reply. I just turned around and walked back inside.

The conference room on the east side of campus was already filling up. Long tables lined the space, surrounded by flawless hair, staged smiles, and the hum of curated laughter.

And there was Elise—perched dead center, a pageant queen in perfect control, binder open, pen in hand. A real hostess moment, perfectly polished. Until she saw me.

Her expression didn't crack. But her grip on the pen did. The plastic bent, a quick snap that only I caught. Panic flickered before she smothered it under the practiced tilt of her chin. Rage simmered in the twitch of her jaw.

Before she could open her mouth, one of the school board liaisons breezed in with a grin plastered across her face. "Oh, Mila! Yes, we've got you now—let me just fix this." She handed me a packet as though it were nothing. "There we go. That was supposed to be corrected earlier."

Corrected. Again. As if we were pawns being shifted, not people with choices.

I didn't miss the vein throbbing in Elise's temple. Neither did Quinn, who dropped her gaze fast, as if she stared at the table hard enough, she could vanish through it.

"That's fine," Elise said at last, her voice tight, smooth veneer stretched too thin. "We can still assign her something… light."

The liaison clapped her hands together, beaming as though we'd solved world hunger. "Programs and welcome table. It's not flashy, but it keeps her in the loop."

Not flashy. Translation: harmless. Forgettable. Easy to erase.

Elise didn't answer.

The meeting dragged anyway—an endless parade of posturing about tablecloth colors and sponsor shout-outs, voices pitched just loud enough to sound important. I stopped listening after five minutes.

Instead, I flipped my packet over and let my pencil wander. The eucalyptus trees outside the window caught my eye, branches bent under the ocean wind. Sharp lines for the leaves. A twist of trunk. Anything to drown out the drone of Elise's perfect diction.

By the time someone motioned for adjournment, half the page was filled with rough outlines of the world beyond the glass—messy, alive, real.

I took my time packing up, not in a rush to trail after their weekend-party gossip. So I lingered, dragging my feet. The quiet stretched—and that was when I heard it. Elise's voice just around the corner.

"No, you don't understand. She shouldn't even be here. I handled it. I—" A pause. "Yes, Mr. Langley, but—" Another beat. Then: "Fine. But if this backfires, don't say I didn't warn you."

The name sliced through me. *Langley*. Darren Langley—my mom's boyfriend, the VP at King Enterprises—lying in a pool of blood. The image tore through me.

I froze in the doorway, pulse skittering. The chill that went through me had nothing to do with the draft sneaking in from the cracked window at the end of the hall. My fingers went numb around the strap of my bag. It couldn't be. I'd seen the body too. But my mother's voice from that night whispered through my mind. *Don't look. Just go.*

I slipped out the side exit before Elise could spot me.

My hands shook as I typed before I could overthink it: *Need to talk. Tonight.*

No reply. Which meant hockey. Which meant I had hours to kill and nowhere I wanted to be.

I didn't go home. I drove straight to the beach instead. I parked by the boardwalk, bought a coffee, and walked until the sky bruised into vibrant reds, pinks, oranges, and gold. The crash of waves almost drowned out the echo in my head. *Mr. Langley*. Over and over.

I kicked off my shoes and sank into the chilly sand, sketchbook balanced on my knees. The pages curled in the damp air, pencil dragging too heavy across the paper. Even the gulls circling overhead came out wrong—jagged, broken, stripped of grace. I stared at the mess of lines until my coffee went cold beside me, forgotten.

When my phone finally buzzed, the boardwalk lights had flickered on, and my throat felt raw from the briny air.

Luke: *I'm starving. Grabbing food for us. Meet me on the roof.*

I stared at the screen, an eyebrow arching on instinct.

Me: *You trying to impress me or bribe me?*

His reply came fast.

Luke: *Can't it be both?*

The rooftop didn't feel like a battleground tonight. It felt... quieter. Safer. A place that remembered us but didn't care what we'd done to ruin it.

We spread the boxes between us, cross-legged on the blanket he'd laid out, ocean wind pulling at loose strands of my hair. The smell of pizza and fries rose warm between us, cutting through the air.

"Still order the same thing?" I asked, peeking inside.

"Half pepperoni, half plain. And fries."

"You don't order fries with pizza."

He shrugged, unapologetic. "No, you don't. I do. And you steal them anyway."

Heat crept up my neck. "That was—"

"Every time." He shoved the carton toward me. "Don't pretend you won't."

I stole one on principle. "Old habits."

His smirk deepened, but he didn't push.

We ate in that same easy rhythm, familiar enough to hurt. Until I told him about the meeting. About the liaison, the "correction," Elise's reaction, and finally, the call.

He froze mid-reach, tension bleeding into the air when I said it. "Langley?"

"Mr. Langley," I clarified. "That's how she said it. No first name."

His eyes narrowed. "Not a coincidence."

My pulse stumbled. "You think Darren's not dead?"

The pizza crust bent in my hand. For a second the rooftop blurred with the possibility of it as I was hurdled back to the night Mom and I'd left town in a hurry.

I'd spotted Mom first—dark hair spilling down her back. Then my eyes caught the prone man on the ground. Limbs bent wrong. Blood spreading. My breath snagged, a scream clawing up my throat.

Mom spun, eyes locking on mine. In two strides, her hand was tight over my mouth. "Not a sound," she hissed. "We have to move."

My pulse pounded so loud it drowned the distant hum of traffic. My knees trembled, barely holding me up.

Because I knew who it was—Darren. The guy Mom had been dating. The VP at King Enterprises. The man whose lifeless eyes—eyes I'd seen crinkle in laughter just weeks ago—stared past us into nothing.

"Mila." My name carried a sharp panic that cut through the fog in my head. I tore my gaze from Darren's face and locked on hers.

"Go. Now. Get in your car and move. I'll meet you at the house."

I ran. Breath scraping, hands white-knuckled on the wheel, headlights blurring into static.

When I skidded into the driveway, she was right behind me. Her car door shut. The front door was open before I'd even killed the engine.

"Pack," she snapped. "Everything. Just move."

"What? No. We need to call the cops—"

"No cops." Her voice cracked like a whip.

"But we didn't do anything—"

Her gray-green eyes locked on mine. "It will come back to us. The people who did this—they'll put it on us. They will make sure we take the fall."

I blinked, pulling myself back from that night where we'd seen more than we should've. The cool air bit into my lungs. Luke was watching me, steady, silent.

"There was a body," I whispered. "I saw it. My mom said not to say anything. We left that night. The blood..." My throat closed. "I don't see how he could've survived that."

Luke didn't flinch. His voice was quiet, grounded. "I believe you. But I'm still going to find out for sure."

I searched his face. "How?"

"I've got a PI. Not one of my father's. He's clean. I used him when you disappeared."

The words hit deeper than I wanted them to. "You... tried to find me?"

He didn't answer. But he didn't need to. The truth was written in the way his gaze held mine.

The silence stretched, heavy but not suffocating.

Finally, I leaned forward, my shoulder brushing his. "I know what you did today. With Elise. The school flipped fast, and that wasn't luck."

He gave a half-shrug. "She tried to humiliate you. I reminded her why she shouldn't."

"Still." My eyes dropped to the grease stain on the box then back to him. "Thank you."

His jaw flexed, but his eyes softened. "Forget owing me. Protecting you isn't up for debate."

The words twisted in me. I shook my head. "I don't want you fighting my battles."

He tipped his chin, gaze unwavering. "Maybe I want to."

My chest tightened. Because that was the danger—leaning

on him the way Mom leaned on men in boardrooms and back rooms, always trading one kind of power for another. I couldn't let myself become her, no matter how much I wanted to lean into him now.

I shifted forward, nudging the food boxes aside with my knee until they slid sideways along the blanket. The smell of hot grease tangled between us as I leaned across the space. Then his breath met mine—steady, warm, and maddeningly patient.

I brushed my lips across his slow enough to feel the catch of his exhale. Not like the last time—when it was all fury and desperation, a collision more than anything. This one was slower. Intentional. I savored his taste, memorized his response. The kind of kiss that dared to linger.

His breath hitched against mine, warm and steady. His hand slid up to my cheek, calloused thumb brushing the skin as if he was memorizing it. My fingers trailed down to his wrist, to the steady pulse thrumming beneath. The warmth of him pressed through his clothes, seeping into my skin. His other arm curved around my waist, anchoring me closer, pulling me past the boxes until there was nothing between us but heat.

The world narrowed to breath and touch and the taste of him. Every time I thought he'd pull back, he deepened the kiss just slightly—enough to remind me that restraint didn't mean distance. His thumb brushed the corner of my mouth when he finally broke away, and I caught his breath on my lower lip, the faint tremor beneath the calm.

We were still figuring out what we were. But in that moment, nothing felt broken—only inevitable.

I rested my head on his shoulder. The stars were bright above us, unbothered by the secrets shifting below. His warmth bled into me, steadying the tremor in my chest.

I slid off his lap until I was next to him, leaning against his side and stealing his warmth. His arm tightened, drawing me in until the world settled around the rhythm of our pulse.

We finished the food in silence, his shoulder solid under my cheek, the wind tugging at my hair. For the first time in too long, the quiet felt safe.

We didn't move for a while, the remainder of food cooling in front of us, the night air damp against my skin. Finally, Luke shifted, brushing his thumb once more over my cheek before he let me go.

Reluctantly, I sat back, fingers skimming the edge of the pizza box. "Guess we should clean this up before the seagulls declare war."

He huffed a laugh, low and tired, and started stacking the box and empty fry carton. I gathered the napkins, our water bottles, anything to keep my hands moving when all I wanted was to stay pressed against him.

We stood at the same time, arms bumping as we crossed over to the stairwell door. He pushed it open and went first, glancing back once to make sure I was there. I was. Step by step, sneakers scuffing concrete, the rooftop slipped away above us, and he walked me to my car.

"Drive safe," he said, quiet, as though the words carried more weight than they should.

I smiled, small but real. "Only if you promise not to eat all the fries next time."

His laugh was low, rough in his chest, and when I leaned in again, the second kiss came easier. Slower. A seal instead of a slow spark. A promise neither of us named.

I gathered my sketchbook, his gaze following every move, and headed for my car. He leaned against the side of his, sleeves shoved up, looking as if he belonged to the night itself. I glanced back once, memorizing the way the shadows caught on his jaw, before I slid behind the wheel.

The drive home blurred—streetlights streaking past, his taste on my lips, the ghost of his hand steady on my skin.

When I pulled into the driveway, another set of headlights

swept across the gravel behind me. My mom's sedan. She must've worked late again; the smell of Dunn's offices would still be clinging to her. Or maybe she'd been out with Principal Miller—the same dinners and evenings that kept my scholarship paid up and my place at Blackwood intact.

We stepped out of our cars at the same time. The silence stretched, thick as the coastal fog. Finally, I said, "Who called to get me reinstated?"

Her fingers tightened around her keys. "It doesn't matter who."

"It matters to me."

Her mouth pressed thin. "It's someone you don't want attention from."

Silence settled between us. She didn't explain. I didn't push. I wasn't sure if she was protecting me—or herself. The night pressed in, thick with questions I wasn't sure I wanted answered.

CHAPTER TEN

LUKE

Mila's words from the roof still scraped raw—Langley bleeding out, her mom panicking, and then them ran because they thought they were next.

I waited until after dinner to approach my dad. Timing mattered with him. Push too early and he would swat me away with, "I have calls." Push too late and he would already be wound tight from the day, more difficult to read under the weight of it.

He'd retreated to his office as usual, phone in one hand and the glow of three monitors painting the mahogany desk blue. The whole room was slick, expensive, and cold.

The boardwalk studio kept circling my thoughts. First Langley disappears. Now the one space Mila ever claimed gets flipped overnight. Different moves, same pattern—erase the past, rewrite the future. My dad was good at that.

Drew had let it slip that morning—casual, as if it was nothing. *Leased.* A restaurant group out of L.A. Better profit margins than the studio had ever pulled. And for Dad, it was about the bottom line.

But it wasn't just numbers. It was Mila's sanctuary.

I leaned into the doorway, my shoulder hitting the wood. "You said the boardwalk studio wasn't being touched."

He didn't look up. "And?"

"It was just leased. Lorne told me recently it was coming, but you swore it wasn't."

A microscopic pause. Then he turned his head, phone still in his hand. "And?"

"Now it's official. Signed off. A restaurant group out of L.A." I crossed my arms. "Better margins than a studio. That's the line, right?"

His jaw ticked. Almost a smile. Almost not. "You've been busy."

"You said we were keeping it."

He set his phone down harder than necessary, the plastic knock abrupt against the desk. "And then I changed my mind." No apology. No reason.

"Why now?" I kept my voice even. "That building wasn't just another property. You told me it was good for the community. We were keeping it."

"Plans change."

"Not without a reason. You went back on your word—what happens to everything inside? The artwork, the history—you just erase it?"

His gaze sharpened, expression flat. "It doesn't matter. End of story." He stood. Slow. Deliberate. His shoulders settled into the posture that killed dissent in boardrooms, radiating *don't push me* without raising his voice. "Back off, Luke. You're playing with fire you don't understand."

The mask slipped for half a second. It wasn't rage or fear—it was colder, control stretched thin. And beneath it all, the edge of guilt. Except my father didn't do guilt. He did pressure points.

"Your fixation," he went on, eyes cutting, "on Mila. On her

family. It's clouding your judgment." A beat. "She's not your future."

The worst part was—he wasn't wrong. In my father's world, Mila could never be my future. She was a risk, a liability, a flaw in the dynasty he was so desperate to cement. But she was also the only thing I wanted that wasn't carved from his blueprint. And if that meant rebellion, I would lead the fucking charge.

Heat flared through my chest. I locked it down. He wanted me to snap. To prove his point. I didn't give him that. I kept my jaw tight. Eyes steady.

When the lack of reaction bored him, he picked up his phone again, dismissing me without saying the word. Conversation over.

I found Drew out back twenty minutes later, leaning on the low stone wall by the pool. His tie was half-loosened, the phone in his hand glowing like he needed a pulse under his thumb.

I didn't sit. "You told me this morning the lease went through."

His eyes flicked up, taking me in. "Let me guess—you already hit Dad about it. Brave."

"Save me the commentary." My arms folded. "Why'd he change his mind?"

Drew slid the phone into his pocket with a sigh. "The new lease is lucrative. Lorne handled the paperwork. Simple as that."

"Better margins don't make him change his mind overnight. Figure out what." Restaurants moved cash faster than canvases. Easier to pad numbers, easier to clean books with volume.

His brow lifted, lazy. "Why me?"

"Because Dad won't tell me. And you've got more access than I do."

Drew leaned back casually on his hands. "And what exactly am I supposed to be digging for?"

"The reason why," I said flatly. "He promised it was staying. What changed?"

Something flashed in his gaze, but it was gone before I could fully take note of it.

He covered it with a twitch of his mouth. Not a smile. Not agreement either. "Fine. I'll poke around. Quietly."

But it seemed too easy. Drew never made anything easy unless there was something in it for him.

"Lorne signed the authorizations?" I asked.

He tipped his head. "If it's a lease, it runs through him. I'll see what paper he buried with it."

"Do that."

We held the stare another second. He looked away first.

Later, I sat in my SUV with the engine off. The driveway was hemmed in by dark hedges and fog.

I opened the glove box and pulled out a fresh burner phone. My thumb hovered a second before dialing a number that I hadn't touched in almost a year.

Marcus Vega. Private investigator. Ex-cop who'd walked off the force with more enemies than friends. Not polished. Not political. That was why I'd kept his number. Because when he dug, he didn't stop for the people who thought they were untouchable.

The line clicked alive on the second ring. Silence. Then a low voice, professional but edged with street: "Who is this?"

"Luke King."

A pause. The faint scrape of breath. "This about the girl again?"

"No," I said flatly. "Something else. Possible relocation. Maybe death. Either way, it was covered up."

"Go on."

"Name's Darren Langley. Former VP at King Enterprises. Disappeared a year ago. I want what really happened to him— and who paid to make it vanish."

Another pause. Then: "Timeline?"

"Yesterday."

Another small silence, as if he was weighing me. "Anyone else know you're digging?"

"No. And it stays that way. Especially from my family."

"Understood." A beat. "You'll hear from me when I have something."

The line went dead.

I leaned back into the leather and stared at the houses generously spaced beyond the driveway, their windows glowing against the dark, the lies loud in my head.

Dad was lying. Drew was evasive. And the boardwalk studio—the one place that was supposed to be left intact for the community but really for Mila—was gone.

It hadn't even been my father's vision. It was mine. An idea he'd once pretended to back, selling it as civic goodwill when it was the only thing I'd asked him to protect.

Now it was another deal on paper. Another promise broken.

Sophomore year, after practice, Mila and I had cut across the boardwalk, skates still clacking from where I'd had them slung over my shoulder. The air had tasted of salt and sugar, funnel cake oil turning the wind sweet. She'd stopped at the corner lot—the shuttered building with the peeling blue trim and sun-bleached sign. And in the window, another sign that read for lease.

"What would you put in there?" she'd asked, hair in her mouth from the wind, pencil already out as though the answer was supposed to be sketched, not spoken.

"Smoothie shop," I'd thrown out.

Her unguarded laugh hit me dead center. "You? Blending fruit for tourists?"

"Better than another T-shirt store."

She'd stepped closer to the glass, breath fogging a small circle. "Art gallery."

"Wouldn't make a dime," I muttered.

"Too perfect," she murmured back, eyes on the empty building, and the way she lingered on it told me she meant more than the space. Then she lifted her sketchbook, angled it against the window frame, and started drawing. Quick lines. The window frames first. Then the door. Then a line of light she imagined would hit the floor at sunset. Half the time, she drew like she could force the world to bend to her lines.

I'd watched the way she bit her lip when a line didn't land exactly how she wanted and how she kept going anyway. Watched her reflection in the glass look braver than either of us felt.

"Gallery's a lot of work," I'd muttered, because vulnerability made me stupid. "You'd have to—"

"—source artists and curate?" She'd shot me a look. "I know what to do with a door when it finally opens, Luke."

I didn't say it then, but I thought it. I wanted this one to open for her. I wanted that building to stay exactly where it was until we could make something out of it that she would stand inside and call her own.

I could still see her there if I closed my eyes. Her hair snapping in the wind. Pencil carving possibility where everyone else saw a tax write-off. She smiled sideways at me, a small curve that let me in on the joke, trusting I wouldn't ruin it.

So yeah. It mattered. She mattered.

Whatever my father erased with that lease, I was going to get it back. Dig it up. Hold it steady. Even if it meant tearing through every wall he built. Because it wasn't just a building. It was hers. Her dream sketched in graphite and painted in oils, her laugh fogging the glass. And if keeping that alive meant burning my father's blueprint to the ground, then so be it.

CHAPTER ELEVEN

MILA

The committee meeting was supposed to be routine—Elise in her element, practiced smile in place, while the school board liaison cooed over her clipboard as though it were the cure for cancer.

My job? Event entry coordination. Stand at the door and smile. A placeholder role, just enough to claim I was reinstated without giving me anything that mattered. Fine. This wasn't how I wanted to spend my time—it was mandated, and that was the only reason I was here. That, and to figure out why someone cared enough to put me back on the list—and who the hell Mr. Langley was. I needed to push Elise for answers but not let her see I wanted them. If she did, she'd twist it into another weapon.

I tuned most of the conversation out. My pencil wandered instead, sketching in the margin of the packet—nothing focused, just lines that spiraled into something almost resembling wings before I pressed too hard and the lead snapped.

Elise didn't look at me once. And somehow, that unsettled me more than if she had. Maybe her silence wasn't about me at all but about who she'd spoken with—Mr. Langley.

Her pen slipped against the page, leaving a streak of ink. She smoothed it like nothing had happened, but her jaw ticked once. The moms around her didn't notice. I did. Elise hated being ignored, and right now, she was pretending I wasn't even in the room.

When the meeting broke, I slipped out the side door before she could think of a reason to pull me back. The sun hit low and gold across the library steps, and the air carried an earthy, damp scent. I adjusted my bag and was halfway down when I heard it.

"Hey."

I turned to find Tori. She hugged her tablet to her chest as if it were armor, strawberry-blond ponytail pulled tight, eyes darting toward the quad before she stepped closer.

"Is Theo avoiding everyone today or just me?" Her voice tried for breezy, but the stiffness in her shoulders gave her away.

I blinked, keeping my tone flat. "Haven't seen him."

She gave a clipped nod. "Right. Must be avoiding me, then."

The wind picked up her ponytail, strands sticking against her lip gloss. She didn't bother fixing them.

I kept my expression neutral. "If you want to talk to him, do it."

Tori scoffed under her breath before brushing her hair back. "Easy for you to say."

I tilted my head. "Why wouldn't it be for you?"

Her teeth caught her bottom lip, a word half-formed, before she swallowed. Then she shifted, weight sliding back. "Just... tell him I need to talk to him."

"Want me to tell him something?"

Her eyes flashed sharp and hard. "No."

Her refusal snapped like a lock clicking shut, and I couldn't tell if she was protecting herself or Elise. Maybe both. Maybe neither. Which made her even more difficult to read.

For a second, though, something flickered behind the edge—

hesitation, maybe even regret. Then she spun on her heel and crossed the lawn without waiting for an answer.

I stood there longer than I meant to, pulse quick and uneven. Tori wasn't on my side. But she wasn't fully on Elise's either. Something was cracking open. I just didn't know which way it would break.

My phone buzzed in my hand before I could unlock it. It was Avery.

Avery: *Survived the meeting?*

Me: *Barely.*

Avery: *What happened?*

Me: *Same circus. Elise still center ring.*

Avery: *You okay?*

I hesitated while crossing to my car, phone still in my hand as I slid into the driver's seat.

Me: *Not really. Can I call you?*

When she didn't immediately answer, I called. She picked up on the first ring.

"Okay." Avery's voice was a mix of relief and exhaustion. "Talk."

I slumped into the driver's seat, keys cold in my hand. "Elise is unraveling. She tried to block me from the committee completely—erase-my-name-off-the-list-level petty. And it almost worked. But someone bigger overruled her and shoved me back on."

Avery made a sound caught between a gasp and a scoff. "Wait—what? She can just do that?"

"She thought she could." My laugh came out thin. "The only reason I was there in the first place was because someone on the board—or one of the companies they answer to—made me. Mandated. And before you ask, I don't know who or why. It's not because anyone actually wants me there. Least of all Elise."

"Okay... guess we'll have to put a pin in that for now. But you're back on the committee."

"Yeah. And Elise is pretending she's fine with it when she's definitely not. I don't even know what game I'm in anymore, except I'm a pivotal piece on the board being moved around at someone's whim."

Avery's silence stretched. Then, carefully: "So… someone out there wants you visible. That's not nothing, Mila."

The words landed in my ribs, a punch I didn't see coming. Because she was right. And I still had no answer for who—or why.

"So that's good, right?"

"Maybe. Or maybe I'm being used. I don't know." I hesitated, breath catching before I forced it out. "And there's something else I haven't told you."

I couldn't keep it from her anymore. Not all of it. The weird committee summons. The whatever-this-was with Luke—close one second, off-limits the next. But the threat against Mom and me? The question of whether Langley was alive or dead? That stayed locked down. I wasn't putting a target on Avery's back.

"What?"

"I kissed Luke." My throat went tight. "Not once. A few times now. But no one can know. We're not… a couple. Not in the halls, not at school. It's safer if we keep distance there."

Silence hummed down the line. Avery's voice came soft but steady. "So, you trust him again. But do you forgive him for how he's treated you?"

The question struck deep, a shove I hadn't braced for. "That's not the same thing."

"No," she agreed. "It's not."

"I trust him." My fingers tightened around the steering wheel. "I have to."

"But forgiving?" she pressed.

I let my head fall back against the seat. "He listened this time. Really listened. He didn't throw what I told him back at me."

"That's trust," Avery pointed out gently. "Not forgiveness."

The silence stretched. I stared out at the line of cars thinning in the lot. "I let him kiss me. That should've been enough. That should've said everything."

Her inhale was sharp. "And?"

"And I kissed him back, Aves." The words scraped out of me. "Because it felt inevitable. Like if I didn't, I'd split in half. And I hate that. I hate that I still want him after everything."

Avery didn't rush in. Just let me spiral.

"I left without explaining," I whispered. "And when I came back, he didn't shut the door on me. He could've. Maybe he should've. But he didn't."

"So he's earned trust," she said. "But, again, what about forgiveness? That's different, Mila. That's letting go of the hurt."

"I don't know if I can. I still feel like he could turn on me and shut me out again. Maybe it's an irrational fear, I don't know."

Her voice was steady now. "Then don't force it. Just be honest—with yourself and with him."

The words settled heavy in my chest.

Finally, I exhaled. "Enough about me. Any news with you and Jax?"

She hesitated. "He walked me to my car today." A pause, softer. "But he's still holding back, as if there's more he wants to say and he's not sure he should."

Protectiveness twined with hope filtered through me. "Give him time. He'll get there."

Her breath caught faintly on the other end, as though she wanted to believe me.

We hung up, but her question still echoed as I started the car and then drove out of the school lot. If I couldn't forgive Luke, then what was left of us?

CHAPTER TWELVE

LUKE

Logan leaned against the locker bank like he owned the place, arms crossed, grin fixed in place. He waited until I was close enough that I couldn't ignore him then fell into step beside me.

"Your old man better watch his back," he muttered, voice pitched low, meant for me alone. "Dunn's going to eat your family alive."

I kept walking.

He matched my pace, sneakers scuffing the floors. "Big empire. Fragile footing. Everyone sees it." His smirk widened. "Guess you'll be the last to know when it falls."

My jaw tightened, fingers flexing around the strap of my bag. The worst part? He wasn't pulling it out of thin air. I'd heard the same tension in my dad's clipped calls, the same unease in Drew's late-night silence.

But a fight in the middle of the hall wouldn't solve anything. It would prove him right—that I was reckless. So I didn't bite.

Logan leaned in anyway, breath hot against my ear. "Maybe Mila should be careful who she ties herself to. Funny, isn't it?

She crawls back, latches on to you, and you're the one headed for the drop. Dunn's going to make sure of it."

I stopped walking. Out of the corner of my eye, Mila stood by the stairwell near the art classroom, watching. Logan caught it too—his grin widened like he'd staged the whole thing for her audience—then he peeled off into the stream of students.

Her brow furrowed for a second before she masked it. But I'd already seen.

I stood there a second too long, fists locked at my sides, every muscle screaming for release. Then the bell shrieked overhead, and the crowd enveloped me again. I didn't give him the satisfaction of a look back. But the words stuck, lodged as if glass under skin.

After seventh period, when I was at my locker, Mila caught up to me. She caught the tension—the way my shoulders stayed tense after class, how I shoved my books in my bag as though they'd wronged me. She brushed close, low enough so only I could hear.

"What was that with Logan?"

"Nothing."

She tilted her head, unconvinced. "Looked like something."

I smirked faintly, too brittle to be real. "I'll tell you later."

It was the best I could give her in a hallway with ears everywhere.

By the time we hit the locker room, it was the usual chaos—gear slamming into lockers, somebody blasting tinny music through a speaker, half the guys shouting over each other as if it were their job. I dropped onto the bench, tugged at the laces of my skates, head still buzzing from Logan's warning earlier in the hall.

Theo slid onto the bench beside me, hoodie half-zipped, calm in a way that felt calculated. But his jaw was too tight, his eyes fixed on the tape as though it owed him something—more guarded than usual, as if he carried a weight he wasn't ready to share.

"Met with Tori," he muttered. "Nothing solid. But she's jumpy. Like she knows something and doesn't want to be the one to say it."

I kept my eyes on my skates. "Define jumpy."

"She flinched when I brought up Elise and changed the subject fast." He leaned closer. "I'll give you the rest after practice."

Across the room, Chase cursed about someone stealing his tape, a couple of guys laughing too loud, the smell of sweat and ice thick in the air. The noise enveloped us. But the weight of Theo's words stuck, circling tighter than any drill Coach was about to throw at us.

Practice dragged. Coach was in one of his moods, riding every play, barking about precision as if we weren't already grinding ourselves into the ice. My legs burned. My head was worse. Theo's message. Elise's silence. My father's clipped dismissal about the boardwalk property, treating it as a case study, and I was supposed to learn the right lesson.

I didn't need a shower after—I needed answers. But I hit the shower anyway. Habit.

I shot Mila a message once I was outside, hair still damp, bag in the backseat.

Me: *You home? Okay if I stop by?*

Mila: *Mom's out. So yeah.*

By the time I pulled into her neighborhood, the sun was gone. Streetlights buzzed faint over cracked sidewalks and patchy lawns. Houses sat too close together, porches sagging, paint flaking, the opposite of the manicured bubble where I lived.

Her place was near the corner—a rental you could spot a mile away. Faded shutters, screen door hanging a little crooked, driveway gravel instead of paved. The porch light flickered yellow across the warped steps where she stood waiting, hoodie pulled tight like she could disappear inside it.

She waited for me on the porch, arms crossed. The light cast her in a soft cone that made her look both fierce and small.

I killed the engine and climbed out, gravel crunching under my shoes. She stood on the porch, arms folded into her hoodie. Her eyes flicked to my hair.

"You're wet."

"Didn't want to stink up your house."

Her mouth twitched. She tried not to smile. Failed. "Considerate."

She stepped back, letting me in.

The house was dim, most of the lamps off, full of old rental furniture—a couch with worn arms, a coffee table scarred from years of use, threadbare carpet underfoot. It wasn't empty, though. It felt lived in. Claimed by her. A sketchbook lay open on the table, shoved against a calculus textbook like it had won the fight.

Her mom's car was gone, just as Mila had said in the text. She tracked my glance toward the driveway.

"She's working late," she explained, tugging open the fridge and handing me a bottle of water. "Or just 'out' is the more likely phrasing."

I nodded and dropped onto the couch, twisting the cap off. Took a pull. My shirt still clung damp at the collar.

"You okay?" she asked.

"Define okay."

She didn't press. Just waited. So I gave her what I had. "Theo met with someone—his sister's friend. She interned at Dunn for a semester last year before transferring to UCLA."

Mila's head lifted, interest flickering. "And?"

"She said most of it was grunt work—copies, coffee runs. Kept out of anything that mattered. But once, she overheard her boss on the phone. Talking to a Mr. Langley. She said his tone changed—uptight, a little panicked. As though whoever Langley was, he carried weight. Enough that just the name stuck with her."

Mila went still.

"Mr. Langley," she whispered. "That's what Elise said. On the phone."

It had to be the same person. But Darren was dead. Wasn't he? Not only that, but he didn't have any living relatives.

Mila sat down across from me, tucking her legs under herself, voice quieter now. "I don't know what they want from me. My mom keeps saying everything's fine. That it's under control. That I shouldn't stir the pot." Her jaw tightened. "But I know what I saw when I met her at King Enterprises. Darren Langley was dead."

I held her gaze. "Are you positive? Because his name keeps surfacing, and yet there was never an obituary. No notice. Nothing public. Doesn't that strike you as—off?"

Silence pressed in.

Her voice cut through it, low and certain. "I'm positive. There was too much blood. His eyes were open—sightless. No sirens. No one coming. And even if they had been, it would've been too late. You don't come back from that."

Then I added, "My PI called me earlier."

Her eyes snapped to mine. "Already?"

"He's fast."

"What did he say?"

"Not much yet. But he found a financial record of a rental storage space in Darren's name. Leased under initials. Closed two months after he disappeared."

Mila's voice dropped. "Closed by who?"

"Don't know. No record of a signature. The payment history ended in cash. The paper trail just... stops."

Her brow furrowed. "So he wanted it hidden."

"Or someone else did."

It wasn't proof—of life or death. Not even that the unit had belonged to him and not someone using his name. But it was a thread—thin, frayed, leading somewhere. And I wasn't about to let go.

She didn't speak for a while, just stared at the carpet, lips pressed together as if she was holding in a hundred thoughts.

Her silence stretched, heavy. Then she shifted, almost to herself at first. "We were brought back here for a reason. Even if Mom doesn't know it—or won't admit she does. And if Dunn, or whoever's pulling the strings, gets wind that we're digging…" Her eyes found mine, voice lower now. "Do you think the same thing could happen to us that happened to Darren?"

Honest question.

"I think if they were going to, they would've already. But I also think they're watching."

Her gaze lifted. "Us?"

"You," I said. "And anyone you talk to. Anyone who asks the wrong questions."

Her throat worked. "Including you?"

"Especially me."

She exhaled, shoulders loosening only to tense again. "Then maybe you should stop."

I shook my head, eyes steady on hers. "You know I won't."

Her fingers brushed mine where they hung between us, light as a breath.

I didn't pull back. Neither did she. The silence stretched, heavy with everything we weren't saying. I shifted, closing the gap, my hand covering hers. She let me. No flinch. No retreat. Just the faint tremor of her pulse beneath my palm.

"You're not alone in this," I said, voice low.

Tension eased from her frame, the faintest shift, and then she leaned into me. Instinct took the rest. My arm slid around her, pulling her closer. Her hair brushed my jaw, carrying that faint salt-sweet scent of the coast.

She tipped her face up. I leaned down, close enough to feel the hitch of her breath, and brushed my lips over hers. Barely there. A spark instead of a flame. It should've been enough—just the ghost of contact—but the second I felt her soften into it, I was gone.

She kissed me back, hesitant for half a beat, then certain, her mouth parting against mine. Slow, searching, like we were relearning each other after too much silence and damage. The taste of her—sweet and intoxicating, familiar and new—slid straight through me, and suddenly, I couldn't get close enough.

Slow didn't last. It never did with us.

Her hand slid up my chest, heat surging in its wake as her fingers pressed into my jaw, dragging me down harder as if she couldn't stand the space left between us. The pressure of it set me on fire. I caught her against me, hand under the edge of her hoodie, thumb grazing skin—warm, soft, alive. She gasped into my mouth, and the sound broke me open, stripped me raw.

The kiss turned frenzied—teeth, breath, the desperate clash of want and memory colliding. Her nails scraped the back of my neck. My pulse hammered in my throat. Every brush of her lips, every tug closer, every frantic gasp fueled the part of me that had missed her so fiercely it bordered on pain.

My hand slipped higher, beneath fabric, fingers splaying against bare skin.

She tore herself away. Our breaths collided in the space between us, ragged, uneven. Her pupils blown wide, a flush racing up her throat, lips swollen from mine. Gorgeous. Shaken.

"Luke—" Her voice fractured. "I'm not ready for more."

I froze, the ache still clawing at me, but I didn't push. Couldn't.

She steadied herself with a breath, words spilling fast, as though she had to get them out before she lost the nerve. "We had everything before, and it still broke. Trust between us is fragile. And we can't even be seen as anything outside rooftops or behind closed doors. I don't want to rush this. Not yet."

Her eyes searched mine, fierce and pleading all at once.

I forced air back into my lungs. Nodded once. "Then we go slow."

Her shoulders softened—barely. But enough.

I lifted a hand, brushing my thumb gently across her bottom lip, still swollen from my kiss. She stilled, breath catching again, but didn't pull away. For a moment, I let my forehead rest against hers, the heat of her skin grounding me, keeping me from pushing for more.

The ache didn't fade. But it steadied.

When I finally stood, she walked me to the door, hoodie wrapped tight as armor. Neither of us spoke—too much still burning in the air. On the porch, she lingered a second, then slipped back inside, the door clicking shut between us.

I crossed the gravel drive, every nerve still wired, jaw tight. By the time I slid behind the wheel, my hands shook faintly on the steering column. Her taste lingered on my lips, the ghost of her body still pressed against mine. Want twisted sharp under my ribs, threaded with frustration I couldn't shake.

I started the engine, headlights flaring across the quiet street. The night pressed in heavy as I pulled away, carrying the heat of her with me and the ache of everything we weren't—yet. And all I could think was how wanting her this much was its own kind of risk—because Dunn, Langley, even my father's empire couldn't cut me down the way losing her would.

CHAPTER THIRTEEN

MILA

My mom was waiting when I came downstairs Friday morning. Coffee mug already drained, jacket tossed over a chair, her car keys spinning once between her fingers before she caught them.

Her long brown hair was pulled in a high ponytail, sunglasses perched on her head. She wore shorts and a loose white tank that showed the strap of her bikini, flip-flops tapping against the tile. A striped beach bag sat at her feet, as if it had been packed hours ago.

I stopped on the last step, blinking. Mom didn't dress like this on a weekday morning—never ready for anything but the office.

"You're not going to school today." No preamble. Her grin tugged wide, a mischievous spark in her eyes.

I blinked. "Uh… what?"

Her gaze was steady, mouth tipped in something between a challenge and a dare. "We both need a break. Hurry and change. I've got a to-go coffee and bagel ready for the road. Let's go."

I stared a second longer, waiting for the catch. For

the but... But you can't miss class. But I've got work. But nothing.

Excitement rushed through me before I could stop it, relief loosening something in my chest. The promise of sun and waves was too good to pass up.

"Give me two minutes."

I bolted upstairs, tore out of my jeans, and tugged on shorts and a tank. I shoved my Sketchbook into my bag and kicked off my sneakers for flip-flops. By the time I clattered back down, pulse already lighter, she was shouldering her bag.

It was unseasonably warm out, the perfect day to play hooky. We were halfway through loading the car when my phone buzzed.

Avery: *Where are you? You're late.*

I thumbed a message back fast. *Taking the day off. Mom's orders. Don't freak.*

Three dots appeared, then—

Avery: *Fine. But you're coming to the game tonight. No excuses.*

Another buzz right after, Luke this time.

Luke: *Where are you?*

Me: *No school for me today. Beach with Mom. Both of us needed it. Play hard tonight.*

No reply came, but I tucked the phone away and breathed easier for having sent it.

We drove with the windows cracked, ocean air shoving its way into the car. The closer we got to the coast, the lighter my chest felt. By the time the sand stretched out in front of us, I'd almost forgotten the mess waiting back at school—the committee, Elise's calculated smirk, Logan's predatory gaze following me down the hall.

We claimed a patch of beach not far from the pier. The air carried a faint chill—it was late autumn, after all—but the sun burned high and fierce, pretending it was still summer. There was not a cloud in the sky, just endless blue fading paler at the horizon.

Goosebumps rose along my arms until the sand's warmth sank in. Golden grains clung to my skin, dazzling like ground glass under the light. The waves moved in shades of slate and turquoise, foam scattering white lace across the darker water.

It felt unreal, skipping school as if none of it mattered. As if I'd stepped out of the chaos and into someone else's painting— broad strokes of sky and sea, too vivid to be real.

Mom sat, sunglasses sliding down her nose, eyes scanning the horizon as though she could read answers out of the tide. We stretched out on the blanket.

"So. College."

Mom dropped the topic I dreaded having with her. Pinching my lips together, I didn't answer. It wouldn't do any good. I could tell by the determined set to her shoulders that she was going to keep pressing the topic.

"You want a different life than this, right?" she shot back.

I groaned. "Fine. College."

"You've got applications due soon," she reminded. "And recommendation letters. Who's on your list?"

"Ms. Lewis." I hesitated. "Art teacher."

That earned me a slow exhale. "Mila—"

"I know what you're going to say." My voice went sharper than I meant. "But she knows me. Really knows me. Not just grades or transcripts or how I look on paper."

Her mouth tightened, but she didn't interrupt. Which somehow made it worse.

So I pushed. "You've always been against an art degree. Against me painting. Just admit it."

Finally, her sunglasses came off. The look underneath was tired. Too honest. "Fine. I have. Because it doesn't pay, Mila. Because you're too smart to pin your future on commissions and galleries that chew people up. Because I want better for you than scraping by on someone else's whim."

The words stung. I sat up straighter. "It's not a whim. It's the only thing that feels like mine."

Her expression softened, but her tone didn't. "I know. I was good, too. Brushes, canvas, the whole thing. But I was just as good with numbers. Better, maybe. That's why I'm where I am."

"You hate where you are."

Silence. Just waves breaking and gulls cutting the air.

Her hair whipped in the breeze as she finally said, "I didn't have choices, Mila. Didn't finish high school, never set foot in a college class. I stacked a résumé with schools I never attended and jobs I never had and prayed no one looked too closely. Then I learned on the fly. Listened to men I dated talk about stocks, spreadsheets, and fiscal reports and tucked it away for later. Taught myself the rest. It worked. But it isn't an ideal life. It's survival. And I don't want that for you."

The confession hollowed me out, her words hitting home. Because wasn't that exactly what Blackwood felt like most days? Elise pulling strings, board members moving me like a pawn. Mom had lied her way into boardrooms. I was being shoved into them whether I wanted to be there or not. "I'm not you," I whispered.

"No," she agreed. "You're smarter. You've got chances I didn't. And I'll be damned if I watch you throw them away."

The fight drained out of me all at once, leaving something more raw in its place. I dragged my fingers through the sand, watching it spill back in golden streams. "But I'm not you when it comes to numbers. I don't think in margins or spreadsheets. I never have. I don't… see the world that way."

Her lips parted, a flash of something similar to regret there. "You're right. That's me, not you."

"So what's me, then?"

For once, she didn't answer right away.

She went quiet. Then, softer: "So maybe you need something else. Something that lets you keep art but doesn't starve you for it. Graphic design. Marketing. You see color, space, angles in ways other people don't. You could sell an image, shape it, and still keep painting."

"Marketing?" I blinked.

"You've got business classes already," she pointed out. "Add marketing next semester. Test it out."

I rolled the idea around, fingers knotting in the edge of the blanket. "It could be… a fallback. If I need it."

Her eyes warmed. "That's all I'm asking."

For once, it felt like a truce.

We talked more easily after that. About letters, deadlines, where I wanted to apply. Then about Blackwood, the move, the fact she was still "dating" Principal Miller.

She grimaced, rolling her eyes behind her sunglasses. "Dating. That's generous. More a PR arrangement than anything else."

I smirked. "And when it's over?"

"When it's over, it's over." She shrugged. "I'll be relieved."

That could've been the end of it, but I pressed. "Anyone else?"

Her gaze cut sideways at me, but her smile shifted—softer. "Edwardo."

"The gym guy?" But I knew exactly who she'd meant. There had always been something easy and natural—electric even— between them. We'd stayed with him last year, but I wanted to push Mom just a little.

"The gym guy," she echoed, and her voice went light in a way I hadn't heard in months. "He was more than that, Mila. A friend. A temptation I couldn't afford."

"Because of where he lives," I guessed.

She nodded. "Too close to where I came from. I couldn't stay there. But…" Her shoulders rose then fell. "Who knows where life will go once you're at college."

Her voice lingered with something wistful.

We ate the bagels she'd packed, legs stretched across the blanket, crumbs carried off by gulls bold enough to circle close until we shooed them. After, we walked the shoreline, the surf rushing in to nip at our ankles before pulling back, daring us to chase it. Our laughter rose with the tide, and for a while, it felt as if the weight I carried had been left somewhere far behind, buried under textbooks and committee agendas.

The beach wasn't empty—there were families with toddlers building crooked sandcastles, a couple of surfers paddling out, office workers who'd escaped for an hour of sun. Not crowded but not ours alone either. By the time noon hit, more people drifted down from the boardwalk, unwrapping sandwiches, soaking up light while they could. The hum of their voices folded into the crash of the waves, a rhythm steady enough to make the whole place feel alive.

We lingered until the shadows stretched long and the sun mellowed into gold. The tide foamed across our feet as we cut back toward the boardwalk, and that was when I spotted Colleen, the woman in charge of the boardwalk art studio.

She stood outside the studio, paint on her sleeve, phone pressed between her shoulder and ear. She ended the call fast when she saw me.

"Mila."

I jogged across the sand. "Hey."

Her smile was warm but tight. "I'm glad I caught you. Our lease isn't being renewed, which means we've got two weeks to clear everything out. I've been trying to reach everyone, but since you're here—"

It hit like ice water down my spine. "What?"

She nodded toward the building. "Come inside. You'll want your supplies. Your work."

My mom and I followed her in.

The familiar smell of turpentine and old wood hit me first. Sunlight spilled through the tall front windows, catching on glass jars and half-finished canvases.

My pieces were stacked against the back wall. Oils. Colors I'd fought for.

My mom froze. I watched her eyes move over the pieces—portraits, beach landscapes, scraps of memory turned paint. Shock flickered there. "You never showed me these," she whispered.

I worried my lower lip. "At home, it's just sketches."

She stepped closer, fingers hovering near the edge of a canvas without touching. "Mila… this is talent. This is more than a hobby."

Colleen overheard, drifting closer with a smile. "She's right. You've developed something real. You should submit. I know a gallery owner who would love to take a serious look. I'll make a call before you reach out. Smooth the way."

I couldn't breathe. The floor tilted beneath me.

My mom looked at me, fierce pride hidden under her usual armor. I wanted to believe. I wanted it so badly it hurt.

We loaded the car with everything—brushes, paints, canvases balanced in the back seat. I hugged Colleen, promised her I'd stay in touch. She brushed it off with a grin, saying she'd be fine, that she usually landed on her feet.

But the hollowness in my chest didn't ease. The studio had been my sanctuary. And now it was gone.

I planned to ask Luke what the hell had happened. Then I sat back, sketchbook balanced on my knees, pencil loose between my fingers, the pages crowded with lines that always led back to him.

CHAPTER FOURTEEN

LUKE

Restlessness crawled under my skin, coiled tight, begging for release. Not the locker room noise, not the sweat and tape and pulsing music—those were static. What mattered was the ice. Me and the puck and whoever thought they could take it from me. I wanted the weight of contact, the grind of blades cutting deep, the sharp snap of the shot leaving my stick. Winning wasn't a hope. It was an expectation.

Plastic blade guards thudded against the rubber floor, the sound swallowed by the rip of tape players wound around their sticks. Sweat and muscle rub hung in the air, trapped in the concrete walls. Someone's speaker bled bass, fighting the rest of the noise.

Jax was a force even sitting still, earbuds jammed in, "One Shot" blasting loud enough that I could catch fragments of the beat from three feet away. He slammed the butt of his stick against the floor in rhythm, as if he was already hitting bodies.

Theo leaned back, legs stretched out, earbuds tucked low, head tilted with that half-asleep posture he wore before games —like nothing touched him until he decided it should. The calm wasn't an act. It was control.

Chase was the opposite. Methodical. His gloves rested on the bench in front of him, laid out with surgical precision. He slid his hands in one finger at a time, adjusting the leather until it fit just right, eyes locked forward on some target only he could see.

I pulled my laces tight until the pressure bit into my ankles then tighter. Flexed forward, testing the give.

Scouts and coaches were in the building—jackets, clipboards, eyes that didn't blink enough. Michigan. Boston. Wisconsin. Ohio. Harvard—to name just a few. Coach warned us before warmups—don't screw around tonight. A few coaches had already reached out, letting me know they'd be there tonight.

The guys didn't talk about it, not really. Jax didn't need to— his game consisted of bruises and intimidation; scouts and coaches knew that already. Theo wore his usual half-lidded calm, as though the suits weren't worth his energy, though I knew he clocked every detail. Chase tuned it out, locked into systems and positioning because that was who he was. And Logan? He looked jumpy, too aware of who might be watching.

I couldn't ignore it. Every name landed, a marker on the ice. Michigan was the one that mattered.

My dad said Wharton. Philadelphia. Business first, last, always. I'd already played out the fights in my head. The lecturing. The spreadsheets. The pedigree speeches. If everything fell apart, fine—Berkeley, Harvard. They were respectable colleges and a degree he could stomach.

But Michigan was mine. One of the top D1 programs in the country, a team built on grit and legacy, the kind of place professional team scouts circled because half the roster ended up in the NHL. Their business school wasn't Wharton, maybe not even Berkeley—but it held its own. More than enough. Michigan didn't care who your father was, only how well you skated and how you did once you hit the ice. That was the weight I wanted. The noise. The chance to carve something that belonged to me.

And it wasn't just mine. Back when things between us weren't broken, Mila had talked about Michigan too—the art program there, the professor she admired, one of those rare names who actually made it in the industry and went back to teach. We'd joked about it, half-plan, half-dream, as if maybe we could end up in the same place without Blackwood tying us down. Now? Who knew what the future held.

I dropped my elbows to my knees and let the buzz sharpen. Mila flashed through me, a clean hit—how one brush of her hand could drop me to my knees faster than any check. She had no idea. Maybe I didn't either until recently. It wasn't weakness. It was the opposite. She could gut me with a look then make me believe I could take on the world anyway.

Coach kicked the door with his heel. "On me." He swept the room from under that worn cap, every line in his face saying don't be stupid. "Keep your heads where they need to be. Crestview's going to come at you hard, but we win by staying disciplined. Don't chase their hits, don't get sucked into their scrums. Clean lines, quick transitions, make them play at our pace. And for the love of God, keep your asses out of the box—I don't want to hand this game to them on penalties."

Last time we played Crestview, Mason—their hammer, their golden boy—was out. The one who never saw a fight he didn't back down from and made damn sure everyone saw him win it. He played as though it were street rules: elbows, bad intentions, no mercy. The kind of guy who'd throw an elbow behind the play then flash a grin, pretending he hadn't just rattled your molars. Coaches let it slide. Scouts drooled over the raw edge. Now he was back, and the whole team played meaner with him on the ice. I didn't care about the hype. I just wanted to hit him hard enough to make him remember who he was up against.

We filed out. Helmets clicked. Sticks tapped concrete, then boards, then ice. The cold hit my lungs, a slap that woke everything up.

Warmups were quick. Edgework. Transitions. One-timers until my hands remembered in a way my head didn't need to. Students pounded on the glass, faces painted, signs shoved up with terrible handwriting. Scouts were visible this time—up in the elevated VIP box, center ice. Suits and quiet murmurs, their gazes locked on whoever they were here to watch. I didn't care if it was me or Mason or someone else. Let them watch. I was already tracking every move Mason made. But it wasn't just him I noticed.

Mila was in her usual seat. Next to Avery, on the other side of the plexiglass behind the bench. Hoodie sleeves pulled over her hands. She wasn't watching Mason. She was watching me.

National anthem. Helmets off, gloves tucked under arms. The arena stilled, breath held in one collective pause. My jaw tightened, lungs working slow, deliberate. Every nerve coiled, waiting for release.

When the last note faded, sticks cracked against the boards. Helmets back on. Gloves pulled tight. I skated to my mark and dragged the blade of my stick across the circle, carving a shallow groove only I would notice. Jax nudged my shoulder once. Ready.

The puck dropped and everything snapped into focus.

Mason lined up across from me.

They came fast. Wings who could fly and a defenseman who loved to pinch, trying to trap us early. My first shift put me on the right side, Theo at center, Jax on the left. Chase anchored the blue line—voice rough as gravel, directing without ever needing to raise it.

Faceoff win. Theo snapped the puck toward me, and their winger clamped me against the boards in a heartbeat—hips solid, stick driving for the puck. I rolled with it, spun, kept my feet, chipped it past and chased, legs chewing up ice. First shot I took was just to send a message—low on the stick side, hard—but their goalie had good eyes. Kicked it into the corner. Fine—note taken.

Next rush, Mason made his move. Stick came down across mine so hard the vibration lit up my wrist. Ref's arm shot up—two minutes for slashing. Didn't bother him. He grinned as he skated to the box, as though he'd already won.

The tempo stayed brutal. We traded rushes. Our student section roared at everything and nothing. Then a bad bounce at our blue line turned into a footrace we lost. Their winger beat our second D pairing wide and slipped the puck under our goalie before he could close his pads. One–zero, them.

I didn't look at the bench. Didn't look at the clock. Took it like a body shot and skated back to center. Next play.

We answered five minutes later. Theo picked a pocket at neutral ice, flew across the blue with me trailing wide. He baited the D, slid it behind his heel. I snapped it without thinking—no dust, no drag. Top right, over the glove. Net.

Glass shook. We were even.

They tried to show off—started mouthing off in front of our net. The next shift, their captain slashed at the back of my legs after the whistle. Jax saw it. He didn't drop gloves—Coach's rule—but he planted the kid three seconds into the next play with a hit you could feel in your fillings. Clean. Shoulder through chest. Boards thundered. Whistles blew but no one called it. Crowd lost its mind.

By the end of the first it was 1–1. My lungs burned clean, the good kind of ache that told me I was in it.

On the bench, Coach leaned down. "They're leaning on your side. Use it. Theo—sell the fake at the faceoff, then pull it the other way. Walker, keep your stick hot."

Theo nodded. "Got it."

Second period opened as if it were a knife fight in a phone booth—tight, vicious, nowhere to hide. Corners turned into scrums, sticks cracked together, legs burned. Crestview got whistled for hooking Jax behind their net. Power play.

I won the faceoff clean and fed it back to Chase. He slid it across, tape to tape, smooth as if the puck was glued to his stick. Theo cut through the middle, drew two defenders, then kicked it out to my wing. I faked low and ripped it high. Off the bar, in. The ping rang in my skull. 2–1, us.

Their coach burned a timeout. Our bench buzzed with the fever of a hive. Student section roared, all noise and chaos, stomping the bleachers enough to shake the glass. I didn't smile. Just breathed.

On my next change, as I glided past center, I let myself look. There she was—halfway up, one hand on the railing, light cutting her face into stripes through the shadows. Avery was beside her, screaming like a siren. Mila didn't scream. She watched then shouted. Eyes locked on me. Steady. Fierce. Pressure and relief at the same time.

My chest went hot then calm. She lifted her chin a fraction. I did the same. Nothing crazy. Just enough. Then the whistle blew, and the world snapped back into motion.

They tied it late off a scramble our goalie never saw. 2–2. The crowd groaned, but our bench pounded sticks anyway.

Back on the bench, Coach pressed clipped words into our ears like bullets. "They're gassed. You can see it. Stay disciplined. Don't go fishing." Across the ice, Mason leaned on the boards, helmet tipped back, smirking as though the whole game bent to him.

Theo leaned in. "You good?"

"Yep," I muttered, barely audible.

Third period turned into hand-to-hand hockey. Every stride felt heavy. Every pass had to be fought for. Logan got a shift to give our other winger a breather—third line, desperate to prove himself. He sprinted behind their net and tried to stuff the puck in from the back side, no chance of it going in, but the scramble he caused bought us ten seconds of pressure we needed. He came off grinning as if he'd scored anyway. Coach barked after him to play smarter, but he didn't tear into him. Not tonight.

Five minutes to go and it felt as though the whole rink had its hand at my throat in the best possible way.

Coach tapped our line. "Last push."

Theo crouched for the faceoff. I lined up on his right. Jax rolled his shoulders, ready to break something. Behind us, Chase and our second defenseman dug their skates in, ready.

The puck dropped. Theo tied up his man then kicked it back with his skate so clean it appeared effortless. I collected, muscled through a shove, felt a stick tug at my hip, and shook it off. Boards to my right, open ice in front—but their defenseman stuck to me, hacking and leaning, body against body.

Jax cut across the lane and slowed just enough to block him off without drawing a whistle. Subtle. Brutal. I had half a heartbeat of space.

Half a heartbeat was all I needed.

I cut inside, faked high—same shot I'd buried twice tonight. Their goalie twitched, bit just enough. I dragged wider, opened my stick, and let it slide low, far side. Under his pad before he sealed.

Net. 3–2.

Sound detonated. Bleachers shook. Students hammered the glass. Jax slammed into me, yelling something I couldn't hear. Theo smirked as though he'd seen it coming the whole time. I tapped gloves, helmet to helmet, let the surge carry me back to the bench.

Next shift, Mason lined up across from me. Crestview's hammer. His grin was all teeth.

"Michigan coach's here for me," he taunted, just for me. "Not you. You're a backup, King." His eyes cut to the stands. "And your little distraction up there? Cute. Easy to spot."

He wasn't wrong. She was impossible to miss, and that scared me almost as much as it steadied me.

The words landed harder than the stick he jammed into my ribs right after. I shoved back. Sticks clashed, elbows, the scrape of cages. The whistle shrieked but too late. His glove raked across my helmet, and I answered with a punch to the chest that sent him stumbling.

Refs barreled in, wedging arms and skates between us, shoving us toward opposite ends. Crowd foamed, half chanting his name, half mine. The ref's arm went up—roughing. Two minutes each.

I hit our box still hot, chest heaving. Across the ice, Mason sprawled in the opposite box, wearing that carve-on smirk like he'd gotten what he'd wanted. He leaned on the boards, jawing at me through the glass. Couldn't hear him. But he got his point across.

Back on the ice, everything collapsed into survival shifts. They pulled their goalie, threw six attackers at us. Chase dropped in front of a shot that thudded against his thigh and still cleared it twenty feet. Theo scraped another faceoff win he had no business getting. I chased down a loose puck and thought about the empty net for one greedy second—then dumped it safe, Coach's voice in my head: don't be stupid.

The horn sounded, sharp and final. For a split second, nobody moved. Then arms shot up. Sticks hammered the ice. Somebody launched into me, and I staggered back, laughing breathless, helmet still on, sweat freezing at my neck. The game was over.

We lined up for the handshake line, and I played it straight. Glove taps, quick words, nothing personal. They'd pushed us. We gave it back. That was hockey.

Back to the locker room, everything hit loud again—steam,

voices, showers hissing, the electric edge still snapping through my muscles.

The hallway on the way in ran past the lower rows. I hadn't planned to look. I did anyway.

Mila had worked her way down a section, close enough that I caught the flush still high on her cheeks. Avery tugged at her arm, talking a mile a minute, eyes locked on Jax. Mila didn't wave—just met my eyes, the hit clean as a pass—straight on, no bounce, no wobble.

That look anchored me in a way I hadn't had since… before.

Inside, the scouts and coaches were already working the room. Hungry with some players, shaking hands, leaning in. With others, their eyes glazed quick, and they slipped out of the conversation just as fast.

One stopped me, asked about the third-period goal, how I read the goalie's pad. Nothing long. Just quick hits. "Good game, we'll be in touch."

Around me, Theo, Jax, and Chase all had their turns. Short talks, the same clipped rhythm. Follow-up calls and emails would come later. Offers were coming.

Theo thumped my shoulder. "You hear them in the stands? Sounded like they were going to shake the glass loose for you."

"Playmaker pass," I shot back, because he'd threaded that feed in the second as if he was passing fate.

He shrugged, pleased without showing it. "You made it count."

Jax's grin cut sideways. "You made them count." He meant the college coaches. "Better not forget me when you're big time."

"You'll be there crushing skulls," I muttered, and he laughed, a sound that promised blood.

Chase, towel draped over his shoulders, didn't say much. But he gave me a look that read pride then turned to strip his pads with the same care he put into killing a penalty.

I sat, helmet in my lap, blades drying, my pulse finally

coming down out of the stratosphere. My phone buzzed in my duffel. I let it go. I knew what might be waiting—Coach's clip, a message from a college coach, a text from my father with some strategic comment about Wharton and optionality. Or nothing at all from him, which somehow said more.

Michigan took up space in my chest as if it were a living thing. The ice, the speed, the demand. I wanted it. Not because it was a resounding fuck you to my father—okay, maybe a little —but because it was mine. A future I could choose that didn't smell of mahogany and compromise. Wharton was control. Michigan was freedom. And somewhere in the middle—her.

Wharton could wait. Or not. He would see my side. Or he wouldn't. Didn't matter tonight.

What mattered was the ice. The win. That look from the stands. The way Mila's hand could undo me and still make me stronger.

I stood and hit the showers, steam enveloping me. Water pounded my shoulders, turned the adrenaline into heat that ran out at my feet. I pictured Michigan's arena—cold, loud, the kind of place that demanded you earn everything. I let myself visualize her there, warm palms, colder glass, that chin tipped up at me, a dare in motion.

For the first time in too long, I believed I could have it all— even with Dunn and my family still circling in the background. The program I wanted. The life I wanted. The girl who made me want it more.

I shut the water off and dragged a hand down my face. Time to choose what mattered, one conversation at a time. I toweled off, got dressed, then grabbed my phone.

Mila: *Good game. That show-off move in the third was unnecessary.*

Me: *Had to show off for someone.*

Mila: **eye roll emoji**

Me: *You still around?*

Mila: *Yeah. By the side exit. Avery's threatening to scale the boards.*

I grinned without meaning to, shoved the phone in my pocket, and told the guys later as I headed for the door. Everything else—college, my father—could wait. Mila was fifteen feet away, and the part of me that bent when she touched me wanted to see her more than I wanted anything else.

CHAPTER FIFTEEN

MILA

Avery didn't need much convincing after the hockey game. I barely got out, "Let's just wait for them to come out"—before she was already nodding, eyes bright, chewing her lip as if she was trying to keep a smile contained.

"It's not like I'm dragging you into anything," I teased, bumping her shoulder as we loitered near the side exit.

"Please." She rolled her eyes. "Dragging me? I'd climb the glass if I had to."

I grinned. That much was true. It wasn't the game she was watching—it was him. Her voice dropped, conspiratorial. "I just need five minutes alone with Jax. Not, like, alone-alone. But away from Chase's death glare."

"That's a challenge."

Her eyes sparkled mischievously. "You think?"

I laughed, softer this time. "You'll figure it out. Just… talk to him. Quit overthinking it. He's a guy. Lower the bar."

She opened her mouth to answer, but the doors swung wide, and the guys spilled out—damp hair, duffel bags slung over shoulders, still buzzing with the leftover energy of a win.

Theo's laugh carried first, easy and careless. Jax trailed a step behind, head bent, quiet in a way that pulled more eyes than Theo's noise ever could. Avery saw him, and her whole face gave her away.

A brunette intercepted Chase before he hit the parking lot. She touched his arm, leaned in too close, and he actually smiled —then let her steer him toward her car. He never even glanced in our direction. The timing couldn't have been better.

Avery snorted. "Hypocrite. He's ready to lock me in a tower, but that? Totally fine." She shook her head then tugged at my sleeve. "Come on. This is my shot."

Jax barely had time to react before Avery was in front of him, suggesting food with an airy confidence I hadn't seen on her in a long time. He hesitated—half a second, maybe less— then nodded. Theo threw his hands up.

"Count me out. I'm allergic to watching people flirt."

I rolled my eyes. "Right. Because you'd never."

He smirked. "Depends who's asking."

I took the opening. "Speaking of which—something weird happened at that committee meeting. Tori actually spoke to me. But not to back up Elise's usual crap. She asked if I'd talked to you."

That wiped the smirk for a heartbeat. "She asked?"

"Yeah. Caught me off guard."

Theo shrugged, casual on the outside, but his eyes flicked down as his phone buzzed. One glance, then he pocketed the phone with a crooked grin. "Guess I'll leave you to it. Enjoy your night, Callahan."

Theo peeled off, no explanation needed. Probably Tori. Which left Luke.

Luke hung back while the others drifted away, until it was only me lingering in the lot. He didn't say anything, just met my eyes, the corner of his mouth twitching like he knew I'd been waiting.

"Hungry?" I asked.

"Of course."

We headed toward our vehicles. I'd parked near him and paused by mine. He caught my eye before heading for his SUV. "Where do you want to eat?"

I shrugged, pretending it wasn't a big deal, even though my pulse jumped. "My place." Besides, I didn't want to trail Avery and Jax. They deserved some time alone.

His mouth curved—half-smile, half-dare—but he didn't argue. "I'll grab the food. Meet you there."

By the time I unlocked the door, the house was dark—too quiet, the kind that pressed in until you noticed every creak. I dumped my bag by the couch and paced once, twice.

It didn't take long until headlights cut across the front window, and my stomach tightened. He was here.

A knock, then the shuffle of his shoes in the entry as I let him in. Takeout bags dangled from his hands, the smell of soy sauce and fried rice filling the room before he even set them down.

"My mom's not home," I told him. "She's got a date and probably won't be back until tomorrow."

His expression flickered—relief threaded with something unreadable I couldn't pin down—but he didn't say anything until we were sprawled on the couch, cartons open, legs tangled in the mess we used to make.

The quiet between us stretched in that warm, familiar way it used to feel when we didn't need words to fill the space. I let myself sink into it, chopsticks clicking against the carton, the low drone of the TV filling the room.

Curiosity itched. "So… college coaches. Did they talk to you?"

He glanced up mid-bite, chewing slow, then swallowed. "Yeah. A couple. Nothing long. Just the usual—good game, they'll be in touch. Follow-ups later."

I caught the way he said it—flat, too casual. As though the

conversations didn't matter, like he hadn't just put on a show for half the arena. His eyes gave him away, though. The focus there. The weight he didn't want me to see. Colleges had been courting him.

"And Michigan? Is it still your first choice?"

"Yeah, it is." He leaned back, arm draped along the couch so I could lean into him. "Best program in the country. Hockey. Business. Everything lines up there."

"Even with your dad?"

His jaw ticked. "Not Michigan. He hates the idea of me going there. Calls it a waste. He's already handed me the list of 'approved' schools—the ones that keep me under his thumb. That's the point. He doesn't want me making choices he can't control."

I didn't say anything. Instead, I pressed closer, and his arm tightened around me in answer.

"What about you?" he asked finally. "Still planning on Michigan too? That art professor you used to talk about still pulling you there?"

I hesitated. "Maybe. I don't know yet."

But I watched him—how easy he was in that moment, guard down, letting me lean into him. It felt the way it used to. Like us. And I loved it. Which is why I told him. "Earlier today, Mom and I went to the beach." He already knew from my text, but there was more to it. "On the way out, we ran into Colleen, the woman who owns the boardwalk studio. She had me take my paintings and supplies home—which I also want to talk to you about. But..." My throat tightened, and I pushed through. "She said I should think about showing my work. And my mom's reaction—God, Luke, she was impressed. It was... surreal." I tried to play it casual, but the heat in my cheeks gave me away. It mattered. Maybe too much.

His eyes shifted down to me.

"She suggested I show my work in a gallery and said she

would make the introduction. I'm going to reach out to the owner after she sets it up."

He grinned, slow and real. "Good. You should. You'll kill it."

Heat climbed my neck, but I forced it down with a smile. "It was weird, though—being seen like that. As if maybe it's not just a pipe dream."

"Not weird," he said. "It's about time."

We ate in silence for a while before the conversation drifted again, heavier this time.

"The boardwalk studio..." My voice caught on the words. "It's closing."

His arm stiffened around me. "Yeah."

"Do you know why the lease wasn't renewed?"

"Lorne's the one who pushed it. They're putting in a restaurant. Smart move, I guess. But that place..." He exhaled in a rough rush of air. "It was meant for you. Dad promised it would stay when I suggested the studio to go in that building. And now, I can't get a straight answer out of him."

I turned, watched the storm in his eyes, and for once, he didn't hide it. I covered his hand with mine. "I know you can't stop him. But the studio being gone—it doesn't erase what it meant. Not to me."

He looked at me, eyes burning, and the distance between us vanished.

His mouth caught mine, a collision that felt years in the making—weeks, maybe a lifetime, waiting to happen. The carton slipped from my fingers, forgotten, noodles sliding onto the coffee table. None of it mattered.

Luke's hand slid to the back of my neck, holding me steady while he deepened the kiss, not rushed, just sure. The way he always kissed—knowing exactly where to push and where to hold back. My chest arched into his, hungry for more.

The couch wasn't big enough for how badly I needed him closer. I broke the kiss and swung a leg over, straddling his lap.

His hands locked at my hips, firm, grounding. His eyes bored into mine, storm-dark, promising damage I didn't care if I drowned in.

His breath brushed my lips. "You're sure?"

"Yeah." Heat curled low in my stomach.

"The house is really ours tonight?"

"All night. She won't be back until tomorrow."

His gaze flicked over my face, memorizing every line, searching for doubt. I gave him none.

His thumb swept under the hem of my shirt, brushing skin, sending heat racing up my spine. I tugged his hoodie over his head, hair mussed, jaw set, fighting for the control he was about to lose. My fingers trailed down the chiseled lines of his chest, over ridges I'd never forgotten.

I kissed down his throat, nipping the spot that made his pulse jump. He hissed, hands clamping my waist, dragging me closer—no mistaking what he wanted. No denial left.

"Mila," he groaned into my hair, the sound guttural, wrecked.

"We said no lies. No games." I pulled back just enough to meet his eyes. "This is real."

His answer was his mouth on mine again, fierce this time. A clash. A claim. My shirt was gone before I realized he'd tugged it over my head. His palms splayed across my back, hot, certain, pulling me flush against his bare skin.

The taste of him filled me—salt, heat, hunger. My body answered without thought, rocking into him, catching friction that had me gasping against his lips. His hand slid lower, fingers curling into the waistband of my leggings, hesitating just long enough for me to nod. *Yes.*

Clothes became obstacles. His jeans hit the floor. My leggings followed. He fumbled for his wallet, tore open a foil packet with shaking hands. The sight—careful, certain—made something in my chest twist. Then his mouth was on mine again, all heat and hunger, as he rolled the condom on.

Skin to skin now, nothing between us but air and a year of wanting.

When he pushed inside me, I bit down on his shoulder to muffle the sound tearing out of me. He stilled, forehead pressed to mine, breath ragged.

"Okay?" he whispered, voice breaking.

"More than okay," I breathed, rolling my hips to prove it.

The pace built—slow at first, then faster, harder—burning through the silence and anger we'd carried too long. His hand tangled in my hair, his other gripping my thigh, anchoring me while we moved together, as if we'd never been apart.

Every sound, every breath, every scrape of skin felt like a promise—this wasn't about winning or losing. It was about us.

The couch creaked under us. My nails raked down his back, his name caught in my throat as heat coiled low and fast. He kissed me through it, swallowing my cries as I came undone against him.

He followed with a shudder, a groan deep in his chest as he buried his face in my neck. For a long moment, we stayed entwined, breathing each other in, refusing the distance that waited beyond the room.

When he finally pulled back, his eyes were softer than I'd ever seen them—storms eased, walls wide open.

"I've missed you." His voice was raw, scraped clean of anything but truth.

I smiled, brushing my thumb along his jaw. "Me too."

This time wasn't about fire or fury. It was easy because choosing him wasn't just a want but trust. And that was the part I hadn't been sure I could give back until now. It felt like we were exactly where we were meant to be—like the stars had finally lined up. We were safe in our bubble for now, but how long would that last?

CHAPTER SIXTEEN

LUKE

Mila's house carried scars if you looked too long—the carpet frayed at the baseboards, paint chipped around the windows, and the blinds leaned crooked. Even a faint water stain had spread across the ceiling. Her dresser drawer stuck just enough that you had to hip-check it to get it closed.

But I wouldn't have been anywhere else. Because she was here. And wherever Mila was—that was where I wanted to be.

She slept curled into me, arm draped across my chest. Her breath was steady against my skin. I hadn't slept much. A few hours, broken. Every time I closed my eyes, last night replayed like a reel spun in my head.

Her skin still burned against mine. Her mouth. The sounds she made when she let go—I felt them in my chest hours later, pulsing as if they hadn't faded at all. Every touch left a mark I couldn't shake. And she'd chosen me—not just for a kiss, not just to let me close, but for all of it. Trusting me enough to go there after everything between us. It told me she was right here with me, even if she wasn't ready to put it into words.

And I wasn't about to tell her how much it meant. I couldn't.

The truth was simple—she was it. The one. I loved her. More with every damn day, whether I wanted to or not. And maybe saying it —even just to myself—was reckless. In our volatile world, love wasn't just a choice. It was a weakness someone could weaponize.

I'd never felt this with anyone else, and I knew I never would. Growing up, I'd had to see too much too fast—shady deals, adults who lied with a straight face, loyalty that cracked the second it was tested. It taught me to hold things close, never hand anyone leverage they could use against me. Handing her that kind of power would tilt everything—make me the one reaching, the one at risk. And if she ever walked away again, I didn't know if I would survive it.

From the first moment I'd seen her, something had clicked. Not just her beauty—though that was enough to knock the air out of me—but her fire. Her stubbornness. The way she carried herself as though she refused to be owned, even when she was cornered. That spirit had lit something in me I hadn't been able to put out since.

Other guys noticed. They always had—the way heads turned when she walked in. They wanted her. But I'd already had her fire, her trust. No one was taking that from me again.

I shifted slightly, my arm numb from holding her all night. The mattress creaked, soft against the worn frame. She stirred, lashes fluttering, before her eyes blinked open.

It was still dark, but the edges of the blinds glowed faint, a thread of dawn leaking through. Her mom could walk in any minute, and finding me here wouldn't play well.

I brushed a strand of hair off her cheek, letting my fingers linger against her skin. Soft. Warm. Home.

Her eyes caught mine, hazy with sleep. "You're still here."

"Yeah," I murmured. "For a little while longer."

"Shouldn't you—" She yawned, voice rough with sleep. "Shouldn't you go before my mom gets home?"

"Soon." My thumb traced her cheek, down the curve of her neck. "Just not yet."

We stayed like that, looking at each other, the silence heavy but not uncomfortable.

"Last night," she whispered finally. "It meant something."

My throat tightened. "It did."

"I'm still… rebuilding," she murmured, fingers worrying the edge of the blanket. Her eyes dipped then lifted to mine. "But I trust you more now than I did before."

"Trust takes time," I said. "We both know that. But I'm here. All in. Even if no one else sees it."

"I get it." Her lips parted. "We can't be open. Not at school. Not with… everything."

"Yeah, for now." I hated it. I wanted to claim her, keep every asshole at bay. But Elise watched for cracks, and Logan lived to exploit them. Enemies were already circling. "Doesn't matter. What we are—it's ours. That's real. The rest of the world doesn't need to know yet."

She leaned into my chest again, her hand spreading flat over my ribs, as if she was grounding herself. "I like it when you say 'we.'"

I kissed her forehead. "Get used to it."

Her laugh was a soft breath against my skin, and for a second, the world outside didn't exist. But the sky was lightening, and I couldn't ignore it. I needed to leave before her mom walked in and found me in her daughter's bed.

I held her a little tighter anyway, stealing one more moment. The house could fall apart around us, and I still wouldn't want to leave. But sooner or later I had to—before her mom walked in, someone noticed, or our secret split wide open where enemies could see. The weight of leaving was more than just her door closing behind me.

CHAPTER SEVENTEEN

MILA

I didn't sleep. Not because of fear or everything circling us like sharks waiting for a drop of blood. It was Luke. The way his arms had wrapped around me without expectation. The steady rise and fall of his chest pressed against my back. The hitch in my breath when he said he didn't want to stop trying.

Even after he left, it lingered. His warmth. His weight. The echo of something I wanted too much. And I hated how much I wanted to believe it was real.

We'd texted on and off Saturday and Sunday—light things, safe things. It was different now, wanting to say more but knowing we couldn't. The space between messages felt heavier than it should have, a kind of distance I didn't love but understood we needed.

Saturday, 6:41 a.m.

Luke: *Home. Didn't get caught. Barely.*

Me: *Congrats on your stealth career.*

Luke: *Stealth is my backup plan if hockey fails.*

Saturday, 6:03 p.m.

Luke: *Did you paint?*

Me: *Sketched. Tried to sleep. Failed at both.*

Luke: *Same.*

Sunday, 4:12 p.m.

Me: *Went to the beach. It was a Mom day. No explosions. Calling it a win.*

Luke: *Send a photo.*

Me: *No evidence.*

Luke: *Coward.*

Sunday, 11:17 p.m.

Luke: *Goodnight, Callahan.*

Me: *Night, King.*

I hovered over a dozen other things that didn't make it onto the screen—nothing about Friday, nothing about the way it rewired something I didn't know how to name. We were careful. It kept us safe. It also kept us at arm's length in the exact place I didn't want distance.

By Monday morning, my limbs dragged as though they were made of lead. I stood in front of the bathroom mirror, toothbrush dangling from my mouth, fighting to keep my eyes open, my chain with the star charm glinting above the deep v of my shirt. I brushed a fingertip over it without thinking.

It felt dangerous. A secret I couldn't tell. A bruise I couldn't stop pressing.

The metal was cool against my skin, and the memory flashed quick—his mouth at my throat, his voice wrecked, the way his hands didn't push so much as hold. Friday wasn't an accident. It was a choice. Mine. I'd told him no lies, no games, and then I asked him to stay.

Want wasn't the scary part. I've always wanted him. The risk was what came after—the part where trust isn't a vow but a muscle that needs reps and rest and the right kind of tension. He'd given me all the checks I needed—steady hands, the pause for my nod, and leaving before my mom pulled in. He didn't take. He partnered.

The mirror held my gaze when I admitted it: something in

me had shifted. Not back to before—there is no before—but forward into a thing I can't define without giving it more power than feels safe. I'm not ready to hand it that name. I'm not ready to hand him that weapon.

But I also wasn't ready for the way my body kept remembering him while the rest of me rehearsed reasons to slow down. Partners. Not lovers. Not publicly. Not yet. Rules were a fence, but they didn't erase what was inside it.

I traced the star again, a pulse under metal. What was my choice, really? To align with Luke's plans, to stay hidden even after everything had changed Friday night? If I accepted that logic, it meant letting the star necklace mean what it used to— trust in us, in our future. Not just a promise I'd broken but a decision to go slow—and about playing it smart.

"Stop it," I muttered around a mouthful of toothpaste before spitting into the sink.

I knew better. I knew what happened when you let Luke King back in. Even if—for one night—he felt like home.

School hit me the second I walked through the doors— bright lights, voices bouncing off lockers, everything turned up too high.

I barely caught half of what Avery was saying when she joined me outside first period. Something about Elise whispering in corners again, someone's name tossed around behind us, but it all slid past like background noise.

"You okay?" Avery's voice cut through, softer than the noise. She slowed near my locker, her thick blond braid sliding over one shoulder as she looked at me.

"Fine."

"Mila."

"I said I'm fine."

She didn't push. But the silence that settled between us wasn't natural. She didn't believe me. And neither did I.

Second period was worse. The air in the classroom was too

warm, pressing against my skin. My pen slipped against my notes, the ink smearing. My brain refused to hold on to dates and formulas, because all it wanted was to replay the night before.

My lips still tingled from the press of his; my heart sprinted with every glimpse of Luke in the hallways. The fragile truce. His crooked smile when he said it back. I'd meant it then, but that was before our so-called truth talk rewrote everything. And the worst part? I wanted to trust it again.

By lunch, I'd had enough of the cafeteria noise, so I ducked out under the oak tree on the lawn. The ground was cool, damp from sprinklers. My back rested against the rough bark, knees pulled tight as I picked apart a granola bar without tasting it.

Somewhere across campus, he was probably laughing with his friends. Hoodie thrown on after morning skate, hair still damp, pretending none of it touched him while I came apart at the seams.

But I knew better. Luke didn't keep things shallow. He went deep, where it got complicated. And Friday night, he let me in.

Which made it worse that Avery found me, still tangled up in him, even when he wasn't here.

"Mila." Avery dropped down onto the grass beside me, stretching her legs out in front of her. She gripped a can of soda in one hand, the straw tapping against her thumb.

"Hey." I tucked the wrapper into my pocket.

"You've been MIA since Friday. I was starting to wonder if I should file a missing person's report."

"Been busy."

"Liar." She nudged me with her shoulder before sipping her drink.

I was halfway to brushing it off when it hit me—I hadn't asked her. I'd been so wrapped up in my own head all weekend, I'd completely forgotten. Heat crawled up my neck. "Wait. You went out with Jax after the game, right? How did I forget to ask you about that?"

Avery's lips curved, amused. "Wow. Took you until lunch to remember? I'm wounded."

I groaned, covering my face with my hands. "I was there when you two decided. I should've asked."

"Yeah, you should've." She leaned back against the tree, smug.

"Well?" I dropped my hands, narrowing my eyes. "Don't make me drag it out of you. What happened?"

Her cheeks flushed, the soda can rolling between her palms. "We grabbed food. Just the two of us. It felt… different. He was easier to talk to than I expected. Funny. Not all swagger like he is with the team."

"And?"

She hesitated then met my eyes. "And he told me he has feelings for me."

The words landed with the weight of a stone in my stomach. "He actually said that?"

"Yeah. Straight up. No games." She fiddled with the straw, restless. "But Chase…" Her voice trailed off.

"What about him?" I asked.

She blew out a breath, eyes flicking toward the football spiraling across the lawn. "He's not going to take it well. Me and Jax. It's the bro-code between them—I'm off limits. To him, Jax making a move is a major betrayal."

I frowned. "It's not his call, Avery."

"Exactly." Her chin tipped up, stubborn fire flashing. "I care about Chase, but he doesn't get to police who I date. I'm not twelve. And honestly, it's a little insulting he thinks he does."

"So what happens when Jax finally steps up? Because he's the one who needs to talk to Chase. He's going after his friend's sister—that's on him."

Avery's mouth twitched, like she'd already pictured it. "He

knows. He said he'll tell him." She hesitated then shook her head. "But even if he doesn't, I will. I'm not hiding. Chase can either deal with it or not."

She wasn't hiding, even with Chase in the way. I wished I could be that bold with Luke, instead of drowning in second guesses. Relief uncoiled in my chest. That was Avery—the girl who didn't back down once she'd decided something.

"You really care about him," I said quietly.

Her smile was small but sure. "Yeah. I do."

She studied me a second then tipped her head. "What about you and Luke? Be honest—what's really going on there?"

I pulled my knees up, wrapping my arms around them. "I feel like I'm drowning."

Avery blinked. "Metaphorical drowning or... actual water involved?"

A dry laugh slipped out. "Metaphorical. It's Luke. It's everything. The pull is still there, same as before, but we aren't the same." Not after Friday night. "And Elise..."

Avery rolled her eyes. "Don't even get me started."

"She's a problem. And she's not going away."

"Nope," Avery said. "But maybe she'll accidentally fall down a sewer grate."

I laughed, some of the tension in my chest lightening. "If only."

She nudged me with her shoulder. "So? Partners? Friends? More?"

I shrugged, staring at the grass between my sneakers. "Right now? Partners and becoming friends again. Maybe more. Friday night was..." The word caught in my throat. I forced it out anyway. "Intense. Like every wall I'd built between us crumbled in one breath. And I hate that part of me still wants to believe it wasn't just heat-of-the-moment."

Avery tilted her head, studying me. "So you're saying it felt real."

My chest tightened. "Yeah. But feeling something and trusting it is not the same."

She didn't push after that. Just nodded, thoughtful, as though she understood I'd already said more than I meant to.

Wanting Luke was one thing. Trusting what surrounded us was another. Which was why I asked, "Do you think things are serious between Theo and Tori?"

Avery tilted her head. "He doesn't talk about it much. They hook up, sure, but I wouldn't say it's anything deep. Why?"

I hesitated. "Tori was weird the other day. Defensive, but also twitchy whenever Elise was around. Almost scared to cross her, but not fully loyal either."

"That sounds about right."

"Do you think she knows something?"

Avery frowned. "Maybe. Or maybe she's just trapped. Elise doesn't let people go without destroying them. And Tori's not strong enough to walk away. Not yet."

I leaned back against the tree trunk, bark biting into my shoulder blades. "Elise doesn't scare me. The only reason she still has leverage is because of my mom. That's it."

Avery glanced sideways. "Then don't give her more than that. You've already walked away once. You could do it again."

I wanted to believe that. I really did. But this time wasn't just about running—it was about staying and surviving. And suddenly, staying didn't feel as risky anymore, because maybe we were finally strong enough to fight back.

The bell cut through, loud and unwelcome. Avery groaned, pushing herself up and brushing grass off her jeans. "Come on. Back to hell."

I followed her inside, her words trailing after me. Chase didn't get a say. Simple as that. I wished everything in my life could be that clear. But the danger wasn't gone. It never was. Which made wanting him feel reckless—and saying yes too easy.

By the time last period dragged itself to an end, my phone buzzed in my pocket. I didn't expect his name on the screen.

Luke: *You've been quiet today. You doing okay?*

My pulse tripped. I thumbed back a reply.

Me: *Yeah. Just thinking.*

Seconds later—

Luke: *Dangerous hobby. Want company later?*

My fingers hovered. The truth was already there, pressing against my chest.

Me: *Not tonight.*

I stared at the message, watched the screen dim. My hand drifted up, brushing the star charm at my collarbone, cool against my skin.

Then I added—

Me: *But maybe tomorrow.*

The screen glowed against the harsh afternoon light streaming through the classroom window, his name still bright in the glass reflection.

I didn't know where we were heading—only that I wasn't ready for it to end. Not yet. Even if I couldn't trust the outcome, part of me still trusted him. And maybe that was the riskiest thing of all.

CHAPTER EIGHTEEN

LUKE

I'd never wanted anything as badly as I wanted Mila. Not a goal. Not a championship. Not even my dad's approval. Just her.

Coach ran us through down-backs until my legs shook. He favored Mondays—the reset, the grind, the way a roomful of guys came in with weekend leftovers they needed to skate out. My calves still shook from edge work. Pucks zipped off sticks with that sharp, satisfying crack. The cold bit at my lungs, and I let it, took it as penance for things I couldn't fix yet. After, the locker room smelled of sweat, tape, and that metallic tang that never fully left your nose.

I showered fast, letting the hot water pound my shoulders until the muscles in my neck loosened. Then I pulled on a shirt from my bag, along with my jeans and boots. I didn't linger, didn't joke with the guys, and didn't even check the mirror. After tossing my gear into the trunk, I slid behind the wheel and gripped it at ten and two, watching my breath fog the cab for a beat before it faded.

Mila had texted earlier in school when I'd asked if she'd wanted company—*Not tonight. But maybe tomorrow.* It should've been enough. But those boundaries were meant to protect her, not trap her. And truth was, I couldn't shake the picture of her from Friday—head tipped back, fierce, mouth against mine, as though she'd already decided. I couldn't forget what I'd told her, low and certain. I'm here. All in. Even if no one else could see it.

I drove. The coast road was washed clean by the afternoon wind, eucalyptus bending over the shoulder and brushing the sky. The ocean flared blue between gaps, flashes of steel and white that hit me behind the ribs and settled there. My SUV ate up the cracks in the pavement, impatient, the way I was too.

I didn't text ahead, didn't ask for permission. I just pulled onto her street and parked where I could see her front step and the slice of the living room window beyond the hedges.

No invite. No pressure. I typed with my thumb. *No pressure, but I'm outside if you want company.*

I could've left it at that—sent the text, driven off, given her space. But I didn't move. My hands stayed locked on the wheel, my heart punching the same spot against my sternum. The porch light was still off. The window only threw back the sky and the tall shapes of the cypress at the end of the yard. No movement. Then the light flickered on, and the door opened.

She stepped into the rectangle of light, bare feet, nails painted a color I couldn't name in this distance. A soft sweater skimmed her shoulders, her hair wound up into a messy knot on top of her head that exposed the long line of her neck. The star charm glinted, catching what the porch light could find. She looked toward the street, spotted my SUV, then lifted a hand in a small gesture—come in.

By the time I walked up the path, the smell of lemon cleaner floated out into the evening. Her hand wrapped around the edge of the door. A dark smudge marked her thumb—graphite, probably.

"My mom'll be home soon," she said, voice low as though her mom would materialize if she talked too loud. "But come on in."

"Thanks." I kept it even, hands loose at my sides, when every part of me wanted to reach for her.

The living room was all soft edges and old furniture, the kind that sagged more from years of use than from any real comfort. A couch with a throw blanket in a knit that begged for a hand to drag across it. A sketchbook on the coffee table, spiral bent as if someone had worried it through a rough week. The window was cracked, letting in the salt and the last of the day's warmth. Somewhere in the kitchen, the fridge hummed steadily in the background.

She folded herself into the corner of the couch, legs tucked beneath her, the blanket pulled across her lap and up to her waist like a shield or a habit. She looked small. Breakable—but not fragile. Mila was forged in fire.

I didn't sit right away. I stood opposite the couch and took her in. The way she held my eyes and didn't. The way her mouth pressed and eased and pressed again.

"You okay?" I asked.

She looked at my chest, then my face, then the window, then back. A slow nod then a head shake. "No. But I will be."

I didn't push. I set my hand, palm up, on the cushion. I'd let her choose. That was the only pressure that worked.

She stared for a second as if it was a question she was answering for herself. Then she put her hand in mine.

Small. Warm. Callus along the side of her middle finger from a pencil that lived there too often. I folded my fingers around hers and felt something settle that hadn't since Friday.

Silence stretched long enough to count. Her breath evened. "Before we do anything else," I said, keeping my voice low, "I need to ask—are you having second thoughts about Friday night?"

The corner of her mouth ticked upward. Barely there. "No second thoughts."

My chest tightened, breath catching. I let my thumb trace her knuckles. "Good."

Her head found my shoulder like it had been meant to be there all along. The weight of it—the trust—hit me harder than any check on the ice. I leaned a fraction into her, careful. Her hair smelled of apples and ocean air, a mix that grounded me more than it should.

She shifted against me, her voice barely above a whisper. "I was quiet today because I was still trying to process. Friday... it changed things. Being with you that way." Her breath caught, soft against my shoulder. "And then today, pretending at school —acting as if we're nothing more than acquaintances—it was more difficult than I thought it would be. Harder because when we're here..." Her fingers tightened around mine. "It's all still there. Intense, but different too."

My throat burned, rough with how much I wanted to fix it. "Friday changed everything."

Her lips curved, faint but certain. "Yeah. It did. Even if it's messy."

"It is," I breathed. "We agree on that. The thing that sucks?" I exhaled through my nose, jaw tight because it wanted to clench. "I can't claim you publicly. Not yet. Not if it puts you in danger." If Elise caught even a whiff of this, she would twist it until it poisoned everything. And if Dunn wanted leverage? All he would have to do was pull the right string and watch us unravel.

Her head lifted. Eyes on mine. There was a softness there that didn't take anything away from the steel. "It sucks for me too."

"I know." The words burned, but I forced them out anyway. "It's killing me. Not being able to tell people you're mine. I want it out there."

Her breath hitched. The star charm rested against the collar of her sweater, a promise for a future I hoped was still within our grasp.

The world I grew up in measured everything in leverage. I learned that early—money shifted from one account to another, promises that sounded clean but always left a film, adults smiling while they lied. I watched, learned, and adapted. I grew up doing mental math, figuring out who would use what, and when.

It hadn't hit me when I first met her. But now I knew—people would try to use Mila against me, against herself. Elise already had. And my dad had the kind of power that could be a problem.

"We can wait if you want. If Friday was too much, or if it feels like moving too fast with everything else going on. But I won't pretend you aren't—" I stopped. The word wasn't ready for the air yet. I felt it under my sternum, stubborn and permanent. "Important."

Her mouth trembled as if she might contradict me, or laugh, or lean in. She did the last one. She rose on her knees and kissed me. Slow. Then not slow.

Her fingers slid along my jaw, found the line of stubble I'd missed with a blade this morning. She traced it as though she was learning a map she hadn't been allowed to study until now. My hand went to her waist and found the edge of her sweater and the heat of her skin where it had ridden up. I didn't pull. I set. I anchored. She made a sound in the back of her throat that took the rest of my patience and turned it to glass.

The kiss turned frantic. Then deep. Then something entirely ours. A rhythm we hadn't invented so much as uncovered, as though it had been under everything since the first time she'd shouldered past me in a hallway a lifetime ago. She tasted of mint and whatever sweet she'd had earlier. Sugar on the seam of her mouth. Confidence in the way she slid closer, one knee bracketing my thigh, the throw blanket tangling between us until I pushed it aside.

The star charm swung and tapped my throat, cold, a tiny

meteor hitting the same spot until I sucked in a breath and laughed into her mouth. She smiled against me like she knew exactly what she was doing.

And as much as I wanted to follow through with where this was going, we couldn't. Not tonight anyway. Her mom already wouldn't approve of me sitting here, let alone what we were doing. I didn't need another roadblock between me and Mila—not one I couldn't fight my way past.

Wanting her lived under my skin—every brush of her mouth flared it, heat racing through me, a fuse I kept trying to pinch out with both hands.

"Your mom," I managed, because it mattered, because it had to matter, because lines made us safer right now. "What time?"

"Soon." Her voice was air and heat and hard edges filed down. "Not yet."

I grinned without meaning to. "Not yet," I repeated, a promise and a plan wrapped in two words.

We didn't go all the way. But we went far enough that the room shifted around us, like it had been arranged for two people before and was pleased to get back to it. Her breath hitched when my mouth found the corner of hers. So did mine when her fingers slid under my shirt and pressed between my shoulder blades.

We found the brakes together—her palms flattening at my chest, my forehead resting against hers until breath evened. She was the first to lift her head. I was the first to step back into my body. Our breathing filled the space, the clock over the mantel ticking loud now that I noticed it.

When we pulled apart, the room felt cooler. The window breathed the night in. I searched her eyes for any flicker of regret, but there wasn't one—only the same steady pull that had been wrecking me since Friday.

Her gaze dropped to my mouth then to my chest like she could see my heart beating too fast. When she looked away, it landed on the coffee table. On the corner of the sketchbook, a graphite fingerprint was smudged across the cover.

"Were you drawing?" I asked, nodding toward it.

A flicker of something crossed her face—hesitation, possessiveness, shyness. She reached out, slid the sketchbook toward us, and hesitated again.

"You don't have to," I offered. "I was just—"

She flipped it open.

The page wasn't a full portrait. It was the side of my face—the hard angle of my jaw, the line of my cheekbone, the curve of my ear. She'd caught the way I looked off to the side, away from her, as if I was fixed on something in the distance. The shading made it sharper than I ever thought of myself, but I knew it was me. She'd even sketched the edge of the henley I'd worn, the collar loose at my throat, the kind of detail only someone who'd been paying too much attention would bother with.

Something inside me sat down and refused to move. I didn't lift my eyes from the page, afraid the moment might break if I did. "When did you do this?"

"Saturday." She tucked hair behind her ear. "After."

"After us."

She didn't answer out loud.

It resonated in a way I wasn't ready for—that she'd seen me this way and put it down in graphite. Every line was proof she carried me with her, even when I wasn't there. I didn't know what to do with the weight of that, only that it shook me all the way through.

Instead, I kept it where it was and let my thumb rest on the margin, careful not to smudge.

"You drew me before?" I asked, not teasing, not fishing. Just —curious. Starved.

Her mouth curved. "Maybe once." Pause. "Twice."

"More than twice," I guessed, because the spiral on the

binding wasn't new, and the graphite on her fingers looked permanent. "You keep me in here?"

"It's easier than keeping you out," she said, so quiet I almost missed it.

I blew out a breath that emptied everything I'd been holding. "You can keep me however you need."

She huffed something that was almost a laugh, maybe to keep herself from doing anything else.

We went quiet again, the good kind. The kind that built something instead of breaking it.

"Things are moving fast with us," she said softly.

I tightened my grip on her hand. "But this time, we don't let anyone tear us apart. No one gets between us."

"Agreed." Her mouth curved into a grin. "How was practice?"

"Loud," I said. "Coach was in a mood. Edge work until we wanted to puke. The guys went at each other as if it were play-offs, and coach finally barked at us to dial it back."

Her mouth quirked. "And did you?"

"Not really." I grinned.

She liked that more than she let on. I could tell by the way she leaned into me.

"I talked to Avery today," she said after a beat. "At lunch."

"What about?"

"Her and Jax. And everything else." A spark lit her eyes, sly. "Avery's going to stand up to Chase. Jax is going to talk to him too."

"He better," I groaned. "It's a blow-up waiting to happen. At least if he's straight about it, there's a chance they'll get through it."

Her smile pulled to the side. "You all have your codes."

"We do," I admitted. "Some of them are worth something."

She tipped her head. "You going to talk to the guys about... us?"

"No." It was too easy to answer. "Not yet. My friends

wouldn't say anything, but Theo could let it slip to Tori without thinking. And if she knows, Elise knows. I'm not giving her that."

Mila's mouth tightened. "Yeah. Elise would have a huge issue with us."

"We need to figure out what her angle is first. Until then, I'm not giving her anything she could use to get at you."

A car rolled by out front, tires whispering over the curb. We both stilled the way you do when you're listening for something particular. The headlights kept going, throwing shadows across the ceiling. It wasn't her mom, not yet.

"How long?" I murmured.

"I don't know. Ten minutes. Maybe fifteen."

"Okay." I sat forward, elbows on my knees, hands clasped, head hanging for a second while the reality of leaving this room in under a quarter hour dug its thumb under my ribs. "Then we use it."

"How?" she asked, mouth tipping up like she knew exactly how.

"This way," I said, turning to her again, taking in the line of her throat, the pulse under it, the way her sweater slipped off one shoulder.

I met her halfway. Her mouth brushed mine once, tentative, before she leaned in again with more pressure. Each shift of her lips felt like a decision—choosing me, choosing this. Her fingers slid into my hair, tugging just enough to pull me closer, and I set my hands at her hips, holding steady.

We didn't push it as far this time, but we didn't need to. It was enough to feel the way she softened—and then didn't, enough to know she was choosing me again and again.

When we finally pulled apart, the room felt cooler, as though the air had shifted around us. I pressed a kiss to her forehead then another to the corner of her mouth because I could, because it was allowed, because her *no second thoughts* had undone something I hadn't admitted was still knotted.

"We're going to be careful," I said.

"I know."

"We're going to be smart."

"Sometimes."

"We're going to be partners."

Her eyes were steady. "Always."

Headlights swept across the living room wall through the half-open blinds, gravel crunching in the drive. I'd parked farther down the street not to be noticed, and I was glad I had.

We moved on instinct. She straightened the blanket, crossed to the door with a practiced ease that almost looked natural. I stood, grabbed my keys, and hesitated anyway, not ready to be on the other side of the threshold.

She paused with me, hand on the knob, eyes lifting. The star at her collarbone caught the overhead light in a sharp flare.

I moved quietly through the kitchen and slipped out the back door just as her mom's car rolled to a stop in the driveway. She shifted so her body blocked the view inside from the street, and it should have been the smallest thing, but I felt it—protection both ways.

I didn't look back until I hit the path. When I did, she was still in the doorway, half-shadow, that star glowing beneath her collarbone, a small lighthouse in the dark. She didn't wave. She didn't need to.

The evening air carried the salt of the ocean. The cypress shifted in the wind. My SUV chirped as it unlocked, steady and familiar.

I got in, shut the door gently, and sat with my hands on the wheel for a beat, mirroring the stillness I'd felt in the rink lot. The porch light glowed behind me. Her mom's car door *thunked*, soft. Voices, low. Normal.

I wanted to shout she was mine, carve it in ice, set it on fire in the language this town understood. Instead, I put the SUV in drive. Not yet. Not until it was safe. But as I pulled away, I knew the truth anyway—Mila was it. The measure of every choice I would make, whether I said it out loud or not.

I glanced at my phone where it sat in the cup holder, screen black, my reflection faint in it. I imagined her sketchbook again —the side portrait, the distant determination carved in my expression. The proof.

The road opened ahead, dark-mirrored where the last sun still clung west. I pressed the pedal and the SUV responded, steady and fast and mine. I drove the coastal road back, palms bending above, the ocean slipping in and out between houses.

And for once, the want didn't eat me alive. It lit me from the inside and dared the world to try me.

CHAPTER NINETEEN

MILA

By Wednesday night, the quiet had started to feel dangerous. Even under the hockey arena lights, it felt as though something was hiding in the dark.

Elise had been suspiciously silent. No more hovering near the guys' row of lockers or draping herself across the cafeteria tables as if she owned them. Apparently, the freeze-out had mostly worked. I suspected it was more her biding her time for the perfect open than anything else.

But the rest of the school hadn't gone that far. No one shunned her the way they had initially. No whispers when she passed. No pointed looks. Instead, people gave her space. Conversations hushed when she passed, eyes sliding away too fast. Not loyalty. Just fear.

Because her dad wasn't the Kings, not even close. But he had money, influence, and connections. And in Blackwood, that counted. Enough to keep Elise relevant. Enough to make her untouchable to anyone who wasn't already brave—or stupid—enough to cross her.

She and her minions had been too quiet. Even Logan had gone still. Too still.

I knew Luke was keeping watch. But so was I. The silence didn't mean surrender. It meant planning. Waiting. They would try something else, soon. We had to be ready, several steps ahead.

That wasn't all that circled my thoughts on loop: Darren. Mr. Langley—or whatever version of him had crawled back from the dead. Why Mom had been called back. Why he'd been slotted into Dunn's side of the chessboard, working for the Kings' rivals after Lorne's betrayal in the form of a gunshot wound. But knowing that didn't make it clearer. It just made me more certain of one thing: we were pawns in someone else's game—and pawns got sacrificed.

For now, though, I held on to the reprieve. I held on to Luke. The time we stole outside of school. The moments when the weight slid off my shoulders just enough to breathe again.

I'd never stopped loving him. Not when I left. Not when I came back. Not even through the worst of it. Luke was larger than life—yes—but more than that, he was mine. He was the one who steadied me when everything else tilted. And even though we'd gone through hell the second I set foot in Blackwood again, things were shifting. Smoothing out.

He'd let me back in. And I'd chosen to do the same. To tell him the truth I had, even if it wasn't everything. What I'd learned about Dunn buying up King Enterprises stock on the sly. Why we'd left. Why we'd come back. At least the pieces I knew.

I leaned against the side of Luke's SUV in the arena's lot. The arena lights burned overhead, a harsh white glow flattening everything into shadow and glare. Each time the doors opened, bright rink light cut across the lot before snapping shut again, shadows elongating once more.

They came in groups, sticks slung over shoulders, hockey bags banging against their legs. Jax tossed me a mock salute on his way past. Theo gave me one of his lazy grins. A couple of the younger guys lifted their chins in recognition. No one lingered. And then Luke.

His hair was still damp from the shower, shirt pulled tight across shoulders worn down by two hours of drills. He clapped a teammate on the back, muttered something that made the guy laugh, then glanced over. His eyes locked on me, and the rest of the lot fell away.

I'd texted him before practice ended—*Meet me outside. I want to show you something.*

So when he spotted me leaning against his SUV, he wasn't surprised. Just focused.

"Hey," he said, voice low when he reached me, as if it was just ours.

"Hey." My pulse stuttered. "Ready?"

"Yeah." His eyes searched mine. "Where to?"

He said bye to the guys, a few of them waving toward me before peeling off to their cars. Luke unlocked the SUV with a beep, but I shook my head.

"Not here," I murmured. "Come back to my house, just for a few minutes. I want to show you something."

We parked a few blocks over, where no one would notice his SUV in front of my house. My mom's car was already in the drive. The glow of the TV flickered blue across the front windows.

Luke raised a brow. "Your mom's home."

"I know." My voice was steady. "Back way."

He followed without question, hands tucked in his hoodie pocket, boots silent on the damp grass. I led him to the side yard, fingers brushing against cold siding as I climbed the trellis. My bedroom window slid open on the second try. I slipped inside first, heart pounding, then turned and reached for him.

Luke grinned—half challenge, half thrill—and hauled himself up with an easy grace that was so him it didn't surprise me at all. He landed inside my room with a muffled thud, scanning the space before locking eyes with me again.

The TV hummed faintly downstairs. A laugh track floated up, cover noise. We didn't speak. Not until I crossed to the easel in the corner and tugged the drop cloth away.

Oil paint—thick strokes, layers built slow until the image came alive.

A night sky, star-salted and endless. A rooftop cutting black against it. Two silhouettes lying side by side.

Luke's breath shifted behind me, heavier. He stepped closer, the heat of him reaching me before his hands did.

His voice was thick when it finally came. "Is that us?"

I nodded. "Painting's just… part of me. I can't turn it off. And lately, all that comes out is this. You. Us."

What I didn't say was that it had been that way ever since he entered my life. When I drew him, it felt like opening a window into his every thought and emotion. I saw things in my art he never let anyone else see.

He was there in an instant, arms wrapping around my waist, pulling me back against him. His chest was solid, his breath hot against the curve of my neck.

"Then don't fight it. Don't fight us."

The words hit something deep. My throat caught. I turned in his arms, searching his eyes.

"Luke…"

"Mila." His hand slid up my spine then cupped the back of my neck.

"I love you." The words broke loose, quiet but sure.

His breath punched out of him. For a heartbeat, I thought maybe I'd broken him.

"You don't have to say it back," I rushed, pulse racing.

"Too late." His mouth curved then crashed against mine, and he kissed me with the kind of intent that left no doubt. We were already home.

Heat sparked low in my chest, spreading fast. His lips moved against mine with a hunger that stole my breath, but it wasn't just urgent—it was steady, claiming, sure. My hands slid up his chest, fingers clutching at the fabric of his hoodie until I fisted it tight.

Luke groaned softly, the sound vibrating against my mouth. His arms tightened around me, pulling me flush against him. His palms at my back, the press of his thighs against mine. His breath caught when I tilted my head and deepened the kiss.

I'd kissed him before. I'd missed him before. But this was different. This was years of want and anger and forgiveness burning down to one undeniable truth: he was mine.

The star charm pressed between us, cool metal tapping against my skin with every shift. Luke noticed. I felt the moment his chest rose harder, the kiss roughening as his thumb brushed the chain where it dipped along my collarbone.

My knees went weak. He caught me, steady and unrelenting. His mouth gentled for half a heartbeat—sweet, coaxing—before it turned fierce again.

I broke away only when air became impossible, my forehead resting against his. His lashes were dark, his eyes blazing in the dim light of my room.

"Say it again," he rasped.

My lips curved, trembling, but sure. "I love you."

His jaw clenched. His grip flexed on my waist, as if he was holding the words inside himself until they broke out. "I love you too."

Then his mouth found mine again, fiercer, deeper, a promise inked into every movement. His hands slid beneath the hem of my sweater, palms hot against my skin, anchoring me in place. My own hands tangled in his hair, tugging him closer until there was no space left between us.

We tipped backward onto the edge of my bed, the mattress dipping beneath our weight. He braced himself on one arm, careful, but the heat between us pulsed wild. His teeth grazed my bottom lip; I gasped.

The murmur of the TV downstairs drifted up, laughter too bright, too out of place. Reality pressed in.

Luke tore his mouth from mine with a groan, his forehead dropping to my shoulder. His chest heaved against me, every breath ragged.

"Not tonight," he muttered, voice rough with want.

My heart pounded erratically. "I know."

His lips brushed the side of my neck, lingering there like a brand, before he pushed himself upright, dragging me with him so I was sitting in his lap. His hands cupped my face, thumbs stroking once across my cheekbones.

"But soon," he said, eyes locking on mine. "Soon, Mila."

I nodded, throat too tight for words. I kissed him again, softer this time—a promise we couldn't keep yet but both wanted more than anything.

CHAPTER TWENTY

LUKE

The house was quiet when I pulled into the drive. Too quiet. I killed the engine, the headlights washing out the garage door before darkness snapped back in. For a minute I just sat there, phone heavy in my palm, my PI's voicemail replaying in my head.

"Luke, it's Marcus. I've dug up a few things. Sending over an encrypted file—should hit your inbox soon. Darren Langley's logs don't add up. Travel records don't match. There's footage too, blurry as hell, but it might be something. Call me back."

I hadn't called him back yet.

Instead, I got out and leaned against the hood of my SUV, the chill of the metal bleeding through my jeans, and opened the attachment.

Falsified logs. Fake travel records. Dates bent to fit an agenda, not reality. And the photo—a grainy shot of a figure leaving King Enterprises the night Darren Langley disappeared.

The face was a smear. The shoulders—broad, sloped—hit a nerve. Familiar enough to make my gut knot. Not proof. Just a shape that wouldn't let go. Couldn't be. But maybe.

I closed the file and opened it again, hoping the blur would sharpen. It didn't. Just suspicion, heavy as stone.

I wouldn't dump the still on Mila—not until I had more than a blurred frame. But the rest—the numbers, the dates—I'd show her. We were past pretending.

The money trail said Dunn was paying Langley. Langley worked at King. That meant someone inside King was feeding Dunn. Not rumor—transactions. And Mila's mom being back at Dunn after working with King didn't read as coincidence; it felt intentional. Dunn didn't just push, he arranged. Put people where he wanted them, then tightened the net. And if I was all in with Mila—and I was, no question—that meant keeping her safe, no matter how deep the rot went.

Things had been quiet too long. Elise keeping her head down. Her dad pulling strings, maybe more than we knew. Elise running her own angles under his. It wouldn't stay this way. Not for long.

I scrolled my phone, thumb hovering before hitting Theo's name.

He picked up after the second ring, voice rough. "What's up?"

"How's it going with Tori?"

A pause. I heard the sound of a TV in the background, muffled laughter. "She's scared of Elise," he admitted. "Not just scared—controlled. They've cut her off. She's not hearing things the way she used to."

I clenched my jaw. "Is Tori willing to push back?"

"She's trying." Theo's voice dropped. "She said she'd feel out Nina, see what she can get from her. But nothing yet. And her internship's a dead end. She's not close to the big players. At least not right now."

I let the silence hang a beat. "Keep at it. Careful, though."

"Always," he said, then exhaled. "And, Luke? Watch your

back. If Elise is quiet, it's only because she's loading the next shot."

"Yeah," I muttered. "I know."

We hung up.

My phone buzzed again almost immediately.

Mila: *Sneaking out. Mom passed out on the couch. Pick me up? Let's go to the roof.*

The screen dimmed in my hand, then turned black. I didn't bother waking it back up.

Because right now? She was the only truth I needed.

I pulled up to the curb outside her house, headlights cutting across the front yard. The TV flickered blue in the living room.

The front door eased open a crack, then Mila slipped out. She wore an oversized sweatshirt and leggings, her hair loose and catching the porch light for a heartbeat before she darted across the grass. She slid into the SUV and pulled the door shut, her smile wide and electric.

"Hey," she whispered, as if the night belonged to us.

"Hey." My chest loosened just seeing her.

We drove a short way before I cut the engine behind the rink. No one would notice us here—only a few staff cars scattered across the lot.

"Side door." I nodded toward the back. "Still got the key."

Mila's eyes flickered with something between mischief and challenge. "Of course you do."

The lock clicked under my hand, the heavy metal door creaking just enough to set my nerves on edge. Inside, the corridor smelled faintly of cold and old rubber, the hum of the compressors deep in the walls. We moved quiet, sneakers whispering against floor, until we hit the stairwell.

The climb felt endless, the echo of each step chasing us up. At the top, another door—this one stiff but not locked. I shoved my shoulder into it, and it gave way. The night air rushed in, cool and welcome.

The roof stretched flat beneath us, tar-black and gritty under the glow of arena lights bleeding from below. The town spread out in the distance, streetlamps glowing soft gold, the coast dark and endless beyond.

I dropped the blanket I'd stuffed under my arm, spreading it across the rough surface. Mila sank onto it, legs folding beneath her, hair catching the starlight. The star charm at her throat winked with every breath she took.

I stretched out beside her, the blanket barely softening the hard roof, and pulled her in close.

We lay shoulder to shoulder, her head tucked against me, my arm curling around her waist. The stars above us were brutal in their clarity, the kind of night sky that made you feel both infinite and small.

"Whatever happens," she said softly, breaking the quiet, "don't lie to me."

"I won't."

"Promise?"

"On us."

She tilted her head, kissed me once. Not fire. Not urgent. This one felt like forever. And it undid me.

I deepened it, turning toward her, pulling her closer until her chest pressed flush against mine. Her fingers curled into the fabric of my shirt, dragging me with her as she shifted, rolling so I half-covered her.

The world narrowed to the heat between us, to the taste of her, to the way her breath hitched when my hand slid under her sweatshirt and found skin—warm, soft, real.

Her lips parted, inviting, and I lost myself there. "Mila..." My voice broke against her mouth.

She only answered by pulling me closer, legs tangling with mine, her body arching up.

We'd shared wild, desperate kisses before, but tonight, there was no rush. No panic. No edge of being caught. Just us, under the sky, nothing in the way.

Her hand skimmed down my chest, slipped beneath the hem of my shirt. My breath stuttered. She felt it, smiled against my mouth, and pushed further.

I braced myself on one hand, careful not to crush her, but she tugged harder, pulling me down until there was no space left.

The stars above us burned, the silver one cool against her throat as the chain shifted. My lips followed it, tracing down the line of her neck, across her collarbone, tasting the salt on her skin.

Her fingers fisted in my hair. A soft sound escaped her throat, raw and unguarded.

And then there were no more brakes.

Clothes pulled aside, skin against skin, the roof hard beneath us but none of it mattering because her warmth erased everything else.

Her eyes found mine in the starlight, wide, certain. "Luke," she whispered.

I kissed her again, harder, and we crossed the line together.

The air between us thickened—heat and want coiled tight, the kind that burned slow before it combusted. Every inch of her drew me closer. My hands slid over her hips. Her breath caught, and she arched into me like she couldn't get close enough. Mila was an addiction I couldn't—wouldn't—quit.

When her lips brushed across mine, going slow wasn't an option. I deepened the kiss so it was both claiming and surrender tangled together, devouring her, invading her mouth until she moaned. Her heartbeat pounded against my chest, wild and certain, matching mine.

She whispered my name, and the sound hit low and hard in my chest. I answered with a promise against her skin, a rough sound that barely counted as words. Everything in me wanted to memorize her—every breath, every tremor, the way she gasped when I moved, and the way her fingers clutched my hair.

The world fell away until there was nothing but the two of us—her warmth under my hands, the scrape of the roof beneath the blanket, the cool rush of night air over overheated skin. Every movement blurred into the next, the rhythm between us tightening until there was no line left to cross.

I slid my fingers down her silky skin and brushed in a teasing caress over her small bundle of nerves. Met by her warm, wet heat, I slipped my finger in, my thumb circling her clit as I pumped inside her. She writhed beneath me, then I curled my finger until she gasped.

"Luke."

Her throaty whisper wrapped around me, sending a rush of desperate need pulsing through me.

I reached for my jeans, fumbling for my wallet. Wrenched free from my pocket, I hastily retrieved a condom, tore the wrapper with my teeth, then sheathed myself. A slow, sensual grin curved her lips. I lined up at her entrance, straining to bury myself deep inside.

Her nails dug into my shoulders, urging me to move. I fed an inch in, and a whimper left her lips before I thrust deep inside. She clenched tightly around me as I withdrew almost to the tip before driving all the way in.

As we moved together, every flicker of her expression pulled me deeper. The way her head tipped back, the sound that caught in her throat—God, she was beautiful.

She pulled me closer, her legs tightening around me, every breath coming faster. Her hands tangled in my hair, tugging as she kissed me, matching my need. When she caught my lip between her teeth and eased the sting with her tongue, I lost it. I wrapped my hand around the nape of her neck. The other gripped her ass as I drove deep. Her hips tilted, and she met my furious pace.

Before I lost control, part of me yelled to pay attention to how fucking right everything about it felt.

I fucking loved how responsive she was. She arched against me, and a wave of lust drove me to go harder, faster until her body convulsed around me, and she cried out.

Two more thrusts, and I followed her. I dropped against her for a second, then shifted, bracing on my arms as we caught our breath. The cool air cut across my back, slipping between us in the space my shift created, waves breaking somewhere in the distance.

We both groaned when I pulled out, and she slid her legs down. I dragged a hand through my hair, still reeling from how badly I wanted her. One touch from Mila could drop me.

I pressed my forehead to hers, both of us caught in the same pull that had always existed.

And when the tension broke, it was all light and silence and the faint hum of the ocean in the distance.

For a long moment, neither of us moved. I felt her pulse against my chest, steadying, grounding. She breathed out, and I caught the sound with my lips—a quiet, content exhale that settled deep inside me.

After, we lay tangled, my shirt bunched under her head, her body curled into mine. The night wrapped around us, stars endless overhead. The roof was hard beneath the blanket, the air cool against my skin, but none of it mattered. She was warm, steady, here.

Her fingers traced the inside of my arm, slow and absent, as though she was memorizing the shape of me. "It feels different," she murmured.

"Because it is." My voice came out rough, low.

Different because her hand was still on my chest, steady on my heartbeat. Because she knew I loved her. And I would burn the world down before I let anyone take her. We just needed to make it out of here, get to college, and the world could be ours.

The truth sat heavy in my chest. Protecting her might mean tearing into my own flesh and blood, uncovering things about my family I'd spent years trying not to see. It might mean exposing whatever Elise and her dad were plotting, cutting the strings they kept pulling tight around us. None of that mattered as much as this—her, here, against me.

Our futures felt close enough to touch. And the only one I wanted was with her. I would find a way to make that happen, no matter what stood in the way.

She must've felt it—the resolve in me, the promise—because her hand slid higher on my chest, palm pressing over my heart. No words. Just the smallest nod against my shoulder, as if she understood I was all in now.

She tilted her head, cheek brushing my shoulder. Silence stretched, filled with the hum of the ocean beyond town, the rustle of palm fronds in the breeze.

Her hand shifted on my chest, flat against the steady pound of my heart. "I used to think I'd never get this again. Especially with how things were when I came back."

"I'm sorry," I said quietly. "For how I treated you. I was pissed, but that's not an excuse. I should've tried to talk to you."

Something in her eyes flickered, the starlight catching the shine there. "And I should've told you the truth before I left. Even if my mom didn't want me to. You deserved that."

I shook my head, thumb stroking the corner of her mouth. "We both screwed it up."

"But we're here now," she whispered.

"Yeah." My voice came rough.

She looked up at me then, eyes glinting faintly in the starlight, the star charm pressed between us.

"Don't disappear on me," I said, the words breaking rougher than I meant.

Her lips parted, soft with regret. "I won't. Not again."

I cupped her cheek, thumb brushing the corner of her mouth. "Good. Because I couldn't take it twice."

Her lips curved then, small and certain. I kissed her forehead, then the bridge of her nose, then her lips, softer this time.

We stayed there, staring at the sky, both of us breathing slower. The stars looked endless, scattered across the black.

She whispered, almost to herself, "It feels like forever up here."

I tightened my arm around her waist. "That's what I want with you. Forever."

Her breath caught, a tiny sound. She pressed her face into my chest, and I felt her smile against me.

And as the night stretched on, with her against me, there was no doubt left. I knew—no matter what waited with Elise, with her dad, with the shadow games between the companies—this was it. She wasn't just my present. She was where it all ended—and began.

CHAPTER TWENTY-ONE

MILA

I woke in my room to the scent of paint and lavender, sketchbooks stacked, canvases leaning against the wall—but the air felt different. It carried traces of him. The memory of his hands, his mouth, his weight braced above me. Mom didn't know I'd slipped out last night or crept back in. I'd spent most of the night on the arena roof with Luke, the stars laid out like a ceiling over us, and let myself be his.

Being in his arms, being with him—it was everything. Safe. Wanted. Desired. Loved. Every touch a tether that steadied me and set me free at the same time. And sex with him... there weren't words. It left me hungry in a way I hadn't known before Luke—every time different, better, as though we were relearning each other from the inside out.

I padded barefoot through the house, the floor cool against my soles. A hoodie hung over the back of a chair, the familiar gray cotton worn soft. Luke's. I pulled it on, the sleeves too long, the weight of it an armor I didn't want to take off.

Coffee in hand, I stepped out into the backyard. The sky was that hazy pre-sunrise blue, morning clinging to the edges. I sat on the old bench swing, phone in my lap, and scrolled.

His messages waited. From last night.

Made it home safe. Still thinking about you. Can't stop.

My chest ached in the best way.

Friday blurred by in pieces. Classes slid one into the next. Elise kept her corner, her minions flanking her, but she didn't make a move. Logan stayed quiet too. Too quiet. It didn't feel like victory, more like the pause before another round.

Art with Avery was the only part of the day that felt truly mine. Charcoal dust smeared across my hands, graphite catching under my nails. Avery leaned over her paper, hair slipping loose from its braid, and shot me a grin when the teacher wasn't looking. We didn't need words to share the relief—that here, at least, we could breathe.

By the final bell, I wasn't ready to go home. Avery wasn't either. So we ended up at the Grill Shack, the burger place near the highway with cracked red booths and a jukebox in the corner that cycled through old rock tracks on repeat. The place was packed—families, a few kids from our school, a couple of old guys at the counter nursing coffee—but somehow, we snagged a booth in the back.

The vinyl seat squeaked as I slid in. I set down the red plastic basket, grease already blotching the paper liner beneath the fries. Avery didn't wait—she swiped one before I even unwrapped my burger.

The question I'd been circling pushed to the surface. I toyed with the corner of the paper then glanced at Avery. "What about Tori?"

Avery's fry froze halfway to her mouth. "What about her?"

"Is she serious about Theo?"

Her expression turned thoughtful, the grin fading. "Hard to say. It's clear she has feelings with the way she looks at him. But I think she's afraid of Elise."

"Do you think she'll ditch Elise? Possibly to our side?" Elise still had tricks up her sleeve, and I bet Tori knew more than she was letting on. If she broke ties, would she give those potential plans up?

Avery shrugged, finally chewing the fry. "If she thought she'd survive it? Maybe."

Maybe. The word stuck like grit lodged in my throat. Maybe was dangerous. Maybe could be betrayal. But for now, maybe was all we had.

I pushed the fry basket back toward her, a small smile tugging at my mouth. "Then we'll take maybe. Until we can make it more."

Avery nodded, and the hum of the diner rose around us again, the world moving on. But beneath the chatter and the grease and the flicker of the neon sign in the window, I felt it— the ground shifting. We were in the calm before the storm. And somewhere out there, Elise was waiting for her chance to make it break. To somehow claim Luke for herself and take down as many of us—me, Avery, possibly my mom—when she did.

By the time the fries were mostly gone, Avery leaned in, voice lower than the buzz around us. "Okay, so I have to tell you something."

My brows rose. "That's never not ominous."

Avery rolled her eyes, but her cheeks flushed pink. "I snuck out."

I smirked. "With Jax." And it must've been the theme of the night.

"Shut up." She bit into a fry, chewing as though it bought her time. "We just... walked along the shore. Talked. He was weird about me sneaking out, but not in a bad way. He just wanted to make sure I was safe. He said he's going to talk to Chase this weekend. After the game."

My stomach flipped. "That's going to go well."

She groaned. "Yeah, I know. But he has to so they don't mess up their friendship. And..." Her lips twitched into a smile she couldn't hold back. "We kissed."

I leaned in, grinning despite myself. "And?"

"And it was… good. Really good." She pressed her hands to her cheeks, muffling her laugh. "I feel ridiculously giddy."

Warmth bloomed in my chest for her, but it was tangled with unease. Chase wasn't going to take it lightly—his best friend with his sister. It could split everything wide open.

"You're happy," I murmured, watching the way her cheeks flushed, the way she practically vibrated with excitement. "Not just surface happy—lit up from the inside."

Her smile softened, her expression glowing under the flicker of neon from the window. "I am."

"Then I'm happy for you." My voice dipped, quieter. "Even if Chase is going to lose his mind."

Avery sighed, slumping back against the booth. "Maybe Luke can smooth it over. Chase actually listens to him."

"Sometimes." I dragged a fry through a smear of ketchup on the paper. "Depends on if Chase is in a mood." I met her gaze. "And Jax? Is he still pretending to be your bodyguard?"

The pink returned to her cheeks. "He's… protective. But not in a suffocating way." She rolled her eyes for effect, but the smile gave her away.

"So you like it." I arched a brow at her, watching her blush give her away.

"Maybe." She shoved the fry basket at me. "Eat before I finish them all."

We both laughed, the sound cutting through the hum of the diner.

"Jax, huh?" Nina's condescending voice dissolved our laughter.

We hadn't even seen Nina slip in—as if she'd been waiting for the moment. My stomach turned to ice. She stood from a booth behind Avery. Her smile was wicked as she came around to stand in front of where we sat. "Didn't think you had it in you, Avery. That'll cause a stir, won't it?"

Nina winked, tucked her phone away, and turned on her heel as she headed out the door, high blond ponytail swinging with every step.

Avery's face went chalk white. "No. No, no, no—"

I shoved out of the booth, my heart pounding. "We have to get to the rink."

We didn't stop to clean up, didn't look back. We bolted into the humid air, sprinting through the parking lot until our lungs burned. Every step drummed with panic. We took my car. Once inside, I peeled out.

Neither of us spoke. The hum of the engine drowned out everything—our panic, our questions, the words we couldn't take back. By the time the rink's lights came into view, my chest was hollow with dread.

We stumbled into the rink. Sweat slicked my palms, and my pulse clawed at my throat. The place was quiet except for the muffled echo of blades on ice. No Elise. No Nina. For half a second, hope sparked. Maybe Nina was bluffing. Maybe she'd just wanted to rattle us.

Then Avery's phone buzzed. Her hands shook as she fumbled it out, eyes darting across the screen.

"Goddammit."

I leaned over. The post was already up, spreading fast: *Avery + Jax. Sneaking behind the Elites' backs. How long before Chase finds out his best friend is hooking up with his sister?*

The blood drained from my face.

"They'll hear it from us first." Avery's voice broke. "We have to tell them."

The guys were still practicing so we had no other option but to wait. We stood where they would exit, our nerves raw, until the guys exited the ice. Steam rising from their skin, jerseys clinging, all of them laughing—still in that bubble where the world hadn't yet shifted.

Avery stepped forward. "Chase—we need to talk."

He slowed, grin fading when he saw her expression. "What's wrong?"

Her lips trembled, but she squared her shoulders. "I like Jax, and you don't have a say in it. I don't care about the bro-code pact between you guys."

The words detonated.

Chase's head snapped toward Jax. The laughter in the passway died, players freezing mid-step.

Jax didn't move. Didn't deny. His eyes held Chase's. And Chase's fist flew.

Chase's fist cracked against Jax's face, the sound echoing down the hall. Jax staggered back into the bench gate, the clang reverberating as the arena exploded with shouts. Bodies scrambled between them. But Jax didn't raise a hand. Didn't strike back. He just wiped the blood from his mouth and stood there, chest heaving, while Chase came at him again.

The second hit landed harder. Jax's head snapped sideways, blood streaking his jaw. His hands clenched, body coiled as if he could break Chase in two if he wanted—then loosened again. He took it. Silent.

Chase roared, shoving against Luke and Theo who were trying to hold him back. Rage poured out of him, hot and jagged. "You—my sister? My best friend?!"

Luke's voice cut low, steady—the kind of tone that usually reached Chase when no one else could. For half a second, I thought it might work. But the rage in Chase's eyes burned right through it, like even Luke's leadership couldn't touch him anymore.

Avery's voice cracked through the chaos. "Chase, stop!" She lunged, fingers gripping his arm, but he shook her off so violently she stumbled back into me.

I caught her. Barely. My chest rattled with every shout, every metallic bang as Chase slammed Jax against the lockers again.

"Hit me back!" Chase spat the words in Jax's face. His fist drew back a third time.

Jax didn't move. He looked at him—really looked, eyes steady, almost pleading without words. "I'm not hitting you, Chase. I've liked Avery for a long time. I would never hurt her. I was going to talk to you this weekend about dating her."

That only fanned the fire. Chase broke loose from Theo's hold. His fist crashed into Jax's ribs, folding him forward with a grunt. Pain etched his face, but still no retaliation.

The hall erupted into a battlefield. Teammates wedging themselves between, shouting over each other. Luke dragged Chase back; Theo stood in front of Jax.

Avery broke then. Tears streaked her face as she shoved forward. "Enough! Please, enough!" Her voice shredded against the walls.

Chase froze at the sound of her sobs. Just for a second. His chest heaved, fury vibrating through every muscle. He wasn't done, but Avery's sobs cut through some of the rage.

I pulled her into me, arms tight around her shaking shoulders. "Stop, Chase. This isn't really about you."

Jax straightened slowly, pressing a hand to his ribs, blood dripping from his mouth. He didn't look away from Chase. Didn't wipe the mess from his face. Just let it sit there, proof of the beating he refused to return.

Chase's hands were still balled, knuckles raw and split. His breathing thundered. For a heartbeat, I thought he'd swing again.

But he didn't. He ripped free of the guys' hold, spun, and stormed toward the locker room, slamming the door so hard the walls shook.

Jax's eyes closed. His chest rose and fell, ragged. Avery wrenched from my arms and crossed to him, hands hovering as if she wanted to touch but didn't dare. "I'm so sorry." Her voice broke on the words.

Jax's eyes opened, softened. He pulled her into his embrace, cradling her head against his chest. "It'll work out."

Would it? I wasn't so sure. I couldn't shake the image burned into my skull—Chase's fist colliding with Jax's face. The sound. The betrayal written across both of them.

The guys slowly cleared out. Theo murmured something about checking on Chase. Luke hovered close, shoulders drawn tight. Before Theo got to the locker room doors, Chase shoved the doors open, fury radiating off him in waves of heat. His eyes locked on us—not just me, not just Luke, but Theo too.

"You knew." His voice was flat, low, deadly.

Luke stiffened. "Chase—"

"Don't." Chase's glare cut as sharply as a blade. "Don't you dare stand there and pretend. You didn't think maybe I deserved to know Jax was hooking up with my sister?"

Theo shifted, weight bracing as though he was ready if this turned physical again. "We didn't know for sure."

"Bullshit!" Chase's roar rattled the stands. His chest heaved. He looked between the three of us, betrayal carved deep into every line of his face. "You all knew something. And you said nothing to me."

My throat closed, words useless. Because he wasn't wrong.

Luke stepped forward, hand half-raised. "It wasn't for us to tell you. And Jax and Avery were probably trying to keep it from blowing up. Trying to protect—"

"Protect me?" Chase barked a laugh, bitter and sharp. "You don't get to protect me. You don't get to make that choice. We made a pack to protect my sister, especially after she fell apart the year Mila left."

The silence that followed was jagged. Too heavy.

Chase's jaw worked, as if he had a hundred more things to throw at us but couldn't pick just one. Finally, he shook his head, eyes burning.

"You think this is a joke? You think it's just about some

code?" His voice roughened, breaking somewhere in the middle. "You didn't see her last year. You weren't here when she fell apart—when some guy she never named messed with her after Mila left and she stopped eating, stopped talking, I could've lost my sister."

Avery flinched, color draining from her face. "Chase, stop," she whispered, voice small and shaking. "Not here."

He didn't even look at her, eyes locked on Jax like he was the only one there.

Guilt twisted low in my stomach. *After Mila left.* The words scraped raw. I hadn't known—not all of it. Avery told me a little when I first came back, in the library—what Elise had done, and how she'd kept if from the guys. *After you left, she harassed me. I didn't handle it well.*

I grasped Avery's hand, twining my fingers tightly with hers. Everyone had thought it was some guy that had broken her down, that made her confidence crack. But it hadn't been.

"She's finally good. And now you—" His hand snapped toward Jax, fingers curling into a fist before he forced them open. "You hook up with girls, Jax. You move on. That's who you are. I can't let you treat her like another one-night stand you'll forget the next day. I won't watch her break like that because of someone I trusted."

Avery's breath hitched, a wounded sound she attempted to swallow. She released my hand and stepped forward, eyes bright with humiliation and hurt. "That's not fair. You don't get to talk about me as if I'm not standing right here."

But Chase was already done listening. He ripped his gear bag off the bench, slung it over his shoulder, and stormed past. The exit door slammed behind him, the sound ricocheting down the hall with the crack of a gunshot.

The room exhaled. Tension bled into mutters, into the shuffle of feet, into skates unlaced with trembling hands. But I couldn't move.

I just stood there, pulse roaring, while the wreckage of friendship and loyalty scattered around me. This—this was exactly the kind of fracture Elise would salivate over. Division she could pry open, rumors she could weaponize. And with Tori still tangled in her orbit, it wouldn't take much for the wrong words to reach the wrong ears. We couldn't afford to be divided. Not when our enemies circled the way sharks do around blood. And still, echoing in my head, the crack of Chase's fist—sharp, final, proof of how fast we could tear ourselves apart.

CHAPTER TWENTY-TWO

LUKE

The fight was still ringing in my ears long after the door slammed behind Chase. The whole place shook with the aftershock.

Jax stood where Chase had left him. Blood streaked down from his mouth, his ribs rising in jagged bursts, but he hadn't lifted a hand. Not once. He'd let Chase beat on him until the rage burned itself out—and he hadn't broken. I wasn't sure if I admired him for it or wanted to grab him by the shoulders and shake him until he fought back.

Avery pressed herself against him as though she could hold him upright by sheer will. His arm wrapped around her— steadying her more than himself. She sobbed into his chest— muffled words I couldn't make out—and he lowered his head, murmuring something softly. His voice was calm, even—the way it got when shit spun out of control.

"It'll work out," he told her. Just like that. Like he could take a shattered friendship, years of loyalty, and a fresh betrayal and call it something that would "work out."

I wanted to believe him. God, I wanted to.

Mila hovered nearby, her arm grazing Avery's back, a steady touch in the chaos. She didn't speak.

Jax lifted his head finally. His eyes found mine over Avery's shoulder, steady but hollow. Then he looked to Mila. "Take her with you. To your place." He wiped his mouth with the back of his hand, smearing blood across his jaw. "That's probably best. For now, anyway."

Avery stiffened. "I'm not—"

"You are," he cut in, but softer this time, brushing his thumb along her cheek. "Go with Mila. I'll see you later."

Her lip trembled, but she nodded. She let Mila guide her away, sneakers squeaking on the floor, until the two of them disappeared down the hall. Jax's eyes followed them until they were gone. His hand curled into a fist, then uncurled, like he wasn't sure what to do with it.

We headed toward the locker room, the weight of the exchange trailing behind us. Inside, metal benches lined the walls, gear bags gaped open beneath them, the cloying stench of disinfectant doing nothing to cover sweat and damp fabric. The room buzzed with low, uneasy mutters. Every eye still carried the imprint of what they'd seen—Chase's fists, Jax's silence, Avery's tears.

That was when the silence broke. A voice I'd been waiting to hear and dreading all the same.

"Well." Logan leaned against the lockers closest to the door, arms folded, his smirk sharp enough to cut. Two of his guys lounged nearby, grins matching. They hadn't been part of the fight, but they'd sure as hell had watched. "Didn't take much for your group to crumble, huh? Family, loyalty…what's next?"

A low buzz went through the guys still hanging back, nervous energy sparking as if the air itself carried a charge.

I didn't even look at him. "Fuck off, Logan."

His grin widened, like he'd been waiting for my reaction. "Hey, I'm not involved in tearing my team apart. That's you,

King." He tapped his temple in mock salute then pushed off the lockers and sauntered away with his shadows.

The muttering followed him, a reminder he wasn't wrong. Every crack in the foundation had just been put on display.

Jax let out a long breath and turned toward our lockers. Theo fell in beside him, quiet as usual, but his shoulders squared, protective without saying a word. I followed, the weight of leadership pressing heavier with every step.

No one spoke as gear fell against benches and pads clattered to the floor. Jax pulled his jersey over his head, wincing when the fabric dragged across his ribs. Red was already blooming beneath the skin.

"You good?" I asked.

His mouth twisted into something that wasn't a smile. "Been worse."

Theo shot me a look as if he wanted to press it, but I shook my head. Not now. Not with the guys' voices drifting in from the other side of the room—half-whispers about Avery, about Chase, about the disaster they'd just witnessed regarding the twins.

We changed in silence. My hands moved on autopilot—untape, unlace, peel sweat-soaked pads free—but my mind was already two steps ahead. Chase was off on his own, probably at home. Furious. We couldn't bring him back tonight, not while his pride was still raw. But we couldn't leave the rest of us hanging in this limbo either.

Finally, I dropped onto the bench, elbows braced on my knees. "Let's go to my place."

Theo nodded immediately. Jax lifted his head, blood cleaned but his jaw started to swell, and gave a single stiff nod.

It would be just the three of us. They knew as well as I did— Chase needed space. Time to burn off the fury before any of us could reach him.

The door creaked, and Logan's laughter drifted faintly down

the hall, a reminder we didn't have the luxury of falling apart. Eyes were on us. Our rivals were circling. And if Dunn was making moves on the business, if word of tonight's fight slipped beyond these walls, we'd be bleeding on more than just the ice.

Jax shoved his gear into his bag, his movements sharp, clipped. Theo's shoulders were tense, but his voice was steady when he finally broke the silence. "We need to figure out how to deal with Chase tonight."

"Yeah." My chest tightened, but I forced the words out. "We do."

We left the locker room as a unit, the three of us. Chase's absence at our backs felt like a missing limb. The girls' cars were already gone from the lot. Good. Avery needed distance from this wreckage.

The night air was cool in my lungs. None of us spoke; the silence carried as we crossed the lot. I hit the unlock on my SUV and tossed my bag in the back. Jax headed for his own car without a word, Theo for his. Engines whirled to life one after another, headlights cutting through the dark as sharply as blades.

I gripped the wheel tight, knuckles aching. Chase's voice still rang in my skull—*You knew*. He wasn't wrong. Maybe we should have told him. But how the hell do you warn about something that wasn't your story to tell?

The road stretched out in front of us, empty and dark. Home waited at the end of it, but peace didn't. Not tonight.

We would regroup at my place. We'd find the fracture lines and try to stitch them closed before the whole thing came apart. Tomorrow we would figure out how to bring Chase back.

Streetlights slid over the windshield in clean white bands then vanished into black as I headed home.

We pulled up the driveway. Inside, the lights were low, the hum of the fridge a constant. I tossed keys in the bowl by the door and jerked my chin toward the kitchen.

"Ice." My voice came out rough.

Theo didn't argue. He moved—cabinet, freezer, a dish towel dragged off the stove. He wrapped two ice packs then slid them across the island to Jax.

He didn't reach for it right away. Instead, he drifted to the sink, gripping the edge as though it was the only solid thing in the room. Blood had dried rusty along his mouth from the cut that stopped bleeding before we'd left. A bruise was forming on his cheekbone. He stared at the drain for a beat, like answers lived there. Then he twisted the faucet, cupped water to his lips, and spat pink.

"You should sit," Theo said.

Jax ignored him and took the ice pack, pressed it to his ribs. He didn't flinch. Getting banged up on the ice was nothing new to us; getting a beat down by a friend was.

My phone buzzed. I glanced down.

Mila: *We're at my place. She's doing okay. I'll keep her here tonight.*

Some tight coil in my chest loosened a notch. I typed back.

Me: *Good. Lock the doors.*

Dots. Then:

Mila: *Will do. Get things straightened out.*

A breath I hadn't realized I'd been holding eased out. I planned to do exactly what she said.

Theo dragged a chair out with his foot and dropped into it, ankle hooked over his knee. His gaze cut to Jax. "Elise texted again?"

We'd seen the text about Jax and Avery in the locker room after getting dressed. Salt in a wound.

Jax shook his head once. "She will. That public shit show just gave her a bullhorn." He kept the ice on his ribs and braced a palm flat against the counter, shoulders set. "Avery told Chase before he saw anything on his phone. That killed the hit she wanted." A beat. "Just not the explosion."

"She tried to weaponize it." Theo's tone was flat. No question in it. Just a fact laid on the table.

"She'll keep trying." I leaned in, pushing the words across the space like a line drawn. "Which is why we get ahead of all of it."

They both looked at me.

My knuckles whitened against the island. "We handle three things. Chase. Tori. The rumors. In that order."

Jax's jaw flexed. Theo nodded once.

"Chase needs time to burn through it," I went on. Saying it didn't make it easier. "We don't hammer at his door. He'll swing again if we do. Tomorrow morning, I go to him. Alone. Neutral ground."

Jax lifted his eyes. They were steady, even through the swelling. "I'm not hiding from him."

"You're not." I nodded. "But I'm not throwing gasoline on a live fire either. You talk to him after I break the glass. Not before."

Silence stretched. Theo watched Jax, waiting.

Jax's fingers tightened on the edge of the counter. "Fine." He nudged the ice higher along his ribs. "Tomorrow, after you."

I let out a breath. One piece set.

"Second." I angled my gaze at Theo. "Tori."

Theo's body went still in that way he had when something mattered. No twitch, no tell. Just a new weight in the room.

"She's afraid of Elise." I kept my voice even. "You've mentioned it. Avery said it tonight. Tori might help if she doesn't think things will blow up in her face. Meaning, you and she are more than a passing thing. Is that a problem?"

Theo's throat worked. "No, it's a good plan." He didn't look away. "Tori's in deep."

"How deep?" I asked.

He took a breath, careful. "She won't sit without clocking the exits. Keeps her phone face down. When it's just us, and I ask about Elise, she whispers like there are ears in the walls."

I hated the way that sounded. Elise's shadow in every sentence.

"We pull her out." The words came hard. "If she wants out."

"And if she doesn't?" Theo's voice was even. Not defiant. Just brutal reality.

"Then we don't force her. But you make sure she knows what's going on between you isn't casual. You go public if you have to. Let Elise see Tori's not a pawn—she's protected. Give Tori a line she can hold if she's ready to take it."

Theo nodded once. "I can get her to meet me. Not at her house. Not anywhere Elise has eyes." He rubbed his jaw, thinking. "There's that coffee place off Grove with the back patio. Nobody from school goes there. We studied there once. She liked that no one bothered us."

"Good." I gave a short nod. "Tomorrow. Early. Before Elise starts her rounds."

"I'll text her tonight. No details in writing—just a time and place. If Elise is monitoring her phone, it reads clean."

I weighed him. "If you want her out, she needs to feel protected. Not like she's sneaking around for nothing."

Theo's eyes flicked up, steady. "I can do that."

"Third." My gaze cut between them. I glanced between them. "Logan's already foaming. The team saw blood. Don't feed the rumors. No posts. No subtweets. We talk to Coach first thing. That's the only conversation we have in public." It was a damn good thing he had cut out a few minutes early to take a call and had missed the explosion.

Theo's eyebrow lifted. "What's Logan got on the Dunn's business, on your family's?"

"Don't know yet." The truth sat heavy. "Mila's got ears where I don't, through her mom. Between them, hopefully we'll know something before it becomes a headline."

Jax studied me, like he could see I was balancing more than I'd put words to. He probably could. He wasn't dumb.

"Now." I straightened. "The part we aren't leaving this kitchen without. You and Avery."

He didn't move.

"This isn't a question about how you feel in the moment because she lights you up." My voice cut steady. "This is me, as someone who cares about Avery, making it clear—are you all in? Not a secret. Not until it's easy. Not when it's fun. All in. Because if you're not, you walk away now. You don't give her half. I won't let you."

Theo's chair creaked as he leaned forward.

Jax shut his eyes, briefly. Opened them. The ice pack had melted to slush against his shirt. He set it on the counter and braced both palms there as if he was taking an oath.

"I'm not walking. I'm in." He drew a breath. "I've been in a long time, if you want the truth."

The tension in Theo's face eased a notch.

Jax kept going. "I kept my hands off because of Chase—because our team. Then everything with Elise went sideways, and it wasn't safe to have anything that looked like a soft spot. And then... it was just habit. Not looking straight at it." He dragged a hand through his hair. "Tonight wasn't a mistake. It wasn't a heat-of-the-moment thing. I was going to talk to Chase this weekend and take the punch he gave me anyway." A humorless twitch of a smile. "Guess we just moved the clock."

"Ground rules," I stated.

Jax arched a brow. "You giving me a curfew too?"

"Don't be an asshole," Theo said, but there was no heat in it.

"Rule one," I said. "No lies. Not to us. Not to her. Not to yourself. You can hold things when safety's on the line, but you don't play us."

He nodded.

"Rule two. No power plays." I held his stare. "You don't use us to pressure Chase. You don't use Avery to get to him. You don't use any of this to punch up at Elise. We do this clean, or we don't do it at all."

Another nod. Slower.

"Rule three." The one that mattered most—even if it made me taste blood saying it. "You don't disappear on her when it gets ugly. You don't go quiet; you don't take space without saying you're taking space." I exhaled, felt the ghost of Mila's text in my chest. "We show up. That's the only way this works."

Resolve settled over Jax. "I can do that."

I believed him.

Theo stood, chair legs scraping. He walked to the sink, ran a hand towel under cold water, wrung it out, and tossed it to Jax. "Your face looks like you tried to kiss a train."

Jax caught it one-handed, pressed it to his cheek, and winced. "You should see the train."

Something small and almost normal loosened the air.

My phone buzzed again.

Mila: *Avery asked if Jax is okay.*

Me: *He is. He's all in with her. We're setting rules.*

Mila: *Good. Then Chase can work with that.*

I slid the phone face down. "Theo—text Tori."

He was already on it, fingers quick, no wasted motion. He typed one line, sent it, then locked the screen.

"What if she doesn't answer?" Jax asked.

Theo didn't look up. "She will."

The confidence there—quiet, iron—made me believe it.

"Coach?" Jax asked.

I rubbed a hand across my jaw. It was a damn good thing Coach had taken a call before we got off the ice. "I'll call him at seven tomorrow. Before the rumor crew has coffee. He hears it from me. Basic. No details about Avery he doesn't need but enough he doesn't get blindsided by whatever Logan's planning to whisper about the fight."

Jax's mouth flattened. "Logan's a vulture."

"Then we stop bleeding where we can. You and Avery stay dark on socials. If anyone asks, we're focusing on the next game. That's it."

He gave me a look. "Avery's not a no-comment kind of girl."

"Then text her before she torches herself in a comment thread," I said. "Tell her the plan. Tell her I said please."

That pulled a faint smile out of him. "You? Please?"

"Don't get used to it."

Theo's phone buzzed. He opened the message.

"Time?" I asked.

"In a half hour. Coffee place on Grove."

"Good," I said.

We let that settle. The plan had substance. It wasn't pretty, but it would do.

Jax leaned back against the counter, eyes on the far wall. "What about Chase tomorrow? Where?"

I pictured him. The version of Chase before tonight—loud, loyal, a fist you wanted on your side. And the version after—fury with nowhere to go. I picked the only place that made sense.

"The pier," I said. "Early. He can see his exit if he needs it."

"You want me there?" Jax asked.

"Not for the first ten minutes. If he's calm, I'll text you. You're close, you walk up slow, you say your piece, and then you let him work it. If he swings—"

"I won't." Not bravado—a line drawn in concrete.

Theo put his phone down, arms crossing over his chest. Silence settled between us. Not hollow this time. Full. Intent spilling into the room carrying weight.

Jax broke it first. "And Mila? You two back on?" His chin tipped toward my phone.

I didn't hesitate this time. "Yeah. We are. But it's not smart to go public right now. Not until we know Elise's next move."

Theo leaned forward, arms braced on the table. "So you keep her in the shadows?"

"For now." The words grated, but they were the only play. "When we move, it has to be clean. Permanent. Not another weakness Elise can spin or a way for her to hurt Mila."

Silence settled, heavy but certain.

We cleaned the kitchen on muscle memory—ice packs in the sink, towels on the counter, lights clicked off. I grabbed my hoodie from the back of a chair and shrugged it on. Theo held the door. Jax walked out then followed.

On the porch, the night pressed cool against my skin. The ocean breathed somewhere out there in the dark, steady and indifferent to our mess.

Jax paused at the steps. "Luke."

I looked over.

He drew a breath, pain flickering across his face. "Thank you."

"For what?" I asked.

"Not telling me to stay away," he said. "Not after that."

I thought of Avery's face when she said "I care about Jax," chin up, eyes bright. I thought of Chase's fist, the sound of it.

"Don't make me regret it."

He nodded once. "I won't."

Theo clapped his shoulder as they peeled off toward his car. "Text when you're home, idiot."

"You too," Jax muttered. He slid behind the wheel, engine coughing to life, headlights cutting across the street. He lifted a hand in a short wave and pulled away.

Theo lingered. "You good?" he asked.

"No," I said honestly. "But I know what to do."

He grunted approval. "Good luck tomorrow."

He left, and the night took him. I stood there another beat, the smell of eucalyptus and brine threading through the air, hands shoved in my hoodie pocket until my phone dug into my palm.

We weren't fixed. Chase was a live wire. Elise was a knife under the table. Logan was circling, teeth out. And somewhere behind all of it, Dunn had his thumb on the scales.

But for the first time since the punch landed, I felt it—the click of something real sliding into place. Tomorrow, we would take the first swing.

CHAPTER TWENTY-THREE

MILA

Avery and I made it to my house without speaking. I got her upstairs, into my room, and shut the door on the rest of it. Avery didn't cry right away. She sat on the edge of my bed with her hands in her lap, staring at the floor, shoulders tight. When the first tear slid, the rest followed—quiet and wrecking.

I folded her into my arms, resting my cheek against her hair. She shook against me until she finally quieted. When she pulled back, the red around her eyes made her look younger and smaller—as though she was the version of her from when I'd first met her.

"My brother hit Jax," she said, voice scraped raw. "And then he talked about me like I wasn't in the room." Her mouth tightened. "As if I'm fragile, incapable of holding my own or making decisions. As if I'll break."

I passed her a tissue. She took it but balled it in her fist instead of using it.

"You don't have to do anything tonight," I said. "We can stay here. Watch TV. Hang out."

"Stay." She mulled over the word before blowing out a breath then finally wiped her eyes. "I'm tired of staying. Of getting moved around like furniture. I mean, Chase tells me I'm break-able, and suddenly, everyone's talking at each other about me instead of to me. What the hell?" Her gaze flicked to the window, to the thin slice of evening beyond the glass. Then her phone pinged. She glanced at it, lips pursing. "I want to *do* something."

I caught the name on her screen. Jasmine. One of Avery's friends.

"There's a party tonight. Jasmine and Margie are there now. It's at Tori's. Want to go?"

I gnawed on my lip for a second. "It's a bad idea, Aves. The guys want us to lay low."

Her mouth pressed into a tight line, eyes narrowed. Some color returned to her cheeks. "I don't care. It'll be a girl's night. Besides, I need to be somewhere loud enough to drown out my brother's voice in my head." Her chin lifted. "It's a good idea. To be seen. Not to let the rumor mill win." She notched her chin higher. "Tonight, I'm not hiding."

I looked her over. Too pale. Hands unsteady when she reached for her shoes. I was going to regret this, but I couldn't say no to her when she wanted to take back the power. "Okay, but we're staying together. I'm not leaving your side."

The corner of her mouth lifted. "I wouldn't let you." She pushed to her feet and glanced around my room. "I just need to wash my face. Then let's head out."

"Bathroom is yours. I'm going to text Luke that I'm going to Tori's party with you."

"Not for permission." Her eyes narrowed in challenge, a spark under the wreckage.

I smiled without humor. "Please. As if we need permission from them? It's a girl's night. I'm making that clear." I fired off the text that stated we were going out, but not where, and then dug my keys out of my bag. It probably wasn't smart, but I was already committed to her plan.

Avery rinsed her face and ran a brush through her long blond hair before pausing at the door, fingers on the frame, like she had one more thing to leave behind before we stepped through. She straightened her shoulders.

"Let's go," she said. "Before I change my mind."

We headed for the car. The night air hit cool on my face. Somewhere down the hill, the ocean breathed steady, indifferent. I tightened my jacket. Avery blew on her hands and shoved them into her sleeves.

"Tori's, for sure?" I asked again, already opening the passenger door. I just needed confirmation as we were invading enemy territory, even if it was an open-door party.

"Yep," she confirmed and climbed in. "It's Friday night. We're not staying in."

When we arrived at Tori's, music bled from the house, rattling into the street in heavy, chest-punching thuds. I'd heard her parents were out of town for the week, and she had a way of turning an empty house into a zoo. Cars lined both sides of the block, light streaming from every window, and bodies pressed against each other in the entryway like the walls couldn't contain them.

Avery didn't hesitate. She was already halfway up the driveway, chin set, shoulders back, every step a dare. "I'm done," she muttered, tossing her hair. "Done with guys calling the shots. Tonight, I'm no one's to control."

I caught up, tugging my jacket tighter against the ocean-cooled air. "And this fixes everything? Trading one kind of mess for another?"

Her grin was razor-thin. "It works for tonight, and that's all I'm focusing on right now."

Inside, heat slammed into me—beer, sweat, perfume and cologne layered too thick. The house pulsed with music, the living room transformed into a makeshift dance floor. Strangers' elbows brushed mine. Someone laughed too loud in the kitchen, bottles clinking. It was chaos but the kind Avery wanted—loud enough to drown her thoughts out.

We pushed toward the drinks table, red cups stacked high beside a jungle of half-empty bottles. Avery shoved a hastily filled cup into my hand before I could argue. She raised hers in mock toast, blue eyes catching mine over the rim. "To cutting out overbearing and out-of-control brothers."

I tapped my cup against hers but didn't drink. While she downed hers, I pulled my phone and shot off a quick text to Luke: *Party @ Tori's. We're fine.* Not because I needed permission. But after the rink, after the way everything felt ready to combust, it was safer to keep him looped in.

By the time we elbowed through the crowd again, Avery's cheeks were flushed, but her laugh was lighter. She grabbed my wrist, dragging me toward the living room where bodies jumped to the beat.

"Dance with me," she ordered, already moving.

I let her drag me into the crush. The floor vibrated under our feet, bass buzzing in my ribs. Avery swayed too close to strangers, every move a rebellion. I laughed, the sound snatched up by music, until she leaned in close, her breath hot against my ear. "See? No brothers, no rules. Just us."

It was weird being at Tori's, and when I glanced around, I couldn't find her anywhere, but people spilled out into the backyard too where I caught a glimpse of a pool.

I felt the shift first—the way a crowded room tilts when someone you know walks in. Then Jax's broad frame cut through the doorway, Theo shadowing him. Luke was a step behind. My pulse stuttered.

Jax's gaze locked onto Avery as if pulled by a magnet. Protective, intense. His eyes flicked to me, a silent question threading between us: You watching her too?

I nodded once. He didn't move closer. Not yet. But he hovered at the edge of the crowd, every muscle wound tight.

Avery caught sight of Jax over the crowd and froze mid-spin. Her mouth parted, and the spark she'd been burning with flamed higher. She lifted her index finger, signaling to give her a second.

I knew how that would go. It was the same with me and Luke. We were drawn to one another. This was a girl's night, though, so I got why she wanted a moment before it was just the two of them.

A moment later, her eyes slid back to him—inevitable. He hadn't moved, every line of him controlled, watching only her. Something in her expression eased, the tension of the night draining. She brushed a strand of hair behind her ear, a small, familiar gesture that felt as though it were a signal: *I see you. Just give me space.*

She didn't reach for him. Not yet. But she didn't look away either. The choice hung there between them—unspoken, fragile—before the music swallowed her again.

I tugged her wrist. "Refill?" My excuse as much as hers. We shoved through the crush until the throb of music dimmed near the drinks table.

Elise slid into the space beside us, Nina at her elbow. She trailed her fingers along the lineup of cups, claiming the space as though she owned it, before drifting closer, lips curved in a smile that wasn't one.

"Nice party," Elise murmured, eyes sweeping the room before pinning Avery. Then her gaze flicked toward Jax, and the smile cut sharper. "Funny. Thought you'd be home crying over your mess." Her gaze flicked to where Jax waited. "Guess you weren't enough for your brother's friend either."

The words landed like glass shattering. Avery's body went rigid. Her grip on her cup tightened until the plastic crinkled.

"Go to hell, Elise."

Elise's smile sharpened, lazy and cruel. "Already there. Want me to save you a seat?"

I stepped forward, but Elise leaned in first, lips brushing Avery's ear. Whatever she whispered made Avery flinch, her hand jerked, and her drink sloshed down her shirt in a dark streak.

"Shit," Avery muttered, fumbling for napkins.

Elise plucked a cup off the table and pressed it into Avery's hand with an exaggerated eye roll. "Try not to embarrass yourself any more than you already have."

Avery took it—cheeks flushed with more than embarrassment—and tipped it back. A defiant swallow, eyes locked on Elise.

I caught the curl of victory in Elise's smile before I saw anything in Avery. She drank deep, eyes locked on Elise as if downing the rest of it was a challenge.

Avery laughed suddenly, too loud for the moment, tugging me close as if we were just two girls at a party. For a second, it almost worked—her cheeks flushed, her grin wide. She even stole a glance toward Jax at the edge of the crowd, chin tilted like she could prove she wasn't afraid.

Minutes blurred—music pounding, Avery pulling Jax into her orbit with a lift of her chin. He'd moved in close, telling Elise to back the hell off. Avery didn't flinch. Instead, she angled her face toward him, daring. "Why are you here, Jax?" She narrowed her eyes at me, but there was no anger. "Did Mila tell where we were going?"

His answer was low, firm. "Where you go, I go."

Her laugh shot past her lips. "Then I'm going to dance."

She dragged him with her, weaving into the crush of bodies. Jax stayed close, a wall at her back, his eyes scanning, never settling. It helped something relax in me that he was on Avery duty, and I scanned the crowd for Luke.

I spotted Theo instead. He'd found a brunette near the wall, his focus fixed on her animated hands more than anything happening with us. Tori was nowhere in sight. I lost track of

Avery in the push of the crowd until Luke's shoulder brushed mine.

"Couldn't stay away, huh?" I muttered.

He gave me that crooked grin, the one that said he knew too much. "You're surprised?"

I tipped my empty cup toward the dance floor. "Tonight's a train wreck."

Then the floor shifted beneath us. The music jolted, not the beat but the way the bodies around us stuttered, a ripple of attention cresting in one direction. Shouts rose over the bass. Cups tipped. The floor seemed to tilt under me, wrong, wrong.

My stomach dipped before I even saw her.

Through the crush, Jax's frame broke clear—Avery in his arms, her head lolling against his shoulder. But her eyes—wide, frantic—fought to stay open, panic skittering for something solid in the blur.

I shoved forward, Luke tight on my heels, the crowd closing and opening around us in jolts of movement.

She blinked hard, unsteady, the motion sluggish. "Dizzy." Her voice caught on the word. "Everything's… spinning."

Elise's laugh cut clean through the music. She raised her voice, pitched just right for the nearest circle to hear. "Wow. Didn't think you'd go that far, Jax. Guess slipping something in her drink was easier than convincing her to sleep with you."

The room shifted. Heads turned. Whispers rippled like sparks catching dry grass. Phone screens lit up.

Jax's expression hardened. "I didn't touch her drink." His grip tightened, steadying Avery against him. "Don't you dare—"

But Elise already had her stage. One arched brow, one tilt of her head, and suddenly, he was the villain in her story.

I shoved through the bodies until I was at Jax's side, Avery limp against his chest, her eyes wide with panic. My glare cut straight to Elise. "Don't pretend that you weren't the one who handed her that drink, Elise."

Elise's mouth curved, wide-eyed innocence dripping from every word. "Me? I wasn't the one hovering over her." Her gaze slid toward Jax, deliberate, cruel. "That was him."

Gasps flared. Whispers coiled through the crowd, sharp as glass. More phones lifted, catching the moment.

Fury vibrated in every line of Jax. But Elise had already done it—slipped the seed of doubt, lit the fuse, another bomb at the guys' already shaky friendship.

And it didn't matter that we knew the truth. Not with half the party filming, not with Elise's poison already spreading.

"Hospital," Luke snapped, suddenly at Jax's side—steady where I wasn't. "Now."

Jax didn't argue. Avery sagged in his arms, her eyes fluttering, breath shallow. He barreled forward, every line of him carved in fury and focus. Luke pushed ahead, his shoulder dropping into bodies, forcing gaps through the throng. Theo appeared on the other side, grim-faced, flanking Jax as though they'd rehearsed it.

All I could do was keep close, stumbling after them, terrified of losing sight of Jax's shoulders cutting through the crush. Avery was a blur in his arms, limp and too still, and every step they took without me scraped raw.

Elise's voice clawed up from memory, sharp as the day I'd caught it in an empty hallway after school. She hadn't seen me. She hadn't known anyone was there. "I'm trying! He's chasing her—what do you want me to do, drug him?"

I'd told Luke. I knew she'd meant him. But now—Avery limp in Jax's arms—that didn't matter. Elise didn't play straight lines. If she couldn't get to Luke, she'd go for someone close, someone easier. And Avery... Avery was the perfect strike. Take her down, and the rest of us followed.

Chase. His name hit like a blow as the door burst open on the night air. If he saw Avery in this state—slack in Jax's arms,

Elise's poison already lighting up feeds—it wouldn't just break them. It would blow us apart.

Luke

We shoved through the night air, panic spurring us forward. Jax didn't stop moving. He carried Avery tight against his chest, her hair tangled across his arm, her head lolling with the car's headlights sweeping over us as we cut toward the curb.

"My SUV," I barked, already yanking the keys free. "We're not splitting up."

Theo didn't argue. Mila dove into the back seat first, making room. Jax climbed in after her, Avery still in his arms, refusing to let go. Theo slid in on the other side, shoulders hunched, silent but braced. I slammed the driver's door and shoved the car into gear, tires squealing as we peeled away from Tori's street.

The drive blurred, traffic lights punching red and green across the windshield, Mila's hand clenched white-knuckled around the headrest. Avery stirred against Jax, a soft, broken sound tearing out of her throat. His grip tightened.

"I've got you," he muttered, voice pitched low like he could anchor her there.

"Hospital's five minutes," I ground out, pushing the car harder than I should.

We pulled into the emergency entrance, but I didn't aim for the main doors. The Kings had built a private wing years ago, an attempt at both philanthropy and privacy. My family's name was still stamped on the walls in brass. I cut the engine and was already out, waving down a nurse at the side door. Recognition sparked in her eyes, and the questions stopped at the look on Jax's face as he carried Avery past.

They swept us into a side room—quiet, controlled. Doctors we knew. Nurses who didn't blink at the mess we dragged in. I filled them in on what'd happened then placed a call to Chase, who tore out of his house immediately at our news. His parents were an hour out but headed in as well.

The air smelled of antiseptic and adrenaline. Gloves snapped. A nurse clipped sensors to Avery's fingers. Blood was taken. An IV line snaked from her arm to a clear bag, fluid already dripping. The steady tick of the monitor filled the silence where panic should've been.

I signed the intake papers, my name opening doors I wished I didn't have to use. By the time I got back, Avery was stretched out on a narrow bed, pale but breathing steady under the monitors.

The nurses had started fluids. Vitals were murmured and recorded, low and efficient—heart rate, blood pressure, nothing I wanted to hear too clearly. Mila stood near the wall, out of the way, her arms wrapped around herself as though she was holding in everything she couldn't fix.

Jax hadn't moved from her side. He sat forward, elbows on his knees, his hand wrapped around hers so tight it looked painful. His head was bowed, the back of his neck corded, but his thumb stroked her knuckles in steady passes.

The beeping steadied—slow, rhythmic. A nurse adjusted the IV drip, checked the monitor, then quietly slipped out, giving us space.

Her lashes fluttered. Then her eyes opened, slow, dazed.

"Jax?" Her voice rasped, raw.

His head jerked up. "I'm here." The words caught, rougher than I'd ever heard him. "I've got you."

A tiny smile pulled at her mouth. "Told you... I can handle myself."

Jax huffed an anguished rush of air and pressed her hand to his forehead. "Don't ever do that to me again."

Mila's eyes cut to mine. "Luke. Do you remember what I told you last semester? About Elise. The phone call in the hallway."

The memory of Mila telling me what she'd overheard came back in sharp focus: *I'm trying! He's chasing her—what do you want me to do, drug him?*

I remembered the way Mila had said it then, tight with fear. And hearing it now, with Avery limp in Jax's arms earlier, it landed different. "Yeah. I remember."

Mila's voice dropped lower. "She shifted targets. It was always about tearing us apart. Luke, she doesn't need it to make sense. She just needs us to crumble."

The truth of it sliced deep. Elise wasn't reckless. She was surgical. Avery had been the easiest way to land the blow.

"Then we don't give her what she wants," I said, though it felt more vow than a plan. "But Jax, her parents and Chase will be here. You need to go before it turns into another scene."

Jax finally turned from Avery, eyes bloodshot, voice hoarse. "I'm not leaving her."

"You can't be here when her parents arrive," Theo said quietly, the first words he'd spoken since the car. "You know what they'll think."

Jax bristled, muscles coiling. "I don't care."

"You should," Avery rasped, her eyes slitting open again. Her voice was weak but steady enough to cut through. "Jax. If you stay, they'll see doubt before they see me. Don't let Elise win twice."

The fight in him broke on that. He looked wrecked, but he leaned down, pressing her hand to his chest. "I'll be outside. Don't forget that."

Her smile read tired but real. "Wouldn't dare."

Jax stood, every movement reluctant, his hand slipping from Avery's only when he had to. Mila caught his arm, steadying him before the fight could flare again. "We've got it," she told him quietly, then her gaze lifted to me. "Luke will handle the rest."

The look she pinned me with left no room for argument. It wasn't a suggestion—it was an order. And she was right. My name was the one on the wing. The one the hospital staff would answer to. The one the Dunns would think twice before crossing.

"Fine." The word came sharper than I intended, but I held it steady. "I'll deal with them."

Theo nodded once, grim, already moving toward the door to make sure Jax didn't circle back.

The room quieted, monitors ticking steady, Avery's breathing evening out. But the relief was paper-thin, already tearing.

The clock was running. Once Chase walked through those doors, careful wouldn't matter—truth would.

I looked at Mila, her face pale under the fluorescent light, but her chin lifted, fierce.

"We need to tell him everything," I said. "Before Elise does."

CHAPTER TWENTY-FOUR

LUKE

Avery had been cleared from the hospital overnight—no lasting damage, just orders to rest. Her parents took her home for the weekend, a reset none of them were ready for. By Monday morning, she'd had enough forced rest and family time and escaped to Mila's before school. That left me with the other fracture to face—Chase hadn't been seen since the hospital.

Gulls cut across a gray sky. The boards beneath me still carried last night's cold, the pier groaning with each shift of weight. Salt stung the air, the tide gnawing at the pylons in a steady grind.

Drew popped into my head, his advice sage in a moment like this: *"Keep your head down. Don't let emotion screw the play."*

I got to the pier first, hands shoved into my hoodie, breath fogging in the morning chill. The planks creaked behind me—footsteps steady, unhurried. I didn't turn until he stopped a few feet away.

Chase looked wrecked—knuckles split, jaw ticking as if he could grind last night into dust. His eyes stayed on the water, anywhere but me.

"You want to hit me too?" My tone stayed even, not a dare—just an opening.

He kept his eyes on the water. "I already swung."

"Yeah. At the one guy who let you. Jax took it so you wouldn't have to carry it afterward. He could've put you on the ground, and you know it. But he didn't."

His mouth pressed thin. "He should've come to me."

"Yeah." No point softening it. "He was going to, but Elise's minions changed the timeline." The old bolts in the pier groaned under my weight. "You know him. You've trusted him for years. He let you land those hits because he respects you. Because he respects Avery. That counts."

A twitch at his cheekbone. "And what about you?" His voice came rough. "You knew and didn't tell me?"

"I knew more than I said." The words came rough. "Enough to know they were trying to handle it the right way. Avery told you before it hit your phone. That was her choice to make. Be mad at me. Be mad at him. But not at her for owning her part."

His head dipped. "Don't tell me you actually trust him with her."

"I do, and so do you. Don't play it that way. I know you're worried because of what happened to her in the past. But she's not the same person. I trust Jax to protect her, to show up when things aren't easy. Is it perfect? No. He waited too long to talk to you. But his heart's aimed right." I angled closer. "Better Jax than any of the assholes waiting in the wings."

He flinched. A wave slammed beneath us, the plank under my shoes vibrating.

"I don't want to watch you bury a real friendship," I added. "Not when the wrong people are counting on it."

Silence. Birds shrieked over the waves. Chase's knuckles flexed like memory still lived in them.

I pulled my phone without breaking my sightline to the water and sent one word. *Now.*

Footfalls hit the wood behind us, steady and measured. I didn't turn, but Chase did, his shoulders squaring.

Jax stopped just out of swing range, hands open at his sides—not submissive, just present.

Chase's stare bore into Jax. "You should've come to me first."

"I know." Jax's voice stayed steady. "And I wanted to. That was the plan."

Chase's mouth twisted. "That's all you've to say?"

"No." Jax drew a breath, lips pressing into a hard line. "It's me owning it. I screwed up. But I'm here now." He stepped closer. "I've had feelings for Avery since middle school. I never acted on my feelings because of our friendship. Because of the team. When Elise had everyone on edge, I kept my distance. It didn't feel safe to let anything show. So I stayed away. Even when it killed me. Then Avery told me she had feelings, and I couldn't turn it off. We kissed, once. That's all."

Chase's scowl cut hard. "Stop. That's my sister." A shudder crawled through him. "I don't need the play-by-play."

"Understood." Jax gave a tight nod. "I haven't told her yet because it's too soon, but I love her. It's that simple."

Chase's glare sharpened. "And you tell me this before you tell her? You think I want to be the first one to know you're—"

"I shouldn't be telling you before her." Jax's voice stayed steady. "I know that. But you're standing here, and I need you to hear it from me. She's always been the one."

Chase stared at him, tension carved into his face. Wind flattened his shirt against his chest. He looked from Jax to the water and back. The muscle in his cheek flexed once. Twice. "Don't hurt her."

"I won't." Jax met Chase's stare head-on.

Chase dragged a hand over his mouth, eyes burning. "I should hit you again."

"You can." Jax didn't move. "I'll still be here when you're done."

Something shifted. Not forgiveness. But maybe the start of it.

I tipped my head toward the line of light where the horizon sharpened. "You two good enough that I can leave you without needing to pull anyone off?"

Chase snorted under his breath. "Yeah."

"Then finish it." I clapped Chase's shoulder once and stepped back. "We're a solid team, not a divided one."

He didn't argue. That was new.

I passed Jax on my way off the pier and brushed his shoulder with two knuckles. The old touch we threw at each other when wins hurt and losses hurt more.

I stepped back far enough to give them space, close enough to move in if it turned again. Their voices carried in pieces over the wind. I couldn't make out the words, but their voices sounded low, controlled.

Minutes dragged. The pier creaked under us, gulls screaming at the surf. When I turned back, they were standing closer. Chase's shoulders had dropped a notch. Jax looked the same, which for him meant steady.

I closed the distance. "At school, we move together. No gaps for Elise to crawl into. No room for Logan to run his mouth. Anyone looking for a show leaves disappointed."

Chase rubbed at the split across his knuckles. "And Avery?"

"Front and center," I answered. "With you both. Not kept quiet. Not a rumor. A fact."

Jax's mouth lifted in a crooked grin. "Public, huh?"

"Yeah." I held Jax's stare. "You go public with Aves. Not with fireworks. With presence. Walk with her. Eat with her. Stand with her. Shut down Elise's meddling."

Jax's nod came slow, deliberate. "I was going to do that anyway."

"Good." I flicked a glance at Chase. "You don't have to like it today. You do have to back your people."

He blew out a breath that fogged in the chill. "I'm not going to hold his hand."

"No one asked you to." I let a corner of my mouth tilt. "We're not building a wedding website—we're closing ranks."

There was a huff from him that might one day be a laugh.

We stood there a second longer. Wind in our faces. Waves crashing below. Holding steady—for now.

I checked my phone—no messages. Mila would be steadying Avery, making sure she walked in with her chin up. School was an hour out, the fallout closer, and the game sat on the calendar as if nothing had changed.

"We meet in the lot," I said. "You two get there first. I'll pull Theo. We walk in, we don't flinch, and we don't feed anything with attention."

Chase rolled his shoulders. "Logan runs his mouth—"

"Coach has him on a leash," I cut in. "And if not, I do."

I stepped back, boots thumping the boards, the ocean breathing under us as both a promise and a warning. "We good?"

Chase gave me a look that wasn't entirely friendly. "We're not fine."

"I didn't ask for fine." My gaze held his. "I asked if you're going to keep your fists in your pockets until we give the school a story they can't twist. Elise doesn't need any more power."

His jaw worked. Then he gave a short nod.

Jax tipped his chin, a silent go. He wanted the last two minutes without me to close the circle. Fair.

I left them with the gulls screaming overhead. The walk back down the pier dragged, but my chest eased all the same.

By the time I hit the lot, engines rumbled, and exhaust hung low in the cold. I leaned on my SUV, waiting for my head to settle. My phone buzzed with a message from Theo.

Theo: *Tori's in.*

Me: *Great. We close ranks at school.*

Theo: *thumbs up emoji

Good. He understood.

Another buzz.

Mila: *Avery's ready. We're heading to school.*

Me: *We're set. Chase and Jax are walking in with us. Jax goes public.*

Mila: *Good. I'll keep her between us through the doors. Let the school choke on Elise's bullshit.*

A grin threatened. I let it live half a second and killed it. Work first.

I looked back toward the pier. Two figures came off the boards, their heads bent, pace matched. Chase's hands stayed open, empty.

We had a plan. Not clean. Never would be. But it would hold if we did.

"Unbreakable," I muttered to the SUV, to the wind, to the morning. "It's time to remind the school what we are."

CHAPTER TWENTY-FIVE

MILA

A very leaned close, her voice still rough from the hospital Friday night and the little sleep she'd managed over the weekend before showing up at my house this morning. "Jax came by before sunrise. Said he couldn't wait for school." Her cheeks held no color, eyes shadowed, but the tremor in her smile betrayed a pulse of excitement. "He asked how I felt about people knowing. Us. He said he's all in."

The words tumbled out faster after that, a breathless rush she couldn't quite contain. "He brought coffee. Said he didn't want me walking in alone." Her fingers tightened around the cup, a shaky laugh escaping. "It feels…good, you know? To have him acknowledge there's something between us, not to hide it from my brother."

Despite the rush of it all, her voice stayed fragile—her pale, tired frame a sign from only being out of the hospital for four hours—but for a second, she looked lit from the inside, as though dawn had broken early just for her.

"I told Jax I wanted to walk in with you," she added quickly, as if the admission needed balance. "Not just him. Both of you."

Something in my chest unknotted at that—her choosing me

as much as him—but worry threaded through it. Jax wasn't half-measure. If he'd decided to go public, he'd burn the whole school down to make it stick—and to make sure no one hurt her. And Avery, standing here pale and trembling, deserved steady, not scorched earth.

I squeezed her hand. "Then we'll do it your way. Together."

Her smile flickered again, a small spark of happiness chasing the shadows from her face.

Jax and I stuck to Avery like glue despite her insistence that she was fine. She wasn't. Her skin was pale, with bruised shadows carved under her eyes, her hands trembling when she lifted her coffee. But she squared her shoulders, and we met the rest of the guys at the curb anyway, chin up, as if daring anyone to tell her she couldn't.

The moment we walked through the doors of the school, everything felt wrong. The rumor mill had already started grinding before first bell—half-whispered, phone-screen lit speculation about last night. But the guys shut it down in the same efficient, ruthless way they'd handled it for me before. Chase wasn't here yet, but Theo's glare was enough to silence whole hallways, and Luke didn't need more than a look to send heads ducking. Jax didn't bother speaking. He just moved with Avery's bag slung over one arm, her tucked against his side—a silent warning in the way his hand never left her back.

They circled the wagons, and this time, I was inside too. Luke had said they would close ranks. He was right.

By lunch, whispers had sputtered out. Phones lowered when we passed. Nobody wanted to be the one caught pushing a lie. Not with the Kings, and definitely not with Jax.

Avery held herself steady through it, stubborn to the bone. She laughed at the right moments, answered when she had to. Only I caught the fade of color in her face by sixth period, the way she clutched her water bottle like it was the only thing holding her upright.

Still, when practice rolled around, she wouldn't admit defeat. Jax ended it for her—steering her straight to his SUV before she could argue. His expression was set; hers was pinched, but she didn't fight him. Not really.

That left me alone when I should've been home, stuck instead in the world of centerpieces and donor lists. Another fundraiser meeting for the gala. Another round of fake smiles.

I arrived early, hoping for a few minutes of silence before the vultures circled. Sunlight slanted through the open windows, carrying in the tang of salt and cut grass from the quad.

Tori was already there, sitting stiff at the end of a table, her phone resting face down as if she didn't trust herself not to check it. When I stepped inside, she glanced up—face unreadable, eyes lingering a beat too long as she took me in.

"She won't be here on time." Tori didn't bother with hello.

She meant Elise. "Good." I slid my bag onto the desk and flipped open my notebook, pen tapping against the margin. Tori and I weren't friends. Maybe not enemies either. Would we be again once she found out Theo was flirting with some brunette at the party last night?

Tori's stare burned into me. "Tell Theo I need to talk to him."

I blinked, the request hanging heavy. "Okay… sure. About what?"

Her jaw tightened. "Not your business."

"And you can just text him…"

She grabbed her phone, thumb flicking across the screen with too much force, and turned her shoulder to me. Conversation over.

The room filled gradually after that, full of people who carried their family names heavier than their backpacks. Pages of agendas shuffled, and chairs scraped, voices layering too sweet to be real.

I tuned most of it out, scribbling notes without registering the words. Flowers. Catering. The usual parade of shallow decisions dressed up as legacy.

Then the door opened, and Elise swept in late—her hair perfect, her lipstick sharper than her smile. She didn't glance my way—not once. But I caught the tremor in her hands when she adjusted her binder. Her eyes trailed down to her phone again and again, like she was waiting for something.

She wouldn't take the fall for what she'd done. Not with Elise's name, her father's reach. But he'd have heard. He had to have. And if there weren't consequences, then what did that mean? Was her dad pulling the strings, approving of her drugging students so long as it got her closer to their end result, whatever that was?

Something was going down—I could feel it.

CHAPTER TWENTY-SIX

LUKE

After practice, I drove straight to Mila's. The sun bled out across the horizon, orange streaks drowning in the Pacific. By the time I pulled into her street, shadows stretched long over cracked sidewalks, the cul-de-sac hushed in that way neighborhoods got when everyone was inside pretending life was normal and not a struggle to make ends meet.

Her mom's car wasn't in the drive. Again.

Mila answered barefoot, leggings and an oversized tee enveloping her frame. Her dark hair was loose, slipping over one shoulder, eyes rimmed with fatigue but steady. She gave me a small smile—brave but worn at the edges—and stepped aside.

The house smelled faintly of cold coffee and laundry detergent, like someone had started things but never finished. We ended up on the couch, cushions sagging under us. She tucked her legs beneath her, curling into the corner. I stretched an arm along the back, and when she leaned into me, the world went still.

I pulled my phone from my pocket, thumbed it open, and handed it to her. The PI file on Darren Langley glowed against the dim light, stark black text cutting through the shadows. "Here."

I handed her the report and stayed on the numbers. I didn't open the still. Not yet. A blur wasn't proof—it was a weapon that hit the wrong person.

She scrolled in silence. Her eyes moved fast, tension flickering across her face, mouth pressed thin. Transaction logs. Timelines. Bank names and dates in neat columns. Then she hit the last section—several large payments from Dunn Industries leading up to that night, then Darren Langley's house sold, the deposit. And then—the sudden stop of all financial data.

Her breath hitched. Her voice came low, barely holding. "So that's it? No record of him elsewhere after that night?"

"No. Nothing. He doesn't surface anywhere." I leaned in, tapping the line with my finger. "The house sold. Proceeds went straight into his account. And not a single withdrawal since."

She lifted her head, eyes darker than the room. "So, he's dead, and that's a cover-up."

"Or hiding."

"Luke." Her fingers hovered over the screen, trembling. "I know what I saw. He has to be dead. And this"—she jabbed at the phone, sharp, frustration bleeding out—"could all be someone's way of making sure we never prove it." Mila's eyes narrowed. "Or maybe his killer doesn't want Darren found. Dead or alive. If he vanishes, so does the evidence tying back to him."

I held her gaze. "Yeah."

The silence stretched. She didn't move. Finally, she sagged back against the couch, the phone slipping into her lap.

"I thought I wanted answers. I thought I needed them. But now... I don't know."

"We're in this together."

She let out a shaky breath, her head tipping sideways until

her temple pressed against my shoulder. "That's what I'm afraid of—that we'll find out something we can't come back from."

I reached over and threaded my fingers through hers. Her grip tightened like a lifeline, grounding us both.

"Then we don't go back," I said. "We build forward."

Her eyes glistened. A silence pressed between us heavy enough to feel. Finally, she whispered, "I want to believe you."

"Then do."

She studied me for a long beat. I could feel her pulse racing through her fingers, but she nodded. "Okay."

And sitting there, her hand warm in mine, the PI's report still lit between us, it didn't feel as though we were circling wreckage anymore. It felt as if we were building something that might actually last. Even if the foundation was cracked.

Her head stayed against my shoulder. She didn't fall asleep, not fully, but her weight eased something in me. Her breathing slowed, steadier, even as her hand clung on, as though letting go might split the ground beneath us.

The PI's file had burned lines of text etched into my head. Darren's name. Last traceable the night Mila swore he died. House sold. Proceeds deposited. And then nothing—no sightings, no calls, no slip-ups.

A man doesn't vanish clean—not unless he wants to. Or unless someone makes him. If Darren was hiding, he was damn good at it. If he was dead, then someone had gone to a lot of trouble to bury the proof. Either way, we were chasing a ghost.

And ghosts didn't move alone. Not this one. Dunn's money in Langley's account pointed one way—Langley was feeding Dunn intel while he worked at King Enterprises. Not only that, but Dunn's daughter was already playing her own games, pushing until someone broke.

Elise—her fingerprints were all over Avery being slipped a drug last night. Dunn had to know. My father knew because I'd told him who was behind it. Elise's dad wasn't blind, no matter how many meetings he buried himself in. Which left two possibilities: he'd sanctioned it, or he was letting Elise spin out on purpose. Either way, she was still dangerous. And to Dunn, the end justified the means.

I thought about Chase. He'd shown up to school this morning, but it had taken all of us to pull him back before he went after Elise—to keep him steady in her crosshairs.

Jax stood at Avery's side, as solid as stone. Theo flanked them, silent but unmovable. Mila blocked whenever Elise drifted too close, her voice enough to keep the wolves back. And me—I drove the truth into Chase until he couldn't dodge it, and Elise's smoke had nowhere to catch.

Chase hadn't forgiven us. Not by a long shot. But he'd stayed in the circle. And for now, that was enough.

We'd moved as one, forming armor around Avery. Every rumor died before it could breathe, every whisper shut down with a look. Elise hadn't liked it. I'd caught her watching, eyes glittering, phone in her hand as though she was already setting her next fire.

We'd won the day. Barely. But tomorrow—?

Mila shifted against me, eyes closed, lashes brushing my sleeve. I bent my head and pressed a kiss into her hair. She deserved a world without shadows chasing her. A world where truth didn't cut her open.

But I couldn't give her that. Not yet. What I could do was hold the line. Keep the walls up until we knew who was trying to tear them down.

Darren. Elise. Dunn. *Lorne.* Too many names, too many cracks in a foundation we were still pretending was solid. And if it all broke—then I'd keep my promise. I would build something new with her. Out of ruins if I had to.

CHAPTER TWENTY-SEVEN

MILA

The smell of coffee pulled me out of sleep before the sunlight did—dark, rich, familiar, promising a normal morning I didn't trust.

I pushed off the couch, my arm light where Luke's weight had been. He'd left sometime in the night, tugging the blanket over me before he went. A line where his body had warmed the cushion cooled under my palm. The house held the kind of quiet that felt staged—no TV murmuring from a bedroom, no clatter of pans. Just the coffee.

Then a hard crack split the silence, followed by an ugly, splintering *thunk*. I flinched—my knee clipping the coffee table. The next sound was fast, steel on something small and breakable. Another. Another. Finality punched into the stillness.

I crossed the hall barefoot, heartbeat lodged in my throat.

Mom stood at the kitchen counter, hair in a knot that had lost the fight, robe hanging open over a tank and shorts. One hand braced on the butcher block. The other clenched a hammer. On the cutting board in front of her, black shards glinted—plastic, metal, the guts of something once whole. Her breath came quick, eyes glassy, mouth set.

She exhaled, shoulders dropping when she spotted me. Then she swept the pieces with her free hand, fingers shaking, and dumped them into the trash as if the can could erase what had existed a minute ago.

Unease slid under my skin, a cold, crawling thing. "What did you do?"

She stilled. The hammer hung loose at her side, as if she'd only just noticed what she held. "Something that needed doing."

"What was it?"

A pause. A small lift of her chin I recognized from every time she wanted me to stop asking questions—don't push me. "Old files—from when I worked for King."

The lie landed wrong. Not the words—those were neat, chosen—but the way she delivered them. Tight. Careful. Not looking directly at me. "Old files on a… thumb drive?"

My gaze tracked the trash—the scatter of black bits on top of a layer of coffee grounds. The hammer clinked as she set it on the counter. Her voice steadied by force. "There are things that shouldn't exist anymore, Mila—things that could hurt us."

Darren's name ran cold through me. The PI's report still burned behind my eyes—deposits from Dunn Industries into Darren's account in the weeks before he went missing. The sale of his house. The money moved neat as a blade. Then nothing. No withdrawals. No sightings. Just silence and a tidy ledger.

"Who would hurt us?" I asked.

Her lips thinned. "Anyone who thought we were in the way." She moved to the sink, turned on the water, and rinsed the cutting board clean of the small, leftover bits of black plastic. Steam curled up. She didn't meet my eyes. "It wasn't mine to keep."

"You kept it anyway." The words scraped out before I could soften them.

A muscle jumped in her cheek. "When I left King Enterprises, I took what I could to protect you. That hasn't changed."

The room shrank around me. The lemon cleaner on the counters burned my nose. Sun found the metal rim of the trash can and turned one jagged shard into a mean little star.

"Protect me from who?" My voice roughened. "From Dunn? From the Kings?"

Her shoulders tightened at the names. "From anyone who thought you were an easy pressure point."

My mind flashed to Elise on the edge of Tori's living room—red lipstick and hunger in her eyes, the way she'd watched Avery crumble. The hissed phone call I'd overheard after school months ago: "I'm trying! He's chasing her—what do you want me to do, drug him?" Back then, the target had seemed to be Luke—or I'd thought it had. Yesterday, Elise had chosen the closest wound, and it had harmed us.

"Was that Darren's drive?" I asked, barely above a whisper.

Her hand stilled on the faucet, but she didn't turn it off. Water ran and ran, drilling the basin. The sound filled the space between us.

"His name is in a lot of places," she answered at last—not yes, not no. "And names get people killed."

"It's already gotten people hurt," I pressed, pulse climbing. "There were deposits into his account from Dunn. Before he disappeared. We saw them—Luke showed me. If that drive had anything tied to that—"

"Then it shouldn't be here," she cut in, sharper than she'd meant to. She shut the water off and turned, finally meeting my eyes. "Do you understand me? It should not be in this house."

"Because Dunn would come for it?"

"Because everyone would." She stepped closer, fingers damp. "You think King doesn't have people who would turn this place inside out? You think Dunn doesn't already have a way to get in?"

The floor might as well have tilted. My back hit the doorframe. "Did you double-cross them?" The question tasted metallic in my mouth. "Did you double-cross the Kings?"

Her mouth parted—offended and wounded at once. "I protected us."

"That isn't a no."

"It's the only answer that matters."

I stared at the trash. The black grit of plastic looked harmless there, almost ordinary. Something a child could pluck out by accident. Something to empty without noticing.

My voice slipped low. "Who was Mr. Langley?"

Mom's face didn't move—only her eyes. "Darren? You knew him."

"No. *Mr. Langley.*"

A slightest flicker—as if tracking a memory she'd buried deep. "Where did you hear that name?"

"Elise," I forced out. "On the phone—she used it when she thought she was alone."

Careful as threading a needle, she said, "You need to leave that alone."

"Was it Darren's?"

"Don't ask me that."

"Mom."

The word shook something in her. She pressed her fingers to her mouth then dropped them. "The more you stay out of things, the safer you are. Do you hear me?"

Safe felt as if it belonged in a children's book—pretty, useless. "You smashed evidence in our kitchen."

"I smashed bait," she corrected, backing away from the counter as if the trash could jump up and implicate her. "You aren't the only one people try to corner."

Her hands shook. She tucked them into the pockets of her robe to hide it, but I saw—I always saw. The tremor ran through me, too.

"Does Luke need to know?" I asked, the question ripping clean even as my stomach knotted. "About what you destroyed?"

Her face softened at his name and went wary at the same time. "If you tell him, you can't untell him."

"He's already in this."

"So are you."

We stared at each other across a tile floor that suddenly felt as long as a runway. Coffee steamed in the pot behind her. A car rumbled past on the street outside, tires humming against asphalt—ordinary sounds in a room that felt anything but.

"If you put this in King hands," she warned, quiet again, "Dunn will know by dinner. That's how these worlds move."

Mom hadn't said Luke specifically—only insinuated that by telling him I would be informing the entire family. "I'm already in it." The truth came out steady. "Dunn made sure of that when he pulled us back here."

She closed her eyes, only for a second, and when she opened them, something resigned had settled. "Then be smart. Be careful. Don't let love make you stupid."

I didn't answer—couldn't. The hammer lay on the counter between us, heavy and dangerous.

When I turned for the door, her voice followed, softer. "I'm doing the best I can."

I paused, hand on the frame. "Me too."

The shards sat in the trash—harmless and not. I left them there and carried the weight of Mom's secret upstairs, where it pressed behind my ribs until school.

School was a blur. My goal was to make it through and corner Luke afterward. When the final bell rang, I pulled Luke aside before he could vanish into the locker room. The late afternoon sun had warmed the quad, heat rising off painted benches and old brick. Our tree gave thin shade, leaves clicking in a breeze that smelled of salt and cut grass. We'd stood here before, pressed up against truths neither of us wanted.

He came without hesitation—just that crooked look he wore when he already knew everything between us was about to shift.

"We need to talk," I said.

His eyes flicked to my mouth then to my hands. "Tell me."

So I did. In pieces at first—coffee, a hammer, plastic splitting, her careful answers that weren't answers.

"Put together," I finished, throat raw, "it looks like Dunn planted Darren, and Lorne eliminated him—or made him disappear. And if Mom destroyed anything tied to it, maybe it was what Darren found. Or what he stole."

Luke didn't move for a beat. Then the air left him slowly, as if breathing had become work. His grip whitened on the branch, tendon standing out in his wrist. His eyes tracked the ground, the bark, my face, then back to the ground, as if he needed somewhere safer to land than my words.

"And your mom," he said finally, voice low, as if not trusting it.

"She destroyed something that shouldn't be here," I said. The words scraped. "Her phrasing."

He braced a shoulder against the trunk. "Lorne—" He stopped. The denial dried up on his tongue. A muscle jumped in his jaw as he forced the rest through gritted teeth. "If Darren was a Dunn plant at King, it's possible that Lorne moved to neutralize the threat."

I swallowed, the taste of metal and coffee turning my mouth bitter. "That's what I'm afraid of."

He stared past me, eyes gone far. Then he looked back—rawness cutting through. "Thank you for telling me."

"We promised," I reminded him, softer. "No lies. No power plays."

His mouth curved—not a smile but an ache. "Partners."

"Not—" I couldn't finish the line we used without feeling the ground tilt. Not today. "Partners," I repeated anyway, and it steadied something in both of us.

"Okay," he breathed. "I'll look into Lorne's potential role."

He stepped in then, forehead to mine—a pause that made the world quiet. His breath brushed my cheek. The tree's shadow cut a wobbly line across the grass between our shoes.

"Be careful," I whispered.

"You too."

We broke apart because we had to. He headed for the rink. I watched him go then pressed my palms to my eyes until the afterimage of him burned away.

If I told him too little, I'd lose him. If I told him too much, I might lose him anyway. Either way, Mom's hammer kept slamming in my head.

I didn't go home—not yet. I stayed until the shade crept over my toes and the wind picked up, rattling the leaves. Then I went to find Avery—because if the world was going to keep swinging, I was going to hold on to what I could.

CHAPTER TWENTY-EIGHT

LUKE

Mila's words, mixed with the PI report, stayed under my skin the whole walk to the rink. Dunn deposits. Darren's house sold. Money tucked away neatly. No withdrawals. Her mom destroying something in their kitchen. And the name—Langley—threading through all of it, thin as fishing line, invisible until it cut your hand.

And there was Avery—slipped a drug at Tori's party. That wasn't rumor. That was one of us hurt, and Elise had been at the center of it.

By the time I hit the rubber mat that led onto the ice, my jaw ached. I shoved my feet into the skates hard enough that my ankle protested. The locker room noise washed over me—sticks rapping benches, jokes tossed around, the humid funk of gear that never really dried. Every step led toward whatever Elise had started—the people she'd attempted to break and the risk she'd put on Mila's shoulders.

Theo clocked my face and didn't ask—just nudged a water bottle toward me at the gate.

"I'm fine," I muttered. But tensions were high. With me. And with Chase. Even though he'd accepted his sister and Jax being together, what had happened to Avery at Tori's party was dangerous. I got it. I just couldn't shake my own frustrations. And from the expression he wore, he couldn't shake his either.

Theo didn't argue. He knew a lie when he heard it. He stepped onto the ice, easy and balanced, and I followed with blades biting.

The cold cut through me, and for a minute, it cleared the noise. The rink stretched wide and merciless under the lights, every inch daring me to slip.

Coach's whistle shrieked. We dropped into lines, drills designed to set lungs on fire.

Chase cut in fast on my left, sharp as a blade turned the wrong way. He didn't look at me. He hadn't looked at Jax all day either unless he had to. Avery's face in the hospital last night had carved through him. I could still see the shadows it left behind.

Chase had seen his sister at the hospital. Elise didn't just hurt one person—she worked a long game to push, isolate, and turn people against each other until someone cracked.

Another whistle. We reset. Start-stop sprints that burned. My chest did too.

The thought landed mid-circle: Lorne would neutralize a Dunn plant within King. Neutralize. What a pretty word for what it meant.

I stumbled out of the turn and clipped Chase's heel. He spun, fist already up. I caught his wrist mid-swing, grip iron.

"Stay in your lane," I ground out. "This isn't about you, Chase. It's what happened to Avery. It's what Elise did to one of ours."

His eyes flared, but the fire banked as he took a measured breath. None of us were angry at each other. We were just bleeding out against what we couldn't fix.

"Enough," Jax snapped from behind us, voice a rasp that cut.

He wasn't near enough to make contact, but it seemed as though he was. "We don't do this here."

We. Don't. The words cooled me half a degree. I let go of Chase, and he yanked his arm back, breathing hard.

Coach's whistle split the air. "Again!"

We went again. Skates cut hard into the ice as it shaved froth under our blades. Sweat stung my eyes. The rink buzzed, lights humming, cold seeping through my pads and still not getting deep enough to numb what needed numbing.

What if Mila's right?

It wouldn't be the first time King hands did something brutal and called it necessary. One wing of the hospital stamped with our name, the other side of town scrubbed clean by Lorne when someone got in the way. Drew wrapped it in speeches about legacy. Dad didn't bother—he just knew which doors opened when you said our name.

Mila had stood under our tree and told me the truth about what her mom did, what she might be hiding. Trust didn't feel clean. It was bleeding out into someone else's hands and hoping they didn't squeeze too hard.

We shifted into scrimmage. I took center, because it was mine. Theo mirrored me on the right, Jax set low on the left, coiled.

The puck dropped. Everything narrowed. Instinct took over. I won the faceoff, tapped the puck to Theo, then cut hard into open ice, calling for it back. He threaded it through traffic, and I caught it on my forehand, snapping a shot from the slot. Crossbar rang. The clang ricocheted off the rafters and back into my chest.

Close. Not enough.

We cycled. Pressure mounted. Chase came in late on a backcheck and clipped Jax's hip. Jax steadied, and Chase caromed off the boards. The two of them locked eyes, and an entire history burned between them—brothers with a fissure running straight through.

"Move your feet," I barked at Chase, breath heaving.

"Get off my back," he threw, voice rough with something that wasn't anger alone.

"Then cover your lane and I won't have to."

He planted his stick across my path, a dare. I should've skated around it. But I didn't. I shoved through. We tangled, sticks clacking, blades snarling, both of us desperate for a fight. Jax cut between us with a shoulder and an expression that promised pain if we didn't drop it.

Coach's whistle shrieked. He didn't say my name—he didn't have to. Doubt rolled across the guys in a wave.

Our bench squinted down the ice. Stands weren't full—it wasn't that kind of practice—but the usual orbit lingered. A cluster of girls near the glass. A handful of parents up top. Elise perched two rows up, perfect profile framed, a phone balanced on her knee.

I made the mistake of meeting her eyes. She tipped her head, smile curved just enough to pass for kind. Not kindness. Inevitability. The look of someone already laying the next landmine.

She didn't need to say a thing. By the end of the hour, those girls near the glass would carry the rumor for her—and by dinner, it would be polished sharp enough to sting: whispers about Mila's family, about dirt buried under King legacy, about cracks spreading where no one wanted to look. Not the truth— just close enough to draw blood.

I drove into the next rush too hot. Puck on my stick, path narrowing, I cut inside a defenseman and felt my edge bite wrong. Skate toe caught. Body pitched. I crashed into the boards hard enough to jar my teeth. The sound went hollow in my skull.

For a second, the ice wavered. Then Jax's glove landed heavy on my shoulder, steadying. He didn't push. Didn't lecture. Just stood there with the weight of a mountain and waited until I got my feet back under me.

"I've got it," I muttered, teeth clenched.

"Then pull your head out," he returned, low enough for me alone.

We finished the drill, practice closing on the fragile effort of holding together what was already breaking apart.

The locker room stank of wet gear and muscle rub. Metal benches rang as sticks hit. No one talked to me the easy way they used to. Words drifted past without resonating. Theo sat opposite, unlacing his skates in sharp, controlled motions, watching through his lashes. A reminder. A warning.

I peeled tape off with jerky fingers. Pulled my shirt over my head and missed the sleeve on the first try. Everything felt off by one degree, enough to make me clumsy.

Chase reappeared from the showers, hair dripping onto his T-shirt. He stopped in front of me, jaw hard. "You good?" he asked.

It shouldn't have sounded like a challenge. It did. "I'm here."

"Doesn't answer the question."

"We're fine," I lied. "You know it's not about us—it's about everything she's stirred up."

Chase studied me, a muscle in his cheek ticking, then shook his head. "Doesn't look that way."

"Rough afternoon. We'll deal with it."

Jax's gaze flicked between us. Theo rolled a shoulder and went back to his laces. The room held its breath around my answer, and I gave it nothing. Chase nodded once—a ceasefire, not peace—and moved on.

I dressed in silence, dropped my gear bag by the door, and got out before someone forced me to sit and talk. The hallway outside the rink ran cold and bright, fluorescent lights buzzing at the edges. The air smelled faintly of coolant and disinfectant—manufactured winter in a town that barely knew the season.

Halfway down, Elise leaned against the wall. She didn't block my path. She didn't need to. Her timing was perfect.

"Tough skate?" she murmured, voice spun sugar, eyes sharp.

I kept moving.

"Must be hard," she continued, "balancing two worlds. Family reputation on one side. A girl who comes with… complications on the other."

I stopped and turned enough for her to see what lived behind my calm. She smiled, as if she'd won something.

"Watch your tongue," I told her.

She lifted both hands, innocence painted in French tips and diamonds no high schooler should be wearing. "I'm just sympathizing. Everyone thought the Kings were untouchable. Turns out, you're…not."

Not subtle.

I closed the distance, crowding her back against the wall. My voice stayed low, steady. "You better be careful. You're making the wrong moves. Enough of them, and all your secrets will be laid bare."

Her smile twitched but didn't slip.

"If you touch Avery again," I added, flat as ice, "I'll end you. This isn't about me and you," I added. "It's about the people you're using as pawns—Avery, Mila, anyone you think you can break."

The smile didn't move, but something in her eyes did—a flare, quick and mean. She leaned in a fraction, enough for me to smell the cloying sweetness of her perfume over the cold.

"Everyone thinks threats solve things," she breathed. "But the thing about ice, Luke? It just needs a flaw to crack."

She turned on her heel and floated toward the exit, leaving me with the arena windows and my reflection fractured across them—too many versions of me staring back.

Outside, the night had dropped hard, the kind of dark that made headlights look vicious. I walked until the glare of the rink lights fell behind me and the parking lot opened up to sky. My hands wouldn't stop flexing.

Mila's face flashed behind my eyes—the way she looked under the tree when truth hurt, the way her shoulders loosened when she decided to trust me anyway. Her mother smashing a thumb drive with a hammer. Darren's name in a report that felt more akin to a ledger of sins. Dad's voice in old memories, low and precise, making violence sound as though it was an order.

If loving her meant exposing what my family buried, what did that make me—a traitor? Or a son who refused to inherit without question?

And if protecting my family meant burying what she'd risked to tell me, what did that make me to her?

I didn't have answers. Only a promise I'd made under the open sky with salt in the air and her fingers tight in mine.

Partners. No lies. No power plays. We don't disappear on each other when it gets ugly.

It was ugly now.

I pulled my phone and hovered over my father's name. The call would go through. He would pick up. He always did when it mattered to the family. He'd tell me the measured version. He'd wrap truth in words that sounded clean.

I set the phone on the hood instead and pressed both palms to the metal until the sting made sense of my body again.

I could hear Coach's voice in my head from years ago, back when the game was simpler: When the ice gets bad, skate lighter. Keep your weight over your edges. Trust your feet.

Trust your feet. Trust the partner who'd met me under a tree and carried a truth to me even when it might destroy us.

I picked up my phone and opened a new message—not to Dad. Not to Drew.

To Mila: *I'm with you. We'll handle this. Both of us.*

I needed to reiterate to her that we were a team. That I had her back no matter what. Her reply came a minute later.

Mila: *Okay.*

I breathed for what felt like the first time since she'd started talking. The breath didn't fix anything. It didn't need to. It reminded me I could still do it.

Darkness stretched in front of me. Elise would keep moving her pieces. Dunn would call someone. Dad would expect answers.

I slid into my car and hit *Start*. The engine growled, steady and alive.

If loving Mila meant pulling truth into the open, then that was where we were going. If protecting my family meant learning where the rot began, then I would find it. Either way, I was done coasting blind.

CHAPTER TWENTY-NINE

MILA

I had my sketchbook halfway out of my locker, graphite from the page smudging my fingers, when the PA beeped and the vice principal's voice went tinny over the halls. "Mila Callahan to the office."

The hallway went quiet in patches, noise skidding around me without touching. I slid the sketchbook back, closed the locker softly so the metal wouldn't clang, and started walking. Students parted in little eddies, eyes flicking away when I looked up. My heartbeat thudded in my chest, steady at first, then harder with each turn.

Outside, the sun shone bright. Inside, the administrative corridor held an old chill, the kind that had nothing to do with weather.

The receptionist's expression told me nothing. She pointed me through. The vice principal's door clicked shut behind me. I was in a small room with three chairs and a table too narrow for comfort. The vice principal sat at the head of the table. To her right was the chair of the disciplinary committee. Both faces wore neutrality that didn't quite hold.

"We've received disturbing information." The vice principal

folded her hands, gaze steady. "Screenshots. Messages appearing to come from you—sent to a media account that covers elite corporate families."

My stomach dropped. "That's not possible." The words came out thin. "I didn't—"

The head of the committee slid a packet across the table. Printouts of emails and blocks of text, timestamps highlighted. I scanned quickly—King Enterprises gala donors, notes on sponsor tiers, bullet points that tracked closer to fact than rumor ever should.

The room tipped under me for a second then righted. It smacked of Elise's handiwork.

"I didn't do this." My voice found its weight. "It's a setup."

They didn't blink. "You understand the severity of this, Ms. Callahan?" The vice principal's tone stayed mild. The words did all the work. "We will need to inform your guardian and begin a formal review. Given the allegations and the harassment this year, expulsion is on the table."

My palms sweated against my jeans. "I didn't send those."

The two of them exchanged a glance that said they had already had this conversation without me. The head of the committee tapped the stack once. "We will be investigating. Until then, you'll stay off gala duties and out of school media rooms."

The floor tilted. My ears hummed with a ring that wouldn't quit. "Am I—" My mouth dried. "Am I suspended?"

"Not at this time." A pause heavy with yet. "But your scholarship may be at risk. We'll notify you when we've completed our initial review."

I stood because my body knew the steps. Open door. Close door. Walk. The corridor back to the hall blurred. What I remembered were faces. Stares swarmed together, as small and relentless as gnats.

Someone's phone lifted, eyes gleaming over the top of it. The sensation of being filmed crawled over my skin. I dipped into the nearest side corridor and pressed my spine to the cool cinderblock, breath shallow.

"Mila."

His voice cut through the noise, and my head snapped up. Luke strode toward me, his hair still damp from the midday lift in the weight room, backpack slung over one shoulder. He didn't slow. His hand caught my wrist and turned me. His body blocked the view from the main hall.

"Come with me."

I didn't argue. He steered me into an empty classroom hardly anyone used, tucked at the far end of the wing where the light hit wrong and left it dim. He tugged the blinds until they gave, and the glare broke into stripes across the floor. Outside, footsteps pattered. Somewhere, a laugh trilled too loud and then vanished.

"You're not going down for this." He didn't crowd. He anchored. The room steadied around his voice.

"How did you find out already?" My throat worked. "It's Elise. She—"

"I know." He unzipped his backpack and pulled a blue folder, corners bent as if he'd jammed it in fast. He set it on the desk and flipped it open. "These are the originals. From her phone."

My brain stalled at that. "What? How did you get those?"

"Look." He slid the first page to me. Rushed, tilted pictures of Elise's phone, caught while someone had access to it. Her chat app open. A thread with the media account. Her handle, not mine. Original timestamps, before she doctored them.

The next pages showed more: sender tags she'd edited, a text message she'd sent to herself under Callahan, then deleted, then forwarded. Beneath that, an export log with her own notes scribbled in the margin: Fix date stamps. Change handle field to MC.

Air came back in a rush. My hands shook anyway. "How did you get this?"

He let out a hard breath. "One of hers finally broke ranks."

"That isn't an answer."

"It was Tori." He tapped a page where her name showed in a printed text thread. A single message, sent to Theo late at night: *I'm done helping her.* No context. No explanation.

"She just passed it to him—and Theo slid it straight to me." Luke flipped to the next printout. "The text came with photos—straight from Tori. Enough to prove Elise doctored the thread." He looked up. "Sloppy. But enough to blow a hole in her story."

My knees went loose, so I braced them against the chair's seat. "So the school—"

"Has enough to slow-roll. They won't pull the trigger on you while this is in review." He watched my face as if gauging where to put the next word. "And I can take this up the chain if they stall."

He could. He would. The realization hit with heat and cold. The King name opened more doors than just those in their wing of the hospital. They could buy attention to whatever issue, or desired outcomes, they wanted.

Relief hit hard enough that I had to sit. The chair wobbled once and then held.

He dropped to a knee in front of me, folder still open, proof fanned out between us. "You okay?"

"No." A fractured laugh slipped out and caught on a breath that wasn't steady yet. "But you being here helps."

His mouth curved, not all the way to a smile. He leaned in, forehead brushing mine, breath warm. He didn't have to say anything. The contact said enough.

Footsteps passed in the hall. Somebody rattled a locker door. A muted cheer rose from the far end of campus—game-day pep in the quad. The school kept moving while my world reassembled in slow clicks.

He pulled back just enough to look me in the eye. "We go public and expose Elise on our terms."

"What does that even look like?"

"Proof first. Then pressure." He straightened, pulled out his phone, and swiped. "Theo handed it to me. I've already locked copies with people Principal Miller can't ignore. He knows she forged this. If they try to pin it on you again, it blows back on them."

"And Elise?"

"She's got a stage to play on—expects to be queen." His eyes cooled, that metallic shift I'd only ever seen when his family name got pulled in. "Let her walk in thinking she still owns the room."

"The fundraising committee?"

"Assembly run-through in the gym. Donors' preview after." He slid the folder back into his bag, movements precise. "You'll be there. She will too. And so will I."

A knot I hadn't known I was holding loosened at that last piece. "Avery?"

"Home. Jax is taking her then going back for practice. He wanted to stay with her after all she'd been through yesterday and last night, but she told him no. Not to miss practice."

My chest pinched at the soft steel in that. "Chase?"

"He'll show. We warned him. He's holding it together."

None of this erased the feeling of being dragged under in the office, my chance at college blowing up in my face. But it gave me something to hold on to before I drowned. I stood. My legs held. "Okay."

Luke's gaze scanned my face once more, a sweep that hit every tell. He lifted a hand and brushed his thumb along my cheek, brief, then dropped it. "Armor up."

I squared my shoulders, stood straight, and slipped my game face on all the way from the classroom to the gym.

The gym had been dressed to impress for the run-through of gala event information sharing. Banners hung crisp against the far wall. The new scoreboard glowed. A scaffold of lights sprouted along the edges for the assembly—soft amber bulbs meant to mimic the gala's mood lighting when the real donors' event hit off-campus. It was to raise awareness, and the faculty thought this was the best place to do it, even though the gala event would be held elsewhere.

Students milled in their assigned roles for the mock event—ushers with badges, check-in kids clutching clipboards, decor committee fussing over centerpieces no one would remember. Principal Miller tapped the mic on the portable stage while the gala adviser sorted note cards.

Elise walked in just late enough to be noticed but not to be called out. White dress too polished for a gym. Hair perfect. Diamonds catching the lights. No binder in her hand. She didn't need one. Her eyes found me and brightened as though she'd been waiting for the moment.

I held her stare the way you regard a yard with an untethered dog—calm, still, ready to move if it lunged.

The guys filed in together, Chase a step behind, Theo peeling off from a group near the bleachers to slot in at Jax's side. Tori slid onto the lower bleachers and didn't look at anyone. She stared at her phone. Her thumb didn't move.

Principal Miller clapped twice for attention. Feedback squealed then settled. The run-through started—a staged version of opening night mixed with a pep talk for the student body, meant to raise awareness for the fundraiser and recruit volunteers for future ones. Welcome remarks, sponsors shout-outs, and a parade of committee leads taking turns at the mic. Each thanked donors and highlighted "opportunities" the gala provided—every line carefully phrased for a résumé.

On cue, I did my part. Walked a mock donor from the

"entrance" at the double doors to the check-in table, handed them an imaginary packet, sent them toward the VIP section. Smile. Thank you. Next. I didn't think about the office. I thought about the folder in Luke's bag and the proof waiting to blow back in Elise's face.

She drifted between groups as if assigned to float. When she reached the mic for her scripted thank-you, she didn't glance at her cards. Elise knew how to make her voice bend into whatever shape the room wanted.

"On behalf of the student committee," she began, posture perfect, "thank you to our sponsors and families for making this possible. It's an honor to be part of a school that believes in legacy."

Legacy. The word lodged.

Her gaze slid across the gym and brushed mine, not a touch so much as a mark. "And thank you for trusting us."

The last two words tasted poisoned.

During the run-through, she lifted the mic, casual as breathing, and smiled out at the rows of students. "Events like these," she said, "take commitment. Hours behind the scenes. Trust. And it only works if everyone is... honest." Her pause was deliberate. Long enough for heads to turn, short enough she could claim she hadn't meant anything by it.

I felt the shift ripple through the space. Theo's shoulders went a fraction tighter. Chase's jaw flexed. Jax leaned forward in his seat, expression flat as steel. A whisper skated down the bleachers, quick and sly. Heads bent together, phones angled low.

Elise only smiled brighter, as if she hadn't just lobbed a grenade into the middle of the room.

Luke stepped forward from the shadows at the edge of the bleachers and walked, not rushed, across the gym floor. He didn't take the stairs to the stage. He took the short leap up, smooth, faced the mic, and put his hand over it so his voice wouldn't boom. He didn't look at Elise. He looked at Principal Miller. "We need to pause."

Heads turned at once. Teachers straightened. One of the sponsors frowned.

Elise's smile barely flickered. "We're on a schedule, Luke."

"We're not." He took Elise's phone off the podium and locked the screen. Small enough to look petty. "You wanted honesty?" His voice carried, flat and even. "Here it is." He held the phone up then passed it to Principal Miller. "There's a doctored thread on this device that frames a student for leaking sponsor information. The originals are already with administration. This is a formality."

His voice carried without effort, tempered steel instead of heat. The gym heard every syllable. He didn't hide behind his last name. He didn't have to. He stood in its center and used it as a shield for me.

Principal Miller scanned the lock screen as if it might bite. The gala adviser reached for it then pulled her hand back. The vice principal had materialized at the edge of the stage without footsteps, pulled by the gravity of crisis.

Elise laughed under her breath, a small, dismissive exhale. "You think you can take my personal device and—"

"Enter it into review?" Luke kept his tone even. "Yes."

Her gaze cut to me and sharpened. For a breath, I saw the razor-sharp edge underneath the gloss. Then the mask slid back into place. "If my phone gets reviewed, so does hers."

"That was already the plan." Luke didn't look away. "But the originals came from your device. And before you argue metadata, those logs are printed too."

Murmurs rolled through the bleachers—not the messy kind Elise spread but contained by the Luke's authority and the weight he carried.

Principal Miller cleared his throat into the mic. "We're going to pause the run-through. Advisers and committee leads, please step into the auxiliary room. Students, remain seated."

The gym loosened in an instant, and at the same time, a different tension sparked everywhere at once. Clusters formed and re-formed. Eyes slid to me then away.

I watched Elise step down from the stage, every movement measured. Her attention landed on me as she passed, lingering long enough for the room to notice.

Luke's shoulders squared, his stare locked on hers. Theo's gaze tracked her, cold and steady. Chase's expression hardened, warning clear in every line of him.

I didn't flinch. I kept my face still.

I felt a pull backward in my ribs, the old urge to run when rooms turned. I took one step toward the door before Jax appeared in my path, not blocking but present. The look he gave me said "Stay" without moving his mouth. Theo took the other side. Two quiet bookends. Close enough to be seen. Far enough not to crowd.

I held. My knees locked and then eased. Luke hopped down from the stage and cut across the floor through a path that opened for him without anyone admitting they had moved. He reached me and stopped so we were chest to chest, and the rest of the gym fell away.

"You okay?" His voice dropped, meant for me alone.

"Trying to be."

His knuckles brushed my shoulder, a brief tap that buzzed through my nerves. "You're not on your own in this."

"Thank you." Two words that carried more than they should.

His mouth crooked, a flash of warmth breaking through the control. "Always."

The vice principal called his name, and he stepped away with a mix of reluctance and purpose. I watched him disappear into the knot of adults by the exit. They closed ranks, voices low. Every so often, I caught a glimpse of him through the doorway—his shoulders squared, his head bent as he spoke, the adults listening harder than they wanted to.

Near the bleachers, I felt someone come to my side before he touched me. Theo's hand brushed mine—just a quick clasp, warm, steady, enough to ground me. He didn't speak.

Jax's gaze caught on it then rose to my face. A nod, no more.

Chase hovered a step away, conflict written in the set of his mouth. His eyes raked the gym—Elise's orbit, the administrators' knot, the cluster of girls already trading whispers—and came back to me. He looked at Theo's hand. He looked at Luke. "We're not losing each other over this," he muttered finally, more to himself than anyone. A declaration. A dare.

Theo gave my hand one more squeeze before letting go.

The exit door shut. The gym's noise rose then flattened as if we'd all agreed to hover in place. Time stretched. When the door opened, the principal entered with the vice principal, Luke a step behind. The gala adviser's face had lost all its color. The principal returned to the mic and didn't bother with "testing, testing." His voice changed slightly this time.

"We will reschedule this run-through," he announced. "Committee leads, check your email for new times. We'll be in touch. Students, you are dismissed."

Elise didn't get her moment under the lights. Not today.

People crowded the aisles and exits in a rush to leave. Luke rejoined me. The look we traded said it all: the office would investigate, the phone would be reviewed, the fallout would come later. The public explosion was over.

We moved as a unit to the doors—Jax, Theo, Chase a half-step behind, Luke and me in the center. Students watched without getting caught. Elise stood near the stage, smile gone tight, fury bleeding through the cracks she tried to keep in place. She didn't come after us. Not here. Not yet.

We cleared the gym, and the sound shifted to the usual din

of the hall. Locker doors clanged. Someone called for a ride. Luke walked me to the end of the corridor and paused where the wall met the glass doors. The sun threw sheets of brightness across the floor. He set his bag down and leaned in, not enough to make a scene but enough to breathe air that hadn't been in a gym.

"Expulsion's off the table," he murmured. "They won't admit it yet, but it is."

"What about her?"

"She'll fight it." His jaw worked once. "But this time, there's a trail."

My throat tightened. "You stood up there and put your name between me and her."

"It belongs there."

He moved into the space between us, and I saw the cost in his eyes—the shadow of his father, the weight of the name he'd just turned into a weapon. Protecting me meant crossing them, and I wasn't going to let him carry that alone. "Does your family know that?"

His eyes cooled then warmed back. "They will."

I didn't kiss him. We couldn't officially be a couple yet, not publicly. I squeezed his hand for a second then let it go. "Thank you."

"You know I've got you."

"Take me outside," I murmured. "In five minutes."

He glanced to the guys, letting them know to go ahead to practice without him; he'd catch up soon. Jax, Chase, and Theo turned as one and headed off in the direction of the arena.

We slipped into the courtyard behind the fine arts building, where the wind cut the heat, and palms brushed against each other. He stood close without touching, heat from his arm bleeding through the breeze. I tipped my head back and closed my eyes until the pressure eased a notch.

"When do they review her phone?" I asked, opening them again.

"Tonight," he answered. "The IT lead doesn't sleep when the principal and review board toss him a bone."

"Elise will spin things before they can act."

"She's already spinning." He nodded toward the campus, toward the networks we couldn't see but felt. "But Tori moved out from under her. That matters."

"Elise is scared."

"She should be."

The breeze shifted. A bell pealed from somewhere off campus—church or clock, I couldn't tell. For a second, everything quieted. It didn't last. "Thank you for today," I murmured again.

He took my hand and folded it into his. "Thank you for yesterday."

"Yesterday?"

"For trusting me with the information you've shared. About what your mom learned while working for Dunn. About the drive she destroyed." His grip tightened. "We're going to figure everything out."

A chime vibrated in my pocket. I pulled my phone out. A new email pinged at the top. From the vice principal. Subject line: Next steps.

I didn't open it yet. I handed the phone to Luke. "You read it."

He scanned fast. His shoulders dropped half an inch. "They're officially clearing the threat to your scholarship and right to stay on campus." He passed the screen back. "The email is just a formality."

"Okay. Good."

He glanced toward the parking lot. "Go home. There's nothing more to do right now."

"And you?"

"Practice." His mouth flattened. "Then home. Then… a conversation."

"With your father."

"With Drew too." His eyes found mine, steady.

I rose on my toes without thinking. He met me halfway. The brush of his mouth was quick. Anchoring. Enough to hold, not enough to feed the rumor mill another meal.

We broke apart. He touched my cheekbone with his thumb, gentle, then lowered his hand.

"Text me when you're home," he murmured.

"I will."

He let me go, and I let him. He turned toward the rink. I turned toward the lot. I pulled up Avery's contact info and pressed the call button.

She answered immediately. "You good?"

"Getting there." I climbed into my car and pulled the belt over my shoulder. "Are you feeling better?"

"Better than last night." She exhaled. "Still not great."

I connected my phone so the audio spilled through the car's speakers and then pulled away from the curb. The school slid by in a rush of brick and glass and banners advertising the donor gala.

"Tell me everything." Avery sounded more like herself.

"I swear this day tried to break me," I started. "Elise—"

"Of course it was Elise," Avery cut in, voice edged with annoyance.

"She nearly had them expel me with doctored screenshots. The system wanted the easy answer, of course, my name on it."

Avery swore under her breath. "And?"

"It didn't stick, thanks to Luke and Tori."

Avery was quiet for a beat, just the sound of her breathing filling the car. "Good. Make her choke on that." Her voice was raw, but there was steel under it. "She doesn't get to win."

Relief caught me off guard. "We'll hold, Avery. No matter what she throws."

"We have to." She blew out a breath. "Because I'm not letting her harm you, too."

The line went quiet again—not heavy this time but shared.

I turned onto the road where the houses clung to the hills and the ocean flashed between rooftops. For the first time all day, the silence didn't feel like an enemy.

CHAPTER THIRTY

LUKE

I pulled into the drive and noted there was nothing out of place, as if life was perfect. The house wore its museum face —lights staged, fountain running. You'd never know I'd spent the afternoon dragging Mila out of Elise's firing line or that practice had felt like skating with sand under my blades.

I killed the engine and sat there long enough to watch the kitchen window go dark then flare back to life. A shadow crossed the glass, profile sharp for half a second. Not staff.

Inside, the air carried the low hum of circulation. I dropped my gear by the mudroom bench and followed the low glow down the hall. The study door stood open a few inches. Dad's voice came through, not raised. Worse. Smooth, controlled, a temperature drop.

"Come in here, Luke."

I pushed the door and stepped onto the rug, preferring to stand. He didn't look up right away. When he did, fury banked behind his eyes as he turned the monitor so I could see it. My checking account. A debit line highlighted in the middle of the page: Marcus Vega Investigations. My hands curled into fists.

"Would you care to explain why you've hired a private investigator?"

I wasn't silent because I was shocked. I was counting to three to breathe around the anger. I made it to two.

His hand came down on the desk—not a slam, just a placement with weight. "Don't insult me. You think I can't see where the money goes?"

"It's my checking account." My shoulders pulled tight. "You had no right to be inside it."

His eyes flicked up, pale and precise. "The account might carry your name, but don't mistake it for independence. I can lock it with one call. If you want to test me, go ahead."

"I don't need protection from the truth." I stepped closer.

His gaze cut through me, and he set his tumbler of whiskey down too hard. The glass rang against the wood, a loud note in the quiet room. "Then tell me. Why the investigator? What exactly are you digging for?"

"I'm trying to figure out what's going on. About Darren Langley. About what Dunn started and what we may have finished. About what Elise did to Avery. About what she's trying to do to Mila."

The explosion came fast, hotter for being contained too long. "Stay the fuck out of it, Luke." He growled. "You hear me? Out. That mess isn't yours to touch."

"What mess exactly?" I forced the words through my teeth.

His hand flattened against the desk, hard enough that the lamp rattled. "All of it. That Mila girl is nothing but trouble. I warned you. Drew warned you. Stay away from her before she drags you under with the rest of them. You don't need to figure out anything," he ordered. "You need to focus on your future. The company that will one day carry you if you don't set it on fire first. That future is not with that girl."

Cold slid through me, clean and surgical. "That's not your decision to make."

"You're risking everything we built—our name, our company—over a girl and your obsession with things you don't understand."

"Maybe I'm risking everything to stop being blind." My hands curled against my thighs. "Dunn deposits hit Darren's account before he vanished. His house sold. The proceeds landed clean. No withdrawals. No trace. And now—today—Dunn's daughter tried to take Mila down in front of the entire school. You think that doesn't touch me? Don't preach risk to me."

His chest lifted, held, lowered. "She's a problem, Luke. Her mother was inside our walls once, too close to things she had no right to touch. Now you're walking the same path."

"Maybe it isn't about them."

Dad's head tilted.

"Maybe it's about what you're hiding." I didn't raise my voice. "About what Lorne did. About what you authorized or refused to stop."

The silence that followed grew teeth. The house hummed around it—the discrete whir of ducts, the soft buzz of recessed lights. His gaze pressed like weight, daring me to flinch.

"You're young," he said finally, a verdict he'd been waiting to deliver. "You think loving a girl makes you immortal. It makes you vulnerable. It makes you stupid."

"Loving her makes me honest." My hand found the doorframe before I knew I was moving. "You want me to stay out of things and away from Mila because you're realizing that I won't pretend anymore."

"You want to throw yourself into ruin and call it principle." His voice leveled, flat again. "Fine. But don't expect me—or this family—to carry the cost."

I turned the knob. The brass felt cold under my palm. Leaving his office was the only answer he'd get tonight.

The hall stretched bright and empty. My reflection walked

with me across dark glass—taller, older, more tired than I'd been this morning when I stuck myself between Mila and a room full of knives. In the kitchen, the under-cabinet lights illuminated the granite in soft strips. I took a glass from the cabinet intent on filling it up but just stood there doing nothing instead.

Of everyone I shouldn't talk to tonight, she was the one I wanted to more than anything. I pulled my phone out and opened our text thread. The tightness in my chest didn't ease as my thumb hovered over the message box.

Loving her was the only thing that made me see straight. It was honesty, and I'd burn down every polished lie in this house before I gave it up.

Footsteps came behind me. I gripped the phone too tight and shoved it behind my back. But it wasn't my father. The steps were lighter.

Drew leaned a shoulder into the door jamb, watching me finish the glass.

"So that mess happened," he said. "I overheard some of it."

"Walked right into it." I set the glass down. "He checked my accounts while he was at it."

Drew didn't flinch. "And you're surprised?"

"No."

He stepped closer, voice low. "Protect yourself. Don't let Mila be the reason you go down."

The instinct to bristle hit, but I swallowed it. "She's not dragging me anywhere."

"Doesn't matter how it starts," he said. "If you're standing too close when it blows, you'll take the hit too." He held my stare. "If you need to worry about someone, don't start with Dad."

A beat. "Who then?"

"Lorne." The name landed hard. "He fixes problems. He doesn't hesitate. And he thinks protecting us means cutting out anyone who dents the family."

Mila's mother with a hammer in her kitchen. Darren's clean

ledger. Elise smiling onstage, carving with a phone. My father forbidding me to have anything to do with Mila.

"Did Lorne do something to Darren Langley?" I asked, knowing I wouldn't get the answer.

Drew's mouth thinned. "If he did, you'll only hear about it when it serves someone else. Don't be the last to know."

"I hired the PI to make sure I'm not."

"That'll get you facts." Drew pushed off the counter. "Don't confuse them for the whole truth."

My jaw ached. "Truth is the only thing I'm after."

"Good." His eyes flicked toward the study. "I'm on your side. Just...don't burn yourself down chasing the truth."

We stood in the kitchen. Drew looked older, not in his face but in the way his shoulders carried weight. He tried to be the polish to Dad's force. Tonight, the polish had worn thin.

"I'm not leaving her," I said.

His eyes sharpened. "Then don't give Lorne a reason to make her a problem."

"Meaning."

"Don't keep evidence on you. Don't let the wrong people hear what you're digging for. Don't give Elise fuel she can spin. Keep yourself clean enough they can't move against you." He paused. "And the best thing you could do for her—the only thing? Stay away. At least for now."

Anger hit hot, sharp. "That's not happening."

"I'm telling you the truth, not what you want to hear." His voice stayed level. "You're tying yourself to her at the worst possible moment. If she goes down, you go with her. You want to protect her? Don't hand them an easy way to use you both."

"Maybe you're right, but she's not the problem."

"I didn't say she was." His gaze cut to the dark window, our reflections layered in the glass. "But her family, our family, Dunn's—those lines are crossing in ways that don't end clean. You're worth more than getting caught in the grind."

"You talk like you're not part of it."

"I am. But I also know what to watch out for." His tone stayed even. "So hear me—keep your head. Don't throw away leverage because your heart is involved. And don't give Lorne a reason to go after her."

"I won't." The weight of it settled, heavy.

"Make sure of it."

He clapped my shoulder once—firm enough to anchor, soft enough to pass as brotherly—and walked out, leaving the hum of the appliances and Dad's words still clinging to the walls.

I leaned back against the counter and swiped out of Mila's contact information to Marcus's then sent my PI a message. *Keep digging into Darren's house sale. Follow the notary. I want the escrow officer, the recorder's timestamp, everything that touched the wire.*

Three dots. Then: *Copy. Already on escrow. Notary looks dirty. Will confirm.*

If the notary was dirty, the rest of the trail wouldn't stay clean for long. I pocketed the phone and went to the window. My reflection wavered over the glass, pale and doubled. Somewhere between the study and the kitchen, the part of me that wanted to be the son my father recognized had left the room.

I heard Drew's warning, but I couldn't make myself heed it. I wasn't stepping back from Mila. And I wasn't giving Lorne a reason to make her his target.

"Protect yourself. Don't let Mila be the reason you go down."

I understood the love under Drew's words. I did. I just didn't agree with it. You could run from a fire or learn where the accelerant was stored.

I killed the kitchen lights and left. Upstairs, the house stretched silent around me, all polished surface and hollow space. I didn't look at the ocean strip beyond the windows.

I lay back in the dark, every nerve wired. If fire was coming, I wasn't running. The flames were already encircling me.

CHAPTER THIRTY-ONE

MILA

Luke's audio hit my phone at 12:17 a.m.

I was in bed on top of the covers, lamp off, house quiet except for the hiss of late-night sprinklers outside and a neighbor's garage door grinding open somewhere nearby. My screen lit around me in a pale glow when the voice message notification slid across.

I thumbed it open, expecting his usual—*home, you okay?*

It wasn't.

Drew's voice filled my room instead. Low. Controlled. "Protect yourself. Don't let Mila be the reason you go down."

My blood iced.

Rustle on the line. Then Luke, so quiet I had to lift the phone to my ear. "Maybe you're right."

"Doesn't matter how it starts," Drew said. "If you're standing too close when it blows, you'll take the hit too."

A breath from Luke, too long, too thin. "She's not the problem."

"I didn't say she was," Drew returned. "But her family, our family, Dunn's family? Those lines are crossing in ways that don't end clean. You're worth more than getting caught in the grind."

"You talk like you're not part of it."

"I am. But I also know what to watch out for." Drew's tone stayed even. "So hear me: keep your head. Don't throw away leverage because you're leading with your heart. If you need to worry about someone, don't start with Dad."

A pause. Luke again, softer. "Who then."

"Lorne." The name came like a blade. "He fixes problems. He doesn't hesitate. And he thinks protecting us means cutting out anyone who dents the family."

Silence stretched, filled with the hum of their kitchen. A drawer opening, a glass against the counter. The audio cut out for a beat or two before Luke's steady but too raw voice sounded close to the phone. "I'm not leaving her."

But there was a beat before it. The hesitation scraped through the speaker—less certainty than fight, as though he was forcing the words through doubt.

Drew pressed anyway. "Then don't give Lorne a reason."

The message cut off with a tiny mechanical click.

I stared at my ceiling until the white square blurred. My pulse banged at my throat as if that could push air back in. He hadn't meant to send it. My name must have been open on his screen; his thumb must have brushed the wrong icon. It didn't matter. It was mine now.

"I'm not leaving her."

The pause before the words burned into my skin.

Luke texted before first bell: *Early film. See you at lunch. You good?*

His message seemed normal. But the shortness of it felt like he was already distancing himself from me, even if he hadn't meant to.

I typed yes and didn't hit send. He didn't deserve my lie. He also didn't deserve my panic shotgun-blasted into his morning. I slid the phone away and chose quiet.

Before lunch, Avery caught me by the lockers. I told her about the recording. "There has to be an explanation," she said, low enough that the hallway noise masked it.

I shrugged, the only answer I had. "Maybe."

She didn't push, just slid me a look that said she didn't buy my shrug any more than I did. In the classes I shared with Luke, I did my best to ignore him—arriving late, leaving the second the bell rang, sprinting ahead before he could catch up.

By the time lunch came, Avery told Jax she wanted to sit with her friends today. Jasmine and Margie waved us over, already staked out at a corner table. Avery dropped into the seat between them, pushing up her long sleeves to her elbows, then shot me one glance too many—a reminder that she knew, that she'd sworn there had to be a reason Luke sounded like that hesitation had come from something deeper.

I stabbed at the salad on my tray and let the noise of their chatter blur. Everyone but Luke sat at their usual table.

Tori was a new fixture glued to Theo's side, which, by the glare locked and loaded on Elise and Nina's faces a few tables away, promised fallout sooner rather than later.

I lasted three minutes. Then I pushed up and mumbled something about needing air. Avery's eyes tracked me, but she didn't stop me. Her hand brushed my forearm as I passed anyway, a press that said *I'm here if you need me.*

I didn't go to the quad. Not today. I took the side corridor between the auditorium and the small practice gym, where a row of narrow windows threw slats of light onto dust and a vending machine whirred. The air smelled faintly of paint and old paper. Someone had taped flyers for the gala along the wall.

I leaned against cool brick and breathed until my shoulders stopped trying to live up near my ears. The message played through my mind again without my permission—Drew's command, Luke's answer, the line that cut.

Footsteps. Not hurried. Confident. Perfume before presence.

Elise slid into the slant of light and paused three feet from me, as if an invisible tape line marked the beginning of my oxygen.

She didn't bother with a greeting. "Rough night?"

I kept my face flat. "Get lost."

She smiled, all pearl and poison. "I could. Or I could offer you a little kindness, Mila. You look like you need it."

"Your definition of kindness and mine don't match."

"Maybe not." She took in the corridor—the shut auditorium doors, the way the light split under them, the emptiness. "Maybe I'm just here to congratulate you."

"On what."

"Surviving yesterday." She tipped her head. Diamonds winked at her ears. "Your mother worked fast with Principal Miller to help get you cleared. Faster than I gave her credit for."

I kept my voice even. "You framed me. Luke dropped enough proof in front of Principal Miller that he had no choice but to act."

"Everyone folds for the right person," she murmured, almost dreamy.

The corridor shrank to the length of my breath. "What do you want."

"To help you accept inevitable things." She lifted one shoulder. "You and Luke aren't built for the long game. You know it." Her gaze flicked to my pocket. "He sent you audio last night, didn't he?"

No one should've had access. Not her. Not anyone. My skin chilled even as my phone felt hot through denim. "Back off."

"That would be a yes." The gleam in her eyes brightened. "Family counsel can be clarifying. Protect yourself. Don't let her drag you into the fire. You heard it, didn't you? And then the part where he agreed the smartest move might be distance."

My throat scraped dry. "You shouldn't know that."

"I know more than you think." She didn't blink. "My family and the Kings make messy stories disappear when they threaten the wrong people. Lorne makes sure it happens. And Luke?" Her voice softened on his name. "Luke was raised to protect the family first. He'll fold into their version before yours."

The world tilted. I forced my feet to stay planted. "Say it enough times and maybe you believe yourself."

"It is true." She stepped closer, careful not to touch. "You want me to tell you he doesn't care about you." She shrugged. "He does. He cares so much it turns into weakness—and weakness that doesn't align with family goals gets cut."

"By Lorne." My stomach churned, and bile splashed against the back of my throat. "Get away from me."

She straightened, as if I'd bored her. "Enjoy your last week. Or month. However long it takes for him to decide the smart move is distance. He'll tell you it's for you. That's his style. It will sound gentle. It will cut the same."

"Leave." The word was steady now. "Before I make you."

Her smile sharpened. "You won't. Because right now you're wondering how much of what Luke tells you is a lie and how far he'll go to give his family the ending they want—with me in it. And you're probably realizing your mom works for my dad, which means I hold more power than you ever will." She pursed her lips. "Or even if I was there when this conversation went down and if Luke and I laughed when he sent it to you."

I didn't move. I didn't blink. I let my stare do the pushing for me. She held it. A beat. Two. Then she broke away, footsteps fading across the polished wood, leaving the air thinner in her wake.

My back slid down the wall, the cold brick seeping into my shoulder blades. Light from the high windows caught the dust and turned it into something I could measure by seconds. I pressed both hands to my eyes and counted to five, then twenty, because five didn't touch it. My chest stuttered—breath, halt, breath, halt—as if my ribs had jammed.

Luke's message replayed in my head, tangled now with the subtext Elise had slipped into the cracks. Was he playing me for a fool? Was she right—that the two of them were inevitable? And how else would she have known about the recording I got last night?

It was hard to swallow, especially with everything Elise had already done—the tampering, the rumors, the quiet dismantling of anything that tied us together.

Footsteps again. Different cadence. No perfume. I knew the weight of them before I admitted I did.

"Don't," I warned, voice raw.

He stopped instantly. The air shifted—less cold, more charged. He left two feet between us and didn't close them, just stood there until my pulse began to steady against the outline of him.

"Mila." His voice was low, careful. "What happened? Why the hell was Elise anywhere near you?"

My throat scraped. Words clung. "She—" I wrapped my arms tight around my middle as though I could stop myself from breaking. "She knows things she shouldn't."

His shoulders went rigid. "What things?"

I shook my head. The words stuck as if caught on barbed wire.

"Mila." His voice cut sharper. "Tell me."

I pushed to my feet so fast the blood roared in my ears. "That recording you sent last night—Elise knew. She threw it in my face like it was some private joke between you two."

"What recording?" His eyes narrowed, lines cutting deep. "What do you mean she knew? And what the hell was she even doing near you?"

"She knew, Luke." Fury burned through my throat. "She said you'll fold the second your family demands it. That you'll protect their version of your future, not anything with me. So, tell me—am I supposed to believe she's wrong?"

His voice dropped low. "You really think I'd choose them over you?"

"You said *maybe you're right* when Drew said *don't let Mila be the reason you go down.*"

His brows rose. "That wasn't the whole conversation."

"Whatever. The point is you said it." Even though there was no way I'd take anything Elise said at face value, I'd had it. I threw my arms up, disgusted. "Forget it."

He caught my arm as I shoved off the wall to storm past him. The heat of his grip seared more than it steadied.

"Let me go, Luke." I forced the words between my teeth. "I need space."

For a second, he didn't move. Then his hand fell away. The heat of his grip stayed even after he let go, a ghost burning against my skin as I hurried through the hall and shoved through the exit doors. I didn't look back, just moved past the glass and the stares, out to the parking lot where the afternoon sun made everything too bright. My keys fumbled in my grip before I shoved into the driver's seat and slammed the door.

The engine roared too loud. Tires squealed as I pulled out— nowhere to go but away. Away from the halls. Away from him. Away from the trap Elise had set that I'd walked straight into.

My hands shook on the wheel, and all I could see was the way his forehead had rested against mine days ago. The memory cut brutal against his silence now.

By the time the coastline unrolled in front of me, the only thing that made sense was the ocean. I parked in the lot and reveled in the wind as it shoved against the car while my pulse tried to catch up.

My phone buzzed in the cup holder. A text from Avery: *U*

okay? I stared at it until the screen dimmed. I couldn't bring myself to answer.

Even with the ocean in front of me, I could still feel the weight of his hand anchoring me. It made the emptiness worse, not better.

Space—that was what I'd asked for. What I thought I needed. Instead, I felt only hollow where certainty should be—and the sharp edge of wondering if everyone else already knew the game, and I was the fool still learning the rules.

CHAPTER THIRTY-TWO

LUKE

The look in Mila's eyes hit harder than the way she left—hollow, like I'd already proven Elise right. Mila wanted space, so I gave it to her. But space didn't mean surrender. It didn't mean letting her believe Elise owned a piece of me she never would.

Fine. Mila could have her distance for now. While she did, I would find out what the hell she meant about the recording.

I pulled my phone from my pocket, thumb flying over the screen until I hit our thread. There was a gray waveform bar above the text I'd sent her this morning. I hadn't even noticed it. My stomach dropped when I hit play.

Drew's voice filled the air, sharp and controlled. "Protect yourself. Don't let Mila be the reason you go down."

Then my voice, lower, clipped in a way that almost sounded resigned. "Maybe you're right."

No wonder she looked wrecked. Out of thirty minutes, she'd heard thirty seconds—the part that colored me in the worst light.

But Elise knowing? That was what lit me up. I hadn't left my phone unattended. No one had touched it. Unless—spyware.

Something slithering through my messages without me seeing. *Dammit*. My battery had been dying faster lately. There had to be something running in the background, eating it up.

The hallway blurred. Fury steadied my stride. People moved out of the way as if they felt it—no one wanted to be caught in my orbit.

The bell rang as I shoved into Econ. Jax slouched in his usual seat in the back, boots kicked under the desk. I dropped into the chair beside him, muscles tense.

"Phone," I muttered.

He raised a brow but handed it over without a question. I punched in my PI's number hard enough the plastic creaked.

I didn't waste time with greetings when Marcus picked up. "Marcus, how did Elise get access to a voice note I never sent?" I cut him off before he had a chance to respond. "If there's malware, purge it."

He didn't ask why—just gave me orders. "Power down. Restart in safe mode. Then trace installs."

That was why he was worth what I paid him. My hands moved fast, following his voice until the screen confirmed it— software buried deep, a program mirroring outgoing files.

I hadn't opened shady links. No attachments. No clicks that could've handed Elise access. Which meant only one thing— physical contact.

Practice. Games. My bag in the locker room. Elise could walk into that place as though she owned it, and if she hadn't done the install herself, she would've found someone who could —*Logan*.

My chest burned. She hadn't played her usual games with Mila this time. She'd crossed a line. She'd dug into my life, stolen my words, twisted them into a blade, and shoved it straight between Mila and me.

The rules that had shielded her just shifted. She'd crossed a line.

But Elise could wait. Mila couldn't.

I snapped my head toward Jax, who'd been watching me as if I was about to combust. "Do what I just did. Now. Then make Chase and Theo do it too. All of you check your phones."

Alarm flickered through his usual flat calm. "Spyware?"

"Yeah." I was already pushing to my feet.

The teacher paused mid-sentence as my chair scraped back.

"Where are you going?" Jax asked.

"To find Mila. Tell Coach I'm skipping. Personal reasons."

No one stopped me.

I hurried through the halls and into my car. The first place I went was Mila's house, but it was empty. The arena was a no. She wouldn't put herself anywhere near practice today. The roof was ours, but she'd know that was where I'd go first.

That left one place since the boardwalk studio was gone. The only one that still gave her peace when everything else was overwhelming—the beach.

It didn't take long for me to drive along the coast and pull into the lot. It was where I found her car, locked and empty. Relief hit first, followed by the hollow twist of knowing she hadn't gone far. I scanned the sand until I saw her.

About half a mile down the beach. Arms looped around her knees. Eyes fixed on the horizon while the waves broke heavy along the shore and rolled back.

I spotted her before she saw me—eyes fixed on the horizon as if daring the water to take her.

I crossed the sand, wind flattening my shirt against me, salt sharp in the back of my throat. Each step sank deeper than I wanted, but I kept going until I reached her.

She didn't look up when I sat, lowering myself into the same pose. Close enough that our shoulders brushed, not enough to trap her.

"I hit the wrong icon," I said finally. "That's how the conversation was recorded in the first place." The words came out harder than I meant, the wind dragging them out to sea. "I won't pretend the conversation didn't happen."

Her voice came out thin. "I listened."

"I know."

"Then maybe the smartest move is distance." She didn't look at me, just at the water, like every wave was waiting to prove her right.

My jaw locked. "You heard one sentence without the rest of the fight." *Maybe you're right.* I knew how that sounded.

"The rest sounded a lot like you letting him push you to save yourself."

"I don't need his permission to protect you." My control snapped, harsher than I intended. I lowered my voice. "I was playing angles out loud. You got thirty seconds of a thirty-minute argument, and what you did hear was tampered with, taken way out of context."

"And he won."

"He didn't." I forced myself to stop short of touching her. "If he had, I wouldn't be here."

Her laugh was brittle. "Your family wants you far away from me."

"That's never happening."

"You sure?" Her head turned then, eyes burning. "You sure when Lorne starts moving chess pieces?"

"Lorne can make moves," I ground out. "Not against you." Heat flared through me, ugly and bright. "What the hell did Elise feed you?"

She hugged her knees tighter, fury breaking through. "Basically, that everyone you love is a liability—especially me. And that liabilities get cut."

I didn't look away. "Everything I love is a liability here. Doesn't mean I drop it."

She didn't answer, just dug her fingers into the sand. The

wind pushed her hair into her face, and she didn't bother to move it.

"Mila," I said quietly. "Elise played us both. She had spyware installed on my phone."

Her head jerked up. "What?"

"That recording—the one you received? It was spliced. She cut sections and layered them so it sounded like I agreed with Drew." I clenched my teeth, the old burn of fury lighting behind my ribs. "I didn't send it. I didn't even know she had access until my PI talked me through how to find the virus and remove it."

She stared at me as if she wanted to believe it but didn't dare. Then she shook her head, a short, disbelieving exhale following. "Why am I not surprised?"

"Because it's her style." I reached for her phone, slow enough so she could stop me if she wanted. "Can I?"

Her eyes narrowed. "Why?"

"Because if Elise tapped mine, she probably got to yours too."

She hesitated then handed it over. My fingers brushed hers —small static contact, too charged for the moment. I unlocked her settings, fingers moving fast, muscle memory and rage in equal measure. A buried file blinked at me in the diagnostics— mirrored connection, same app.

"You have it." I showed her the screen. "Same spyware. She's been copying our messages, maybe tracking locations too."

Mila went still. "You can get rid of it?"

"Yeah." My voice came out rougher than I meant. "Already did." I swiped through the final line of code, cut the connection, and dropped the phone back into her palm. "You're clean now."

Her hand closed around it slowly. "So this is how she's been getting everything."

"Not anymore." I met her eyes. "Nothing is going to come between us."

She exhaled, a shaky sound that could've been relief or heartbreak. "Until the next thing."

I didn't argue. Because she was right. But at least for now, we'd caught one of the knives before it landed.

The fight drained out of me slowly, leaving only the ache of everything we still hadn't talked about.

Her shoulders shifted, as if the movement steadied her a fraction. Elise had aimed to leave her bleeding long after she walked away, and she had. I saw it—the doubt, the fear—and forced myself closer to center. "You've told me you don't think your mom's been honest since before Blackwood."

"She hasn't." The word scraped her raw.

"Then maybe I'm not the only one raised on half-truths and threats dressed up as protection." My tone dropped, steady, the one I used when I needed her to hear me without breaking apart. "Maybe the only good thing in this is us choosing each other anyway."

A sound tore out of her that wasn't a laugh and wasn't a sob. "You make it sound simple."

"It isn't." I let my knee brush hers in the sand. "But this part is."

We sat breathing the same air until her grip loosened on her legs. Her hand drifted, fingers finding the edge of my shirt. I looped an arm around her back, pressing my palm into the sand —close enough to cage, careful not to.

"I'm not walking away," I said, slow enough to nail down each word. "Not for optics. Not for my father. Not for Drew. Not for Lorne. Not because Elise thinks she knows the angle I'll take."

"Even if it gets worse?"

"It will."

"Even if Dunn moves?"

"He already has." I leaned in until there was only an inch between us, breath heavy enough to count as contact. "Tell me to go if you want distance. I'll give you that. But I won't take it from you."

Her eyes burned into mine. "That's what you really want, isn't it?"

I closed the space until there was nothing left to take. "That's the last thing I want. I want this. Us. No one coming between you and me."

The words landed heavier than I meant, but I didn't pull them back. Her breath caught, sharp in the space between us, and for a second, it felt as though the ocean and the whole damn sky had gone still to hear the answer.

We shifted, facing one another. Her hands slid up to my neck. My grip drifted to cup her cheek, instinct fighting control and losing in the only way that mattered. The pull between us was tidal; you could step back from water, but you couldn't stop the moon.

We broke because we had to. Her eyes stayed locked on mine, wide and wrecked in a way that mirrored me.

"Then tell me—if your father pushes, if Lorne stares too long, if Drew warns you again—what do you do?"

"I tell them distance isn't protection," I said. "It's surrender."

"And if they make you choose?"

"I already have."

Her lips parted, eyes flashing as if she wanted to call me a liar but didn't have the proof.

I leaned closer, the words dragging out of me rougher than I meant. "I don't care if everything implodes around us. I can't stay away from you."

The space between us collapsed. No hesitation this time, no slow control. Just heat, anger, need—everything that had been chewing at us breaking loose. Her mouth met mine hard enough to bruise, my hands in her hair, her fingers fisting my shirt as though we were both trying to keep from shattering.

It wasn't careful. It wasn't safe. It was real.

When we tore apart, breathless, her forehead pressed to

mine. I still heard the ocean crashing and the wind tearing, but none of it felt bigger than what was happening right here.

"This is messy," she whispered.

"We're allowed messy." I kissed the corner of her mouth, grounding us. "We're not allowed lies."

The ocean roared. The sand shifted. But we held steady as my mouth crashed into hers. Her lips parted under mine, until I couldn't tell where the sea ended and she began. She tasted of wind-whipped air and defiance. My thumb dragged along her jaw, memorizing the line of it, while her nails scraped into the back of my neck as she threaded them into my hair—pain and want sparking through the same wire.

She gasped when I angled closer, and I caught the sound against my mouth, swallowing it as if I'd been starving for it. Every shift pressed her into me harder—the push of her chest, the catch of her hip against mine, the way she didn't retreat, not an inch.

Control was a word that didn't exist in this moment. I was fists in her hair, rougher than I should've been, softer than I wanted to be, caught between dragging her closer and remembering she was breakable. She didn't let me choose—her tongue brushed mine, pulling me deeper, making the decision for both of us.

The world pitched under us, but none of it broke the grip I had on her. On this. On the proof that distance had never been an option.

When we finally ripped apart, breaths ragged, foreheads locked, my chest heaved like I'd just gone three rounds in the ring. Her pupils were blown wide, lips swollen, hair tangled from my hands.

Her voice broke through, wrecked and unsteady. "We're going to burn for this."

I didn't blink. Didn't let go. "Then let it burn. Nothing else matters if I have you."

"Then we face whatever comes our way together," she whispered and placed her hand in mine.

I tightened my grip, the sand cool against our knuckles. For a second, it felt as if that promise might be enough to hold everything steady. I exhaled. "There's more."

Her brows pulled together. "More?"

I reached into my back pocket for my phone and swiped the screen awake. The glow cut across both of us, queuing up the grainy photo, the timestamp burned into the corner. "My PI sent this earlier."

She leaned closer, squinting. The picture was blurry—night-shot—but the shape was there.

"Who am I looking at?" she asked.

"It's the night you and your mom left. See the timestamp?"

"Oh." Her lips paused slightly apart as the pieces fell into place. "Is that...?"

"Yeah. It looks like Lorne." The outline was unmistakable.

"And that's the night Darren was last alive."

"Yeah. But I'm not sure he isn't still breathing. You told me about overhearing Elise mention a Mr. Langley, who I can only assume works at Dunn. Darren had no known relatives."

"So you're saying this picture doesn't prove Lorne was the murderer, even though it places him at the scene?"

"Pretty much. There's no body, no weapon, nothing that can tie him to Darren's death. For now, we don't do anything. All we really have is a blurry picture and conjecture."

"And if he's not alive—if someone's using his name?"

I felt her fingers tighten around mine, her pulse quick against my palm. "Either way," I said, "we stay quiet until we know which." The ocean crashed before us, steady and merciless. Whatever truth waited out there, it was already in play.

CHAPTER THIRTY-THREE

MILA

The beach stretched quiet, heat fading as the day slipped into that hour before dark. Waves broke and rolled back, steady and unbothered—the only witness to the fight we'd had, and the way we found our way back. My mouth still carried his touch—the salt on his skin, the press that left my lips tender. But more than touch, I remembered the way his breath mingled with mine, how it quieted something restless inside me. The memory throbbed high in my chest—longing and the sense this was where we'd always end up.

We didn't go home. We swung by the little strip past the cliffs, the one with salt-stained windows and faded awnings. The place we used to go to when we didn't want the night to end. The door creaked open, wood swollen from years of sea air, and the smell of baked bread and roasted vegetables spilled out. Luke knew the order without asking—avocado stacked on grainy bread, tomatoes still warm from the grill, sandwiches wrapped in butcher paper, and cold bottled water. He didn't look away when he paid. Didn't reach for my hand either. Everything between us felt too live to touch.

He carried the bag back to the car and set it in my lap before sliding behind the wheel. The paper crinkled under my hands as we pulled out. The drive to the arena was short—cliffs falling away to flat streets, the ocean flashing silver in the rearview before the buildings closed in again. When we pulled into the lot, cars lined the wall, silent and empty.

He popped the trunk. A big blanket lay folded there, edges frayed from use, waiting for nights like this. He slid me a sideways look. There was a question in it and something that didn't need one.

"Practice is still on," he muttered, lowering his voice as a group of kids clattered past the side door with helmets swinging. "We'll go up the back."

I nodded. "We can make it without anyone seeing."

"We always do."

Parked in the far corner, we headed out with the food and the blanket. The back hallway was colder than the outside air. Voices carried through—muffled by distance and white noise— the scrape of blades, the crack of a puck, his coach's bark. I let Luke lead. Not because I couldn't find the stairs on my own, but because I wanted to watch him move in his place. Broad shoulders I knew too well. The shift of muscle under his T-shirt, easy and unhurried, as though he trusted every inch of this space. He pushed the service door open with a hip press, balancing the food with a hand. Calm, efficient, as if nothing could rattle him here.

We climbed concrete stairs that smelled of dust and old rain. He set the pace, steady and measured, and I stayed a step behind. My heart beat against my ribs like it wanted to get ahead of me. At the roof access, he paused, angling his body to block the gap as he pushed the door open.

The horizon caught me first—skyline shifting, the last threads of light bleeding into deeper blue. The ocean stretched wide to the left. Above, the stars hadn't surfaced yet, but I knew they were there, waiting. Observing. A promise suspended just out of reach.

The arena roof spread flat and dark beneath it all. We'd been up here enough times for it to feel both stolen and ours. The wind tugged hair into my mouth and lifted the hem of his T-shirt, flashing a strip of skin and the tight line of muscle at his side. I watched his knuckles as he spread the blanket. Cuts marked them, faint and healing. Leftovers from last week's practice brawl? A drill gone wrong? With Luke, fights were language. A way to burn off pressure when words failed. He rarely threw the first punch. But when someone else did, he never walked away.

He glanced at me when I didn't move immediately. Checking. An old reflex that at the beginning of this year used to fire resentment through me. Tonight it landed lower. Warm. Steadying.

"Hungry?" He tilted his chin at the bag.

My stomach answered with a low ache. "Starving."

We sat cross-legged facing each other with the bag between us, the blanket soft and warm beneath me. I unwrapped my sandwich, the paper crackling, the smell of grilled bread and roasted tomatoes rising. Avocado pressed smooth against the crust, herbs seasoning the air. The first bite was warm and messy, juice running down my wrist. We ate without talking at first, our shoulders brushing when we reached for napkins. My knee kept finding his. He didn't pull away. I didn't either.

With the door shut, the rink noise dropped to a low hum. Every now and then the whistle cut through, sharp and thin, carried up through vents. Luke huffed a laugh through his nose, more at the reminder than the sound itself.

"You should be down there," I murmured around a bite.

"I should be a lot of places." He wiped his thumb along my lip where avocado had smeared then stared at his hand before licking it clean, slow and thoughtless.

Heat circled low. I set the sandwich down before it slipped. My hands didn't feel reliable. Neither did my breath.

The kiss on the beach had changed something between us and also dragged up everything that hadn't. I could feel both. A shift in the axis while the planet still spun. We had spent months pretending we were only partners, that the fire edging every fight was temporary, controllable, a symptom of proximity. Partners, not lovers. A line I was okay with because I needed walls to keep my life from sliding. The wall had cracked the second his mouth met mine. Not a collapse. A fracture that let in light.

Luke watched me the way he did when the ice was loud and the world went white around him—fixed and focused. He'd hated me for leaving without telling him why, and I'd earned that. But the year apart had broken my heart as much as it had his. He was still both—the boy I walked away from and the one I couldn't let go. The difference was me. What I believed. What I was willing to lose.

Gentle tufts of wind rustled the edges of the blanket. Shadows lengthened across his face. I waited for the panic to spike, the familiar free fall that hit every time I let him into any place I couldn't control. It rose. But it didn't drown me.

He leaned back on his hands and stared at the horizon. His jaw worked, the kind of movement that meant words were close but not ready to leave him. "I'm done pretending I don't walk into rooms and look for you. I'm done acting like it's safer to keep you at arm's length. It isn't. It never was."

"We're really doing this," I breathed. "After all of it."

"Yeah."

A muscle fluttered in my throat. I could hear my mother's voice somewhere in the edges of that wind. Her warning lingered, low and dark, the way a bruise shadows skin. Dunn never let go of an angle. She hadn't said it to scare me or to explain why we ran—after the murder at King Enterprises, after everything blew up. And why, later, she was pulled into Dunn's pocket. Not by choice. By threat. He wanted her under his thumb, and keeping her there meant keeping me close too. Survival wasn't clean. It was leverage.

I drew my knees up and wrapped my arms around them, my thoughts shifting to what we would face at school. "Elise will go nuclear."

"Let her," he muttered. No hesitation. No bravado either. He flicked his gaze toward the arena door as the hinges rumbled, but no one came through. His shoulders eased. "Her opinion doesn't matter."

"She hates that you're with me," I said. The words cut, but I didn't pull them back. "And she knows where to hit. She'll try to come between us."

"You already chose."

My lungs stuttered. "Did I?" I was still half living on borrowed time, a cover-up stuck to the bottom of my shoes. Dunn Industries buying up King stock, piece by piece. I'd told him that already—out in the arena lot, where he turned his back on me before circling around. Where we called a truce on the arena's rooftop. I thought saying it out loud would free me. Instead, it chained me tighter.

Luke didn't flinch from any of that now. He didn't know everything. But he knew enough to be hurt. I'd told him on the beach what I hadn't managed before—that I ran after hearing him and Drew on that recording, after Elise cornered me with it and left me no room to breathe. That was why I needed space. I'd expected him to throw it back at me. He hadn't. He'd listened, expression tight, hands open. And then he kissed me instead.

His thigh pressed into mine now, a warm, heavy line. "You choosing me doesn't erase the rest. I'm not asking you to pretend it does." He set the food aside and dragged the blanket higher so it folded over our knees. "I'm asking you to do this with me. No lies between us. If it gets ugly, we give each other the benefit of the doubt. We don't disappear."

The words held weight. My throat closed around them. The last time I disappeared, I had ripped him in half and stitched myself with guilt so tight I couldn't breathe for months.

I reached under my shirt and found the chain at my collarbone. The star charm sat cool against my fingers. I had worn it every day since he'd returned it to me. I slid the star off the chain and set it in his palm. "It's a gesture of commitment, not a sign of divide." The charm looked small there. Almost fragile. His hand wrapped around it, and his mouth went a little uneven. The kind of expression that would never be visible to anyone who didn't live under his skin.

"I can't promise I won't be afraid," I murmured. "That I won't screw it up. I can't even promise I won't feel the urge to run when things get too much. But I can promise I'll stop at the door. I'll turn around. I'll look at you. We do this or we don't. Not halfway."

He nodded. Not once. Slow, as if the agreement had to settle into his bones. He gently tapped my knee. "Partners," he murmured. Then his eyes sharpened. "And more. Don't make me pretend we're only one thing."

My laugh caught. "I'm not pretending anymore. At least while we're alone." The admission slid out of me and left a clean ache behind. "You and me. No matter the cost."

Something eased in his shoulders then. A held breath released. He leaned in and bumped my temple with his. Not a kiss. A contact point that felt older than our new vows. I breathed him in—cedar and spice and wind and the faint smoked bite of the grill that clung to his shirt.

"Say it again," he whispered.

"No matter the cost."

Below, a whistle shrilled. The sound overshot the roof and spun out over the parking lot. A gull screamed back, offended.

Luke huffed another short sound. "Coach hates double whistles. Someone's getting bagged." The sound had carried up through the vents, thin against the wind. He didn't get up. He didn't even shift his weight toward the door. He stayed angled toward me, hand still cupped over the star. He didn't pocket it.

"Keep it," I told him. "For now."

His thumb moved over the point. He didn't thank me. He didn't make a joke. Instead, he reached for the chain at my collarbone. My breath caught as he slid the star back where it belonged, fastening the clasp with careful fingers.

"It means I'm with you," he murmured, his eyes steady on mine. "And what we want—it's ours. We'll get there. The things we're fighting for don't stay out of reach."

The words sank in deeper than the white-gold charm against my skin.

We ate the rest of the sandwiches after that, hunger returning now that the fear had a shape. I licked juice from the ripe tomato from the corner of my mouth, missing a spot. Luke reached over, thumb wiping it away, his knuckle grazing my lip. My eyes stung, too full of everything I couldn't name out loud.

"Tell me the worst thing in your head," he murmured, eyes still on mine.

The ocean kept breathing as though it would never stop. "Elise will put me against a wall. She'll use my mom to do it. She'll find the place I'm softest and press." I kept my voice flat. Anything else and it would shake. "She can't touch you directly. But she can use me, Avery, or the guys to get to you. That's what she'll try."

He stared at our hands. He didn't pull his away. "She can try. But it won't work. And you and I will be side by side when she does."

Below, a door banged. Voices spilled out—laughs, curses, the usual chatter. We both stilled. A car alarm chirped once then stopped. No one took the stairs up. The roof stayed ours, a secret no one else knew.

I turned my face into Luke's shoulder and breathed him in, loving the scent that clung to him no matter how many times he showered.

"I don't want to wait until we're safe to be close," I whispered into his shirt. My voice scraped, raw. "Safe doesn't exist. It's just a word people use to make rules they later break."

His chest rose under my cheek. Fell. His hand curved to the back of my neck, thumb pressing lightly into that soft place beneath my ear—the spot that made my eyes close. He knew where I unraveled. And he never tugged at it unless I let him.

"We don't wait," he said. "We don't put us off. Not anymore."

From anyone else, it would've sounded like a line. From him, it resonated.

I pressed closer. His thumb brushed the star at my neck, the charm catching the faint light as if to seal it.

"You're my girlfriend," he said—steady, certain, leaving no room to argue. "And everyone will know it soon. We'll pick the right moment, and when we find it, there will be no more hiding. You hear me?"

I let out a shaky breath, almost a laugh. Flutters burst through my stomach, and elation pressed hard behind my ribs. "I hear you."

"The fundraiser is in a few days. We'll announce it then. My family won't be able to do shit. They'll play nice in public."

I worried my lip. *Public* didn't mean their hands were tied— just maybe restrained. Slightly.

We stayed until the arena lights clicked off in sections, shadows crawling across the lot below. We didn't move. When we finally gathered up the bag, Luke cleaned the area with that same quiet efficiency he brought to anything he could control. We didn't talk about what came next. Tomorrow had its own reckoning. Tonight was ours.

On the way down the stairwell, our shoulders brushed the whole flight. He didn't pull away when a door slammed somewhere below. I didn't flinch when laughter carried up through the shaft. The steady thing between us held, enough to carry us out into the hallway and still feel intact.

At the last landing, he snagged the edge of my hoodie and tugged. I turned. He didn't crowd me. Didn't make a show. He brushed his mouth across my temple, then the corner of my lips, then lower—to the pulse at my throat, slow and deliberate, as if he were marking every place he planned to memorize later.

"You're mine," he murmured. Not a claim for anyone else. A truth he'd built with me. "And I'm yours. What's between us doesn't belong to anyone else."

My chest hurt in a good way—the kind that told me I was finally using the muscle as it was meant.

We slipped out by the equipment room and hugged the wall. The building had gone quiet—practice over, players gone. No one looked up. No one saw us pressed too close in the shadow.

In the lot, he folded the blanket into the trunk. On the drive back, windows down, his hand rested easy on the wheel. Streetlights smeared gold across his arms. The roads felt familiar again, worn by everything we'd survived on them.

"I'm scared," I admitted. Pretending otherwise would only slow me down. Tomorrow was its own challenge. We were making our relationship public. Elise would go ballistic, up her endgame to levels I couldn't predict. And then there was his family—and hers. What would happen when they found out? According to them, we were the last two people who should be together.

His hand slid from the wheel, fingers brushing mine before

catching the belt loop at my hip. An anchor. "You don't have to be. Not with me." When he parked, he didn't kill the engine right away. He looked at me in the half-light from the streetlamp. "We'll make rules," he said, voice low. "Not to cage this. To protect it."

"No lies," I echoed.

"No power plays."

"And if we disagree, we say it then—not later," I said.

"Agree." A spark darkened the blue of his eyes. "And if it gets ugly—"

"We don't disappear." We said it together. Not planned. Not rehearsed. My throat tightened anyway. He exhaled as though I'd taken the weight off what he'd been carrying too long.

We sat parked at the curb a few feet from the house until headlights swept past and faded. Moths battered the streetlight's glass, chasing heat they'd never reach.

"I'll have Jax or Theo meet me at the beach and drive your car back here before morning."

I nodded, but my car was the furthest thing from my mind. "Come inside," I whispered.

He didn't ask if I was sure. His eyes did. I nodded. The knot behind my ribs loosened enough to make space.

The house met us with cool air and laundry soap. Shoes off by the door, his dropped next to mine because he knew me now, knew the small things mattered. His keys hit the bowl. My hand found his. Not to guide. Just to take with.

We didn't rush. The couch caught me when my knees went unreliable. He steadied me and then lowered beside me. Heat radiated from him.

"I don't want anyone else," I whispered. Words scuffed up my throat. Not denial. Honesty. "Just you."

His features sharpened, eyes softened. "That's enough."

It was. For this night, it was enough. We were done pretending.

He tugged me across the space. The kiss wasn't safe. Wasn't reckless. It was alive, a thing growing under my ribs now that I'd stopped starving it. His fingers slid beneath my hoodie, brushed bare skin. My breath stuttered. I caught his wrist, pressed him closer. He didn't push past the boundary my hand made. He listened to my body better than anyone had ever listened to my words.

He tugged me forward until I was practically in his lap. The weight of the day still pressed against my ribs, but the second his hands framed my waist, the pressure shifted—lighter, sharper, dangerous in a different way.

I climbed over him, my knees braced on either side of his thighs. His hands tunneled into my hair, palms spreading heat down to my scalp. My pulse tripped hard.

"I can't stop wanting you," he murmured, but the words were barely out before his mouth found mine.

The kiss wasn't gentle. It didn't need to be. It was a collision —his frustration and my fear, finally uncontained. My fingers locked behind his neck. His hair curled between them, grounding me when my whole body felt like it was breaking apart.

The taste of him—warm bread, salt, and something entirely Luke—filled me as he deepened the kiss, pulling me tighter, until I was squirming against him and couldn't tell if the sound that left me was mine or his. Heat sparked low, demanding, and my shirt lifted under his touch.

I broke away just long enough to breathe. My lips tingled, swollen, and I saw the storm in his eyes—hunger held back by a thread. The restraint only lit me up more.

"Not here," I whispered, voice scraping like it had to fight through every nerve. The idea of someone finding us—of Mom coming home—had me half panicked, half reckless.

His hands fell back to my hips, heavy and reluctant, but he let me shift off his lap. My chest ached at the loss of contact. He didn't push, didn't force. Just waited, eyes locked on me like I was the only thing in the room.

I stood, breath still ragged, and grabbed his hand. My grin felt shaky but real. "Come with me."

The look he gave me before rising—dark, steady, ready—hit harder than any kiss.

I pulled him up the stairs and down the hall, my pulse rattling so loud it felt as though it shook the walls. My room waited, familiar but suddenly charged. I closed the door and twisted the lock. The sound echoed, final. My chest tightened— not from fear. From the weight of choosing this after all we'd been through today. But that was the thing—I chose this. Not that it was easier, but because it was ours.

Luke was already there, close enough his breath ghosted my cheek. His hand slid under my chin, tilting my face up as if he needed me to look him in the eye before he kissed me again. When his mouth claimed mine this time, it was fire breaking through old walls. No hesitation. No pretending.

I pressed into him, and he backed me up until the back of my knees brushed the mattress. His hands anchored at my hips, then he lifted me onto the bed. He followed, the heat of him pushing me back against the pillows. His shirt was gone in seconds, and I let my palms roam across hard muscle, the ridges I'd memorized in glimpses finally mine to trace.

The air between us thinned, heavy with need. My clothes came off in a clumsy pull, laughter spilling between our mouths before dissolving into another kiss. His hand found my ribs, sliding up until his thumb brushed the underside of my breast. The touch sent a shock through me, sharp and undeniable.

"Tell me to stop," he rasped, breath catching. His forehead pressed to mine, eyes burning.

"I won't." My voice was hoarse, my body already answering. "Not tonight."

That broke him. His mouth crashed into mine, rough,

desperate, and my fingers clawed at his jeans until he got the hint. Zipper down, button loose, fabric shoved out of the way. I felt him hard against me, straining, and the ache between my legs turned urgent. Skin to skin, finally, no more barriers.

I guided his hand where I needed him most. The groan he let out when he felt me slick and ready nearly undid me. His fingers worked me slow at first, deliberate circles that made my breath hitch, then deeper, harder, until I arched against him with a strangled sound.

"Luke—" I gasped, nails biting his shoulder.

"I've got you." His voice was raw, steady even as his body trembled with restraint.

He paused only long enough to grab a condom from his wallet, rolling it on with shaking hands. Then he looked at me again, one last check.

I nodded, throat tight, heart hammering. "I want you."

He slid inside slowly, a groan breaking from his chest as I gasped at the stretch, the fullness that stole my breath. For a second, we just stayed there, pressed together, breathing the same jagged air. His hand threaded through mine, grounding me as much as I anchored him.

Then he moved. Every thrust stoked the fire higher, building fast, relentless. His mouth claimed mine between gasps, between curses muttered low against my skin. I clung to him, hips rising to meet his, the rhythm pulling us under until nothing existed beyond the heat, the pressure, the sound of my name breaking from his lips.

Release tore through me first, sudden and consuming, a cry muffled against his shoulder. He followed seconds later, his whole body shuddering as he pressed deeper, lost in me.

We collapsed together, sweat-slick, tangled in sheets that smelled faintly of us. He kissed the corner of my mouth, then my temple, then just held me while our breath evened out.

The house crept back in by inches—the AC kicking on, a car

driving down the street outside, his phone buzzing once and then going quiet wherever it was on the floor. I tugged the sheet higher and pressed a last kiss to his shoulder before we reached for our clothes. He pulled on his jeans and found his shirt. I slid into mine, fingers clumsy and content.

"Water?" he asked, voice rough.

I nodded. We padded down the hall then the stairs, the floor cool under our feet, and the kitchen tap thundered into a glass. We shared it, passing it back and forth until it was gone.

On the couch, the room reset around us. Streetlight cut a pale stripe across the rug. The quiet shifted from intimate to real—tomorrow pressing at the edges.

He kissed me once more then leaned back to look at me fully.

"We're not alone in this," he murmured. "Elise will make moves. Dunn will too. My family won't stay quiet. We choose who gets our time. We choose where the story goes when we can."

"We choose each other even when we can't," I said.

"Especially then."

He stretched, shirt lifting just enough to tease. I reached without thinking, tracing the line of muscle at his side. He caught my wrist lightly, his mouth curving. "Careful. Keep touching me that way and I'll be ready for round two."

"Maybe I'm trying to memorize you before everything changes again. And I don't want you to stop. Not anymore."

His mouth brushed mine, brief, hungry, as though he wanted proof. Then he bent and kissed the inside of my wrist. "I'm not going anywhere," he murmured. "If you run, I'm chasing you. If I push, you pull me back. Deal?"

"Deal."

No contracts. No words carved in stone. Just the press of skin and breath, a promise heavier because we knew exactly what it would cost.

CHAPTER THIRTY-FOUR

LUKE

The room had gone still as dawn approached, the air heavy with that in-between quiet before morning fully wakes. I couldn't resist her touch. One brush of her hand, and I'd followed her back upstairs. Mila shifted in my arms, her head resting on my chest, breath warm against my skin. A thin line of gray pressed at the blinds, hinting at daylight but not yet breaking through. I lay there, tracing idle circles against her shoulder, my mind refusing to stop spinning.

She stirred, voice muffled against my skin "You're thinking too loud."

I huffed a quiet laugh. "Didn't mean to wake you."

"You didn't," she mumbled, eyes still closed. "You just do that thing where your brain starts pacing."

I smiled into her hair. "The University of Michigan wants me," I whispered, fingers tangled in her hair. "Full ride. Their coach made that clear."

"Congratulations, Luke." Her lips brushed my collarbone, voice soft with sleep. "I'm not surprised, though. What are you thinking?"

"It's everything I wanted." I kept my voice low. "Or was. Because without you, it's just a school. Another hockey team."

I glanced down, needing to see her expression, but her eyes stayed closed. A faint smile curved her mouth—there, then gone.

"Mila?"

She didn't answer, her breathing already evening out. I stared at the ceiling, her weight warm against me, the word *future* sitting heavy on my tongue.

Mila was asleep when I reluctantly slipped from the bed. Sheets tangled around her waist; her bare shoulder caught the light leaking through the blinds. Her hair fanned across the pillow, lashes casting spiked shadows across her cheeks. Her lips were still swollen, cheekbones pronounced even in sleep. She had a natural beauty that didn't need polishing—it just was. Inside and out.

I didn't want to leave her. Every muscle told me to climb back in, bury myself in her warmth, stay there until the sun forced us to move. But her mom's car could pull in at any minute, and the last thing Mila needed was another fight on her doorstep.

What we had wasn't something I could name. It was more than I'd ever let myself want and nothing I'd felt with anyone else. The pull to her was constant. She walked into a room, and every part of me turned toward her. She didn't even know how much power she held over me. One touch of her hand could bring me to my knees.

At the door, I stopped. I looked back at her one more time and let myself memorize the curve of her full mouth, the shadows over her cheek, her dark hair spilling across the pillow.

She's mine.

Soon, everyone would know it. No more hiding. No more half-truths. She was my girlfriend, and I wasn't pretending otherwise. The school, our families, and, of course, Elise would know. Let them come for us. Let them try to split us. I would tear their world apart before I let them touch her.

I slipped outside, pulling the door until the latch caught. The night air cut cool against my skin. My SUV waited at the curb, a little way down the street. I slid behind the wheel just as her mom's headlights swung into the driveway. Timing down to seconds.

I sat there for a while, engine cold, hands on the wheel. The weight of everything stacked against us pressed in.

Dunn's takeover stalled only because Mila warned me. Her mom traced the shell companies back to him—quiet buys of King stock, one percentage at a time. My dad and Drew moved fast, snapping up shares before Dunn could. They called it a Pac-Man defense—eat or be eaten. For now, it was working. But none of it mattered if Mila wasn't beside me. Every defense, strategy, and share was empty without her in the middle of it.

There were deeper cracks. The reason Mila and her mom left Blackwood hadn't gone away. Darren Langley's probable murder and cover-up. Maybe at Lorne's hands. Maybe not. Secrets like that don't stay buried. When they surfaced, the fallout would hit everyone—my family, Dunn, the town. And when it hit, it wouldn't be containable.

I started the SUV, pulled away from the curb, and headed home.

Elise had her own plans for me. But they wouldn't work. Not now. Not ever. Logan was the one I had to watch—every move, every shift on ice, every sideways word. Trust was currency, and Logan was bankrupt. Tori claimed she was with us, but trust wasn't a given. Avery and Jax were solid, and Chase was learning to live with it. Theo keeping an eye on Tori helped keep her in line.

I drove through the empty streets, lights flashing across the windshield, thoughts turning heavy.

The truth could destroy us. But so could the lies. For once, I'd rather burn with her than survive without her.

CHAPTER THIRTY-FIVE

MILA

The days blurred after Luke and I had spent the night together. We didn't talk about what would come next at the event. We just kept moving—practice, classes, meetings. The world kept spinning as though nothing had changed, but everything had.

By Friday, the Blackwood Foundation Gala had dominated the calendar. Every message thread, every hallway conversation, every *see you this weekend* carried the same undertone—money, image, control. King Enterprises and Dunn Industries were jointly hosting the event. It would be interesting, or terrifying, to see which way the balance tilted.

Luke texted once that afternoon: *I'll be late to the fundraiser. Don't let Charles Dunn near you before I get there.*

I didn't answer. There wasn't much I could say. Why would Mr. Dunn come near me? That was more my mom's nightmare than mine. But Luke would arrive later, as he didn't have to be there as early as Mom and me.

By Saturday night, the event already felt close—its presence threaded through the air as if charged with static. Mom moved through our rental with quiet purpose—hair pinned, perfume lightly misted, expression steady. She wasn't going with Principal Miller as her date and said it was better to keep things simple. I knew what she meant—no attachments, no witnesses, no one else to pull into whatever this night might turn into. When she turned to zip my dress, she paused for a second, then met my eyes in the mirror.

"You don't have to go," she said quietly. "You've done your part."

"I know. But I'm going."

Her reflection softened. "Okay. Just...be careful."

The car ride was mostly silent except for the radio droning as background noise. The town slipped by in streaks of light until the building came into view—marble, glass, and enough security to pretend this was about charity instead of two companies trying to rule.

The driver—courtesy of Dunn Industries—eased the vehicle to the curb. Flashbulbs popped near the entrance, cameras pivoting toward names that mattered. Mom and I got out of the vehicle and moved forward together, through the glass doors and into the wide, gleaming space.

Inside, crystal caught the glow and fractured it, refracting across glass and gold. Chandeliers dripped as though made of diamonds over marble floors. Waiters in black moved as though choreography through clusters of silk and tailored suits, champagne flutes flashing in their wake. The air smelled of perfume and polished wood—money dressed up as elegance.

My dress wasn't made for this room. Silver, low-backed, catching the light in places I didn't want noticed. Mom said that was the point.

When she gave it to me, I couldn't stop staring. The fabric moved like mercury—fluid, alive. I'd loved how it skimmed my skin, caught the light, and made me feel as though maybe I could belong among the wealthy at the event. But here, under chandeliers and cameras, it felt like standing in a spotlight I hadn't asked for.

Mom's emerald dress was sleek, high-slit, designed to turn heads. Every line of it deliberate. The kind of beauty that didn't ask for attention—it took it.

Her hand brushed mine as we stepped through the archway and into the room's pulse. I felt the tremor in her fingers, which surprised me.

"Stay close," she murmured without moving her lips. "Don't stare. Don't react. If Dunn comes near you—"

"He won't." The words tumbled from my mouth without invitation. She'd been a wreck while we'd gotten ready, convinced something would go down at the event and we'd be caught in the crosshairs. Dunn, King, Lorne… they were all here tonight. Predators in tailored suits, lying in wait, and neither Mom nor I wanted to be caught in their sights.

Her eyes snapped to mine. "Don't say that like you know."

Then her expression reset, mask snapping into place. She took a steadying breath, then smiled—a smooth, practiced upturn she used on headmasters and donors. "We're fine," she said lightly, louder this time. "You worked check-in, remember? Stick close to people you know from school. Smile, be polite, then eat something. Shoulders back. Chin up."

I nodded as though I was listening, pulse already cataloguing exits.

The press line was gone. Twenty minutes since the last camera flash. The room had settled into low conversation, laughter and champagne flowing freely. A string quartet played in the corner, notes drifting through the air as if they belonged to someone else's night.

Security was thicker now that the cameras were gone. Not bulky bodyguards but quiet suits, hired muscle, who didn't blink enough. One near the side hall. One by the double doors to the service corridor. One near the Dunns.

My name badge was off. Student liaison was over. I was just a girl in a silver dress who didn't belong.

"Breathe," Mom said softly.

"I am."

"Breathe quieter."

I almost smiled. Then Luke walked in. No announcement. No warning. The air just... shifted.

He moved through the doorway and into the space as if he owned it. Black custom suit that accented his broad, muscular shoulders, white shirt, no tie. Hair still damp at the ends, evidence of a quick shower. Every motion was deliberate, quiet. Controlled. He didn't glance around, but his presence demanded attention.

And then he looked at me. Full focus. No hesitation. The noise behind me dulled to a hum. My chest loosened so suddenly I almost swayed.

He came straight to me. Not rushed—intentional. Each step closing the distance that never really existed. I felt it in my chest before I saw it in his eyes—the familiar pull that said neither of us had ever really let go.

His hand settled on my waist, sure and warm. "You look—" His voice hitched, then steadied. "Dangerous."

"To you?" I asked.

"Every time."

Mom murmured something polite and stepped aside—close enough to hear, far enough to look casual. Her way of keeping me safe without showing it.

Luke leaned down, lips brushing my ear. "You good?"

I nodded. "You?"

"About to be."

And then we were moving—his hand still low, guiding, not pushing. Through the center of the ballroom as though the space had always been meant to clear for him. Heads turned. Polite greetings followed. He didn't stop. A nod here. A handshake there. Controlled efficiency. He didn't play the room—he ran it. A product of his heritage, the wealth attached to his last name, the power his family wielded and what he'd grown up in —rooms full of power players who smiled while they drew blood.

The Kings stood near the center table. Grant King's stance was pure command—broad shoulders squared, a dangerous presence radiating from him as he spoke with another man. Beside him was his wife, Eleanor, in cream satin, beauty weaponized by poise. Her smile polished to perfection, but the cunning in her blue eyes impossible to miss.

Luke's hand flexed against my waist, a silent warning—or reassurance. Then we were moving. Each step felt deliberate, threaded with all the history waiting in their eyes when they finally turned toward us.

"Dad. Mom." Luke's voice was polite, clipped. His grip on me tightened by a fraction. "This is my girlfriend, Mila Callahan."

Grant's eyes dragged over me once, cataloguing details. "Mila." No warmth. Just an assessment.

Eleanor stepped forward when he didn't. "Thank you for your help with the student coordination." Her voice was smooth, practiced. "The turnout's wonderful."

"I—" My voice barely found shape. They'd completely skipped over Luke's announcement, but maybe that was a good thing? "I'm glad."

Grant extended his hand. I took it because not taking it would've made a scene. His palm was cool. His stare wasn't. "A Callahan at my table." His gaze cut to Luke. "Interesting."

Luke went still beside me. His thumb moved lower on my waist—firm, possessive.

"Why wouldn't she be?" His tone was even, controlled. "She's with me."

Eleanor's smile tightened. For a second, the conversation paused.

Then his brother, Drew, slid in, smooth as ever. "Wow, territorial pissing already?" he said, half-laughing, kissing Eleanor's cheek. "That's faster than usual. Mila, you look stunning. Claire, come here. You remember Mila, right?"

Claire moved beside him, pale and tense in light-pink silk, clutching her purse like armor. Her gaze met mine—steady, kind, seeing too much.

"Good to see you again." Her voice was low, careful. Her fingers wrapped around mine—quick, warm. A warning wrapped in grace. Something in her eyes said she understood exactly what it cost to stand here with Luke against his parents.

Grant exhaled through his nose, jaw flexing. "We'll talk later," he said to Luke.

"Yeah." Luke's tone was calm. Dangerous. "We will."

A man called Grant's name from across the room. He turned toward it, the conversation already dismissed. The spotlight shifted with him, and the air between Luke and me finally eased.

Luke's hand squeezed my waist. "Come on," he murmured. "We're not done."

He wasn't wrong.

Lorne stood near the entrance, tie black, grin sharper than the edge of his cufflinks. The woman on his arm looked ornamental, her expression bored.

"Lorne," Luke said.

Lorne's eyes cut to me. "And this must be Mila Callahan." He smiled, lazy. "You have your mother's eyes. I hope they're finally seeing clearly."

Cold slid down my spine.

Luke shifted, subtle—his stance angling, hand settling at my hip, body between me and Lorne. Not blocking me. Claiming space.

"Careful," Luke growled.

Lorne laughed. "Always."

Then the room's air thickened again—because Mr. and Mrs. Dunn had arrived.

He didn't need to raise his voice as he responded to greetings. Presence did the work for him—polished suit, quiet menace. His features carried a pit bull's intensity, all clenched focus and restrained force. His wife was still stunning, though time had softened the edges. Her eyes were slightly unfocused, his arm looped around her waist as though a tether keeping her upright.

Mr. Dunn lifted his glass. "Luke. Good skate last weekend."

"Thank you." Luke's reply was steady.

Then Dunn looked at me. The smile was polite. The eyes—calculating.

"And this must be Mila Callahan. Your mother's been helpful too, hasn't she?"

My throat went dry.

Luke stepped in before I could open my mouth. "And my girlfriend."

Dunn's smile didn't move past his mouth. "Of course. That must be why you're here."

That was it. We were public—and to one of the big players. Metal hit the back of my tongue.

Mom appeared at my right, clutch shielding her ribs. "Good evening, Mr. Dunn." Her voice was smooth, practiced. "Mila and I were just heading for a drink." She smiled—polite, thin. "Excuse us."

Luke looked at me with a question in his eyes.

I nodded. "I'll be right back."

His thumb brushed my hip as he let go, slow, deliberate. A promise.

The bar was tucked under a tower of glassware, half-shadowed. The music shifted—softer, meant to soothe. It didn't.

Mom ordered water instead of champagne. Before the glass even hit the counter, someone called her name—one of the board members, older, polished, smiling too wide. She hesitated then turned toward him, clutch now gripped tight in her hand.

I leaned against the end of the bar, waiting for when Luke could break away from his conversation and join me. That was when Elise made her move. She cut through the crowd as though she'd been trained for this. Red lipstick, jet-black hair pined in an elaborate updo, black dress, and a calm that looked rehearsed. She didn't bother pretending we weren't already watching each other.

When she stopped in front of me, she held out a thick envelope. "For you."

I didn't want to take it. I did anyway. Then I opened it and withdrew a stack of papers. A quick scan told me the contents had something to do with King Enterprises, and at the top, a stamp of my mom's credentials. The world tilted on its axis, my vision tunneled, and my stomach hollowed out as I read. "What is this?" But some part of me knew, and holy shit it wasn't anything good.

Elise leaned in, her voice almost gentle. "My dad asked me to make sure you got that."

"Why?"

"Because he didn't want to embarrass you and your mom with the feds swarming the place and arresting her in front of everyone." Her gaze flicked toward Luke, now talking with his father. Then to Dunn, her dad, who gave her a slight nod. "He's being generous, Mila, and giving you both time to get the hell out of here—and town. You should appreciate that."

My pulse hammered. "What is this supposed to be?"

"A bargaining chip." Her lashes lowered, then she tapped the top page with one manicured nail. "Your mom accessed restricted King files over a year ago—files that my father later acquired—her credentials, her time stamp, all neatly recorded. And then there's you, who disappeared with her right after. Convenient timing, don't you think?" Her gaze flicked toward Luke before settling on me once again with venom dripping from the cold depth. "You're with the wrong person—Luke is meant to be mine—and it's going to cost you and your mom more that I think you want to give."

I couldn't feel my hands.

"That's not what happened. My mom hasn't done anything." But the flash drive—the memory of Mom in the kitchen, smashing it with a hammer—swam to the forefront of my mind. It had to be a mistake. Mom was capable of a lot for our survival, but not that. It wasn't her style.

"Maybe," she said. "Maybe not. But the board won't care. Grant King won't. And the feds definitely won't. So here's your out." Her tone went deceptively soft. "Walk away from Luke, tonight."

My throat locked. "And if I don't?"

"My father makes your mother the story instead, and she goes down for espionage." Her gaze didn't waver. "You get painted as bait. Luke gets dragged into a scandal for falling for you that will cause his family to lose faith in him. With Luke and I back together, a peaceful merger is inevitable. If not, the merger burns. Everyone loses. Except us."

Except us—because Dunn was planning a hostile takeover, buying up King's stock with shell companies. No matter the outcome, they would come out ahead.

The swish of fabric pulled my gaze. Behind Elise, Mom's hands shook, the water in her glass sloshing over the edge, tiny drops painting her emerald dress to deep jade.

"My dad already showed your mom the files," Elise added. "The story's already been written for her, too. So don't pretend this isn't real."

Everything went soundless.

Her perfume hit next—sweet, cold, poisonous.

"This is me doing you a favor," she whispered. "You walk,

this dies quietly. You stay, they will take you down and call it protection."

I almost laughed. Because of course she called it mercy.

But the worst part was, I believed her. Not emotionally. Strategically. From what I knew of her father, he didn't bluff. He built outcomes.

Was this why they'd called Mom back? To set her up? I dropped my gaze to the papers. If so, they'd succeeded. But still, my voice scraped out. "This won't fix things for you. Luke is never going to—"

"This isn't about me," she snapped. "It's about trajectory. Luke and I belong to the most powerful families in this town. Your mom's collateral. Don't make it messy."

She stepped back, perfect composure sliding into place. "Be smart, Mila." Then she vanished, absorbed back into the fold of donors and secrets.

Mom stepped forward, crowding me. Her lipstick was still flawless. Her voice wasn't. "This is bad, Mila. And way too soon. I haven't—" Her hand shook before she steadied it. "We don't have options. Not yet."

My throat burned. "What do you mean?"

"You need to let him go," she whispered. "Tonight. Quietly."

Her voice broke.

And I hated them. Every one of them. For making Mom beg. For making this the only way to protect her. For calling that love.

Across the room, Luke turned from his father. Drew shadowed him. Claire close, pale, but steady. Then Luke's gaze found me—and everything in him snapped taut. His posture shifted, easy confidence gone. Shoulders squared. His eyes cut across the space, fast and assessing, landing on Elise as though he could tear her down with a look. For a second, no one else existed. Just the two of us—his fury colliding with my fear across the polished floor.

Every cell in my body wanted to move, to meet him halfway.

Mom's fingers pressed into my arm. My hand tightened around the papers until they crinkled in my palm, pulling everything into focus.

If I stayed, I wasn't just his. I was leverage—the weapon Dunn could use to gut him. To destroy her. To ruin both of us.

If I walked, I saved Mom and Luke, but in return, I lost him. Either way, they won. Either way, I died inside.

Luke took a step forward but stopped when Dunn's gaze slid his way. His fists curled at his sides, as if it took everything in him not to cross the room. The look he gave me wasn't a plea—it was a vow.

Behind him, Dunn watched. Lorne leaned close, murmuring to a man in a dark suit. Grant's jaw locked. Claire's mouth shaped my name, silent. Mom trembled.

I glanced down at the open file, the stamped pages trembling in my hand. Every line of data—dates, access logs, her name—felt like a bullet headed straight toward us.

Our future wasn't speculation anymore. It was evidence. And if I didn't walk away now, they wouldn't just come for me —they'd come for everyone I loved.

***

Want to know out what happens between Luke and Mila? To find out, continue reading the Blackwood Blades series with SUDDEN DEATH.

If you liked Cross-Check, check out the Hidden Valley Elite Series.

Thanks so much for reading my work. If you enjoyed reading CROSS-CHECK, I hope you'll consider leaving a review or rating.

Looking for your next book to read? Check out more books by Amy McKinley/Isla Vaughn here:
https://www.amymckinley.com/pages/reading-order

ALSO BY ISLA VAUGHN

Hidden Valley Elite Series

Savage Start

Savage Lies

Savage Truth

Brutal Days

Brutal Nights

Cruel Start

Cruel Hate

Cruel Love

Wicked Games

Wicked Ends

Fall Lake Ballers

Quarterback Keeper

Pump Fake

Red Zone

Power Plays & Pucks

Shattered Ice

Pucking Power Plays *(coming soon)*

Blackwood Blades *(coming soon)*

Iced Out

Cross-Check

Sudden Death

Breakaway

Isla Vaughn also publishes under *USA Today* bestselling author Amy McKinley.

Mafia Elite

No Way Out

Blood Oath

Born in Darkness

Savage Secrets

Ruthless Heir

Collateral Damage

Rivals

Gray Ghost Novels (Former Navy SEALs)

Moments That Define Us

Broken Circle

Eye of the Storm

Beneath the Surface

Vantage Point

Covert Threat

Marked for Death

Deadly Isles Special Ops (Navy SEALs)

Twisted Secrets

Bound by Secrets

Forged by Secrets

Standalone Titles

Shattered Melody

Siren's Call: Cursed Seas

Fake Fiancé (A Second Chance Office Romance)

Moonlit Destination Series

Moonlit Whisper

Moonlit Kiss

Moonlit Mirage

Five Fates Series

Hidden

Taken

Bound by Blood Mafia Series *(coming soon)*

Hidde Enemy

Stolen Prize

Secret Pawn

Broken Vow

Buried Rival

Tarnished Crown

ACKNOWLEDGMENTS

Some stories whisper. Others crash in like a slapshot you never saw coming. Cross-Check was definitely the latter—loud, insistent, and determined to pull me back into Blackwood with Luke and Mila whether I felt ready or not. I couldn't have made it through this second leg of their journey without some truly incredible people in my corner.

To my family—thank you for loving me through the chaos. You've gotten used to the thousand-yard stare that means I'm not really in the room, I'm in a scene, and you still give me space and fresh coffee. You roll with the looming deadlines, my brain being half off in fictional drama, and I don't take that for granted for a second. Your steady support is everything.

To my critique partners—there are not enough words for how grateful I am for you. You listen to the messy brainstorming, help me untangle plot knots, and gently (or not so gently) nudge me when I'm avoiding the hard emotional beats. For this book, you went all in again, even when time was tight and life was busy. Candace Irving, Emily Albright, Kristin Kisska, and Jessica Riley Miller—thank you for every chapter read, every note, every "you've got this" message. Your insight makes these books sharper, but it's your friendship that makes this whole journey feel less lonely.

To my editor, Taylor Anhalt—thank you for your sharp instincts and endless patience. You spot the things I'm too close to see, ask the questions that push me deeper, and help whip these pages into shape so the story on the page matches the one in my head. Your care, talent, and dedication shine through every round of edits, and I'm so grateful to have you on this team.

To my illustrator, Audrey Anhalt—you brought Luke and Mila to life again in a way that feels both familiar and brand new. Seeing them on this cover—reaching for each other but still holding space between them—is pure magic. And to TE Black Designs—thank you for turning that artwork into a finished cover that fits this series so perfectly. Your eye for detail and design continues to blow me away.

To Colleen Noyes and the team at Itsy Bitsy Book Bits—thank you for shouting about these books with so much enthusiasm. Your passion for connecting readers and authors doesn't go unnoticed, and I'm incredibly appreciative for every post, share, and bit of behind-the-scenes work you do.

And to you—yes, you holding this book—thank you. Whether you started with Iced Out and came back for more, or you somehow landed here first, I'm so grateful you chose to spend your time with Luke, Mila, and the rest of the Blackwood crew. Your messages, reviews, and excited reactions are what keep this series alive. If you haven't already, I'd love for you to join my newsletter so you don't miss what's coming next for them.

With all my love and gratitude—thank you for reading. 🖤

ABOUT THE AUTHOR

Isla Vaughn writes steamy sports romance packed with fierce women, irresistible alpha males, and all the emotional chaos in between. She's the author of the *Hidden Valley Elite* series and several other sports romance series. When she's not writing, she's probably reading, drinking too much coffee, or dreaming about life in a beach house.

instagram.com/islavaughnauthor
facebook.com/author.IslaVaughn
tiktok.com/@islavaughnauthor
bookbub.com/profile/isla-vaughn
goodreads.com/islavaughn_author